ROTTING UPRIGHT

VOLUME 1

ROTTING UPRIGHT

Volume 1

Edited by Aaron Crocker
Cover Design Leslie Safford
Formatting by K H Formatting

TABLE OF CONTENTS

The Price of Progress____1
The Fellowship of Eternal Resurrection____________________63
Phantom Flu____119
Jack and Alexandra's Sea Trip into Hell: A Zombie Tale______207
About the Authors____________________________________247

Dear Reader,

Our team cannot thank you enough for joining us around the campfire for "Rotting Upright, Volume 1"—the first in a three-volume anthology all about zombies.

In his work, *Keep the Aspidistra flying,* George Orwell might not have been referencing zombies when he said, "This life we live nowadays! It's not life, it's stagnation, death-in-life. Look at all these bloody houses, and the meaningless people inside them! Sometimes I think we're all corpses. Just rotting upright." Nonetheless, I feel this quote clicks. A zombie, in its very iteration is a meaty (pun intended…) metaphor that has managed to not only survive but surpass its folkloric roots; we see this in their ravenous hunger, a constant pursuit of *devouring* in many iterations, regardless of the amount they've previously consumed.

So, what is it about zombies that make us so uncomfortable? Sheer gore? The threat of a zombie apocalypse? Or the point where their very existence all too easily juxtaposes how we sometimes feel with our own—decomposing shells, traveling in groups, emotionless, fighting to simply survive.

Rotting Upright is about more than just death and decay; a common theme that weaves its way through each story is desperation. From a family so ravenous to find a 'miracle cure' for their neurodivergent son that they resort to deception, peril, and bootleg pharmaceuticals to a grieving son willing to do anything to ensure that he and his mother are never faced with another loss, *Rotting Upright* explores society's tendency to overlook small details, like caterpillars or the very human desire to love and to be loved and to want this with such conviction that one would be willing to die alongside that love.

As we sit together, on this oh-so-apocalyptic eve, as the undead yet unalive descend upon us, I'd ask us all to consider what these stories offer about what it means to be human. Are we mindlessly wandering, controlled by our desires, obsessions, and longing. Or, do these stories speak to *why* we keep going? Maybe, just maybe, each story offers hope and makes a compelling case on why we should keep on going, embracing the 'little' things, finding satiation in what *is* as opposed to what *is not*.

Without further pomp and circumstance, I present, *Rotting Upright, Volume 1*.

Gratitude Always,

Aaron Crocker

The Price of Progress

Shawn Putnam

1. Every family has its ups and downs.

Rusty Jenkins liked to walk downtown Rockford every night around twilight. He liked the way the fading sun reflected off the gleaming windows of the few buildings that stood over ten stories tall, sending shimmering pools of orange onto the dark, cracked pavement in front of the newly renovated library on North Church Street. He liked walking down the roads bordering the Rock River to the Burpee Museum, people watching all the way.

More than just the scenery, he enjoyed the feelings the walk awoke within him even more. The library, for instance, had always been one of his favorite places as a kid. The smell of uncounted pages was just as intoxicating now as it had been the first time his parents had taken him. And then the short walk to the Burpee Museum, where a life-sized model of a river crocodile called out to young Rusty to clamber up the creaking wooden stairs to the second floor and come touch it – priceless. The Burpee Museum of Natural History had expanded quite a bit over the decades, and for the better, he was sure, but it couldn't compete with the rosy glow of nostalgia.

Rusty supposed that, most of all, the cozy memories of childhood chased away the very grown-up concerns that plagued him nowadays. Ultimately, that was the purpose of his nightly sojourns into the darkening shadows of Rockford's downtown. It wasn't so much *remembering* that he wanted to do. He wanted to forget. Forget the son he'd had with an ex-girlfriend, a son that he hadn't seen in over thirty years. Forget the daughter that he and his wife Carol had conceived eighteen years ago. Oh, how happy they had been when they'd figured out that they were pregnant again. They'd both seen this new pregnancy as a chance to erase the mistakes of the past. How they'd labored over what they would do differently, how they'd watch for certain signs more closely, get *this* newborn to the doctor more rapidly. They'd stayed up late into the night, his work schedule and her classroom times be damned, fantasizing about how this time, things would be different.

And different they had been. After all, a stillborn daughter was much different than their first-born autistic, retarded son.

Rusty knew that "retarded" wasn't the politically correct terminology. He was quite careful not to use the word when dealing with Jacob's teachers as they painstakingly went over his IEP year after year. But then again, Jacob wasn't in school anymore. He was twenty-one years old. The mind of a three-year old clumsily stuffed in the body of a fully grown man, and wasn't it just a treat to know that the only child he'd had the opportunity to raise would be living with he and Carol for the rest of their lives?

Thus, the nightly trips from their tidy house on Auburn Street to what he had once known as the bike path, but now knew as the larger Sinnissippi Gardens, which did indeed have a bike and walking path that ran from North Church Street all the way into Loves Park. He always started at the midway point of the path, right near the greenhouse and the overly large, flower encrusted outdoor analog clock, but he always headed straight south toward the library and then onto the Burpee Museum. Sometimes he needed a longer walk, and he'd head to the Discovery Center. He never went in, though. Hadn't since Jacob's first public meltdown, during which he'd trashed several exhibits and hit Carol when she'd tried to calm him down, the incident that had finally convinced Rusty and Carol to medicate Jacob.

They'd had Jacob relatively late – they'd both been in their early thirties – and when Jacob had melted down, he'd been thirteen. In the throes of puberty, not knowing his own strength, he'd broken Carol's nose. He hadn't meant to, of course, but he never meant to do anything that he did. Broken TVs, snapped Xbox discs, laptop shaped holes in living room walls – in the end, Jacob was innocent of all of it. He truly couldn't control himself, and while it was difficult, Rusty and Carol understood that fact.

And to be fair, the medication had helped. The combination of Clonidine, Aripiprazole, and Amantadine had calmed Jacob right down, and at the relatively cheap cost of his waking hours. Since Jacob had gotten out of school, and the transition program that followed, he sometimes slept until nine, ten, even as late as eleven o'clock. But Jacob supposed he couldn't begrudge his son the descent into unconsciousness. What did the boy have to look forward to, after all, when he was awake? When in high school, Jacob had enjoyed unaccompanied walks around the neighborhood (unmolested, thank you very much, FBI statistics) but that had come to a shattering halt when Covid hit during Jacob's senior year. Auburn Senior High School's special ed teachers had broached the topic in *just* the wrong way for a boy of Jacob's mentality, which was very much all or nothing. When they'd introduced new protocols such as social distancing and mask wearing, Jacob, who hated change at the best of times, decided if everywhere but home was potentially dangerous, then at home he would stay.

To be fair, the global pandemic had been uncharted waters for everybody, and Rusty wasn't sure he could have done any better than the teachers in introducing the concept to his mentally challenged child. Still, he resented them to this day. They had basically turned his walk loving outdoor playground enthusiast into an agoraphobe.

Treks around the neighborhood where Jacob had been, according to their neighbors, a somewhat fondly regarded fixture? Gone.

Weekend trips to the two nearby fast-food restaurants, where Jacob would walk (by himself!) and order a simple lunch (by himself!)? Distant memories.

Instead, Rusty and Carol were left with a son, a grown-up son, who rarely left the house. When he did, even three years after the worst of the pandemic had passed, it was with a mask firmly pressed over his nose and mouth and a pair of disposable gloves slipped over his hands. Once something new was introduced into Jacob's routine, it *stayed* in his routine, no matter how his mother and father tried to convince him it was no longer necessary.

Rusty's nightly walks had begun at roughly the same time that Jacob's walks had ended. At first, Rusty had thought if he could show his son that walking was safe the teen would join him, but those hopes had been dashed rather quickly. It had only taken a few refusals and the near reappearance of the meltdowns the meds had so neatly eliminated from their small family's routine to show Rusty the futility in his reasoning. But Rusty quickly grew to enjoy the solitude. The first time he realized he had gone for two miles without once thinking about his son, guilt fell upon him, followed closely by something akin to relief.

For that brief moment in time, the stress of raising a special boy like his son, the years in front of them that would see no maturation, no mental growth, faded into the background. And so, he went back, night after night, earbuds affixed in his ears with music blaring or a podcast playing and temporarily walked away from his problems.

After almost thirty years of marriage, Carol understood. She had her own methods of escaping the realities of living with a boy like Jacob. When they'd bought their house on Auburn Street, it had been with the tacit understanding that of the three bedrooms, one would be her exclusive domain. Scrapbooking, a hobby that she'd let fall by the wayside in the mad rush to get Jacob the care his condition demanded, had made its reappearance in her life to an almost obsessive degree. She'd bought software to convert snapshots to digital images, and had invested in a Cricut, a device Rusty barely understood and didn't really care about. But it made her happy, and once Jacob no longer had any obligations to school or his post-graduation program, Carol spent hours in her "study", filling scrapbooks with photos from their little family's past.

The situation wasn't perfect, but it was livable.

Rusty had his walks, a job that he hated, and his dreams of what could have been.

Carol had her scrapbooking and her students.

Jacob had his high-definition radio and the bedroom where he spent most of his time.

They weren't deliriously happy, but they were content. And things would have most likely would have continued on in this fashion for an indefinite amount of time if it hadn't been for the street shouter Jacob met in front of the library one fine Autumn evening.

2. Haven't I heard this one before?

"**I** know that you've looked at your life and thought to yourself, there's got to be something more!"

The voice was just loud enough to slip under the cacophonous sounds of Five Finger Death Punch, and as deafening as Rusty liked to play his music, that meant that the man in front of the Rockford Public Library must have been talking very loudly indeed. Well, there was nothing for it. Rusty hunched his shoulders, pretended he hadn't heard the man, and tried to hurry past him.

"You, sir," the man said, and almost against his will Rusty glanced in the stranger's direction, certain that the man couldn't be addressing his comments at him but almost as certain that he was.

"That's right," the man continued. "You, in the red hoodie. Don't you want to know how much better your life could be?"

Yep. The man had been talking to him, just as Rusty had been afraid of. He'd been in this type of situation before, and he found that the solution consisted of just one word: ignore. If a further solution was needed, just rinse and repeat. Eventually, these types of people got the hint and went after easier prey. Rusty did remember, with the slightest hint of a smile, that one time a pair of Jehovah's Witnesses had followed him for three or four blocks. To this day, he was certain it wasn't out of malice, but because they honestly thought he hadn't heard their earnest entreaties.

"Don't pass me by, my friend," the man said. "Maybe it's not you that needs us but your friends. Possibly your family?"

At that, Rusty finally paused. With the speed of a retreating glacier, he turned back to face the street shouter, and just as slowly, he began to walk back to the man.

"Ah, I thought that might get your attention," the man said, his tone jovial and yet somehow conspiratorial. "Even when you were walking by,

I thought to myself, here is a selfless man. He won't care about helping himself, but his loved ones? That's the way!"

Rusty stepped in front of the man and slipped the hood of his red zip-up sweatshirt from his head, exposing long, greying hair that had come partially untucked from the black elastic band he used to keep his hair tied into a ponytail. He popped the earbuds from his ears, grabbed the charging case from his front jeans pocket, and tucked them inside. He did all of this with a sort of scrupulous fastidiousness that hid the very real, irrational anger that he'd felt at the man's last words.

"Thanks for stopping, friend," the street shouter said. "So very few actually do. They don't understand the changes that they're passing up, but you? You seem like a man who could do with some positive changes."

"What's your name, boss?" Rusty asked. "I like to know who I'm talking to."

"My name is Matthew, friend," the man said. He was clean cut, blond hair trimmed closely to his scalp and nary a hint of stubble to be found on his square jaw. He was dressed simply, in a pair of blue Dockers and a black polo shirt. It was a relatively cool autumn for Illinois, but the man wore no jacket. Rusty recognized his sort – most likely he kept himself warm with delusions of his own righteousness. A petty thought, maybe, but as it was close to his stillborn daughter's eighteenth birthday, he readily forgave himself.

"Hmm. Well, Matthew, you are right about one thing. I could do with a positive change."

"I thought so," the newly named Matthew said. "And we can help you achieve those things; I promise you that."

"Oh, I know you can," Rusty said.

"So, you've heard of us, then?" Matthew asked with a grin.

"Of course I haven't," Rusty snorted. "You haven't said who you represent, and before you do, I don't give a shit."

The grin was erased from Matthew's face as efficiently as if it had been drawn in chalk. He took a step back in the face of Rusty's sudden anger, but Rusty grabbed his arm.

"Where you going?" Rusty asked. "You wanted my attention. You gonna do a fade now that you've got it?"

"Hey, man," Matthew said, and Rusty knew that he was hearing the man's real voice, not the glad-handling huckster he'd been just moments before. "It's a free country. You got no right to put your hands on me like this."

"Like I said," Rusty said as though the other man hadn't spoken. "There's a positive change only you can help me with. You can shut the fuck up. Think you can handle that, champ?"

Rusty abruptly let the man go, and Matthew stumbled backwards, only staying on his feet through sheer luck. There was guilt in the back of Rusty's mind, but he pushed it down into the oblivion of his darker thoughts. "Who're you with?" Rusty snarled. "Jehovah's Witnesses? Baptists? By God Scientology? Fuck, it don't matter. You're all the same. You all say you've got the answers to life's problems, but you don't know jack shit. What it comes down to is, you promise the world, and you don't deliver nothing."

Rusty wasn't sure why he was engaging with the man, and with such anger besides. In a way, as the anniversary of his daughter's death drew closer, he'd found himself seeking a confrontation with someone. He'd never blamed Carol for their stillborn child, any more than he'd blamed her for the way that Jacob was, but if he couldn't blame her, and he couldn't blame himself, then all he was left with was just anger. Most years around this time, he found himself growing morose, less talkative than normal, but this year, he had found himself helplessly navigating a directionless fury; a missile without a target. It could have been anyone – a coworker at one of Rockford's few remaining factories where he'd punched a clock for over thirty years, a cashier who'd been just the slightest bit too slow, a drive-thru attendant who'd handed him the wrong order. In the end, it seemed he'd found a scapegoat who deserved it, just the tiniest bit.

"You sound like you've got some experience in broken promises, friend," Matthew said, and oh great, the huckster was back.

"Yeah, that's one way to put it," Rusty said. "And I'm not your friend."

"Well, I've given you my name, but you haven't done me the same courtesy, so what else am I to call you?"

"Look, it don't matter," Rusty said. "I'm sorry I grabbed you. I'm sorry I snapped at you. Just…man, just be careful about the kind of shit you peddle. Maybe you think words don't hurt, but they do. Sometimes, they hurt more than anything."

"A decent piece of advice. Might I give you a piece of advice in return?"

"Why not?" Rusty said, already dismissing the man in his mind. He slipped the hoodie back over his head and grabbed his earbuds from his pocket. FFDP seemed a bit heavy all of a sudden. Maybe Justin Timberlake or Ed Sheeran instead? One wouldn't know it to look at him, with the iron-grey beard that fell almost to the bottom of his chest and the ponytail that fell to his waist, but he was a not-so-secret fan of pop singers as well as heavy metal artists, and he found that the surest way to find his way *out of* a funk was to find his way *into* the lyrics of a pretty female popstar. For a while, Avril Lavigne had been his jam, and then Christina Aguilera, but lately, Sabrina Carpenter had been his go to mood reliever.

"Just because someone, maybe a lot of someones, have let you down before, doesn't mean that everyone is full of shit. Something to keep in mind, Rusty. For Jacob's sake, if not your own."

The earbuds dropped from Rusty's suddenly nerveless fingers, and he turned his attention back to Matthew. The man stared into his eyes with a knowing gaze, a tiny smirk playing on his lips.

"Now you're ready to listen," Matthew said, and Rusty found that he was.

3. Promise the moon, but shoot for the stars.

"I do have an organization behind me, Rusty. You're right about that," Matthew said. They sat in a corner booth at the Olympic, a small but well-regarded restaurant on Auburn Street just a mile and some change from Rusty's home. "But it's not religious."

Matthew took a bite from the burger on the platter in front of him and wiped his chin with the restaurant-provided white linen napkin right after. It seemed to be a ritual with the man. First a bite of food, then a napkin wipe to the mouth, then another bite of food. In contrast, Rusty had only a glass of ice water on the table. He wanted nothing more than a nice, frosty beer but had decided that to partake would not be in his best interest. He knew himself well enough to know that one beer would turn into two turn into three, and he needed to keep a level head.

"I'm sure you have questions," Matthew continued. "I can't promise to answer everything, but I'll answer what I can."

"Questions," Rusty said. "Yeah, I've got questions, all right. Starting with, how the hell do you know my name? My son's name?"

Matthew chuckled a good-natured laugh that revealed his utter lack of surprise at Rusty's opening gambit. "You know, you'd be surprised at just how often that's the first thing people want to know. Not what we want. Not even how we can back up what we claim we can do. Just "how do you know my name?". And I'll tell you the same thing I've told everybody else we've approached. Why shouldn't we know who you are?" He spread his arms in a genuinely perplexed gesture. "Are you a deeply undercover agent of the government? Maybe under the auspices of Witness Protection?"

"I'm not, and it sounds like you goddamn well know I'm not," Rusty said. "And you also know that's not what I mean."

Matthew nodded. "No. That's not what you mean at all. The question you really want to ask is this. How do we know about your situation? Your son's condition. Is that more accurate?"

"Yeah," Rusty said. "That's exactly what I mean."

Matthew shrugged. "Well, Rusty, I hate to disillusion you, but medical records? They're easily accessible to someone determined enough. And really, neither you nor Carol have ever been secretive about Jacob. In fact, some might say that you've been more upfront than necessary about his condition. Playing martyr, less understanding people might say."

Rusty sat back in his chair, briefly considering the other man's words. Disregarding the man's claim of martyrdom, he supposed it was true enough that he and Carol had never hidden the difficulties they'd had in raising Jacob over the years. He'd actually lost track of how many days he'd had to take off to get Jacob to various doctor's and psychiatrist's appointments. How many specialists they'd seen to nail down Jacob's diagnosis. How many IEP sessions he'd sat through during Jacob's scholastic career. And hadn't Carol, at one time, told him that she'd specifically requested from her principal at Auburn not to work with special needs kids because she dealt with it enough at home? He was sure that she had. But that raised another, more pertinent question.

"So what," he said, "you've been spying on us for God knows how many years?"

"Nothing so sinister," Matthew said, shaking his head. "My organization has, hmmm, I guess you could call them agents, in most of the schools in the city. Not many, really. Just one or two per school. We don't really need that many people, because, as you know, relatively speaking there aren't that many *real* special needs children per school. More than there used to be, certainly, but we're not sure if that's because certain conditions have become easier to diagnose or because there's been a true uptick in affected children. That's one of the things we're still studying. It's been a real debate amongst some of us, believe me."

"You keep saying 'we'," Rusty said. "Who are you?"

Matthew smiled, waving the waitress who approached them away. "We don't need anything else right now," he said to her. "Unless you changed your mind about eating something, Rusty?"

Rusty shook his head. He'd never been less hungry for food in his life. But hunger for answers? That he had in spades.

"Just flag me down if you need anything, hon," the waitress said, and retreated. It seemed to Rusty that she recognized Matthew. Maybe as a good tipper, or…A question bloomed uncomfortably in Rusty's mind.

Just how many times had Matthew been here, having this same conversation with other parents in Rusty's plight?

"*We* are the solution you didn't know existed," Matthew said. "I know you'll find this impossible to believe, but we can fix your Jacob. Make him whole for the first time in his life."

"Bullshit," Rusty said, and he couldn't believe how steady his voice was when inside, he wanted nothing more than to rant and rave. "Autism can't be cured, and even if it could, there's still the…cognitive disability to deal with."

"You mean the mental retardation," Matthew said. "Call it what it really is, why don't you?"

"Yeah, fine," Rusty spat out. "My kid's a retard. 60 points off of the average IQ, I think one of the sped teachers told me once. You know what that means?"

"Why don't you tell me what it means to *you*?" Matthew suggested.

"It means Jacob's got an IQ of about 40, that's what it means to me. My kid's got the mind of a toddler in the body of an adult. And that's not something any sort of therapy or combo of pills can fix."

"You're right. Neither of those things will fix your son. But I'm telling you right now that we can. Wouldn't you like that? Wouldn't it be wonderful to see your son go off to college? Get married? Hell, even get a dead-end job like yours if it meant that you could have a normal conversation with him?"

"Yeah, you know what?" Rusty said, getting up from the table. "Fuck you. I should have beat the hell out of you when you first talked to me. I don't know what kind of a scam you're trying to run, but you can leave me the hell out of it."

"We will, of course, respect your wishes, Rusty," Matthew said, getting up from the table as well. He approached Rusty, pressing a business card into Rusty's hand. "But think about one thing. If medical science can only go so far, is it so wrong to ask for a miracle, instead?"

4. A night in the life.

When Rusty got home that night, he was the least relaxed he'd been since starting his walks several years earlier. But he hid it well, not wanting Jacob to sense anything amiss. And that was the thing; despite his condition, Jacob could be remarkably empathetic on occasion, at least when it came to his mother and father.

"Hey Jacob," Rusty called out as he entered the kitchen through the attached garage. It was a nightly habit. Jacob liked to know where he and Carol were at all times, and Rusty always made sure to announce himself when he got home. "You in the living room?"

"I'm in the living room, Daddy," Jacob confirmed.

"Where's your mom?"

"She's in her bedroom," Jacob said. "Where's Maggie?"

Maggie was the Jenkins' family dog, a Basenji that Rusty and Carol had bought to try to bring Jacob out of his shell when he'd been younger and they hadn't understood his condition as well as they did now. They'd only been able to relate to him through the lens of their own experiences, and they'd thought that Jacob might be lonely.

"Where's Maggie?" was the question that had prompted Rusty and Carol to bite the bullet and buy the puppy. They'd dithered for weeks, but when they'd realized that Jacob had already named his hypothetical dog and was actively looking for her, they finally understood that Jacob had wrested the decision from their hands.

Jacob had taken to the responsibility of raising a puppy in a way that he had taken to very little else in his life. He was the one who fed the dog every morning and evening. He was the one who played with her most every day. As he couldn't quite get the hang of getting the leash and harness on Maggie, he never took her for walks but he was the one who let her out to the backyard. Didn't clean up the yard, though. That was Rusty's job, but he didn't mind. Small dog equaled small poops.

"Well, I don't know," Rusty said, walking into the living room and flopping down on his recliner. There were three pieces of furniture in the living room – his recliner, Carol's recliner, and Jacob's couch that he shared with his bestest girl. The ownership of each item was strictly delineated, and woe betide anyone who forgot the division. "Where's Maggie?"

Jacob raised the lightweight blanket covering the lower half of his body with a slightly dull-witted grin. But only slightly – if one didn't know any better, one might have thought Jacob was only a bit scatter-brained, and not…what he really was. Curled tightly at his hip was a bundle of brown and white fur. Maggie blinked her dark emerald eyes at the sudden intrusion of light before slipping back to sleep as Jacob covered her again.

"That's good son," Rusty said.

"Maggie is ten years old now," Jacob said. "I've had her since I was eleven."

"That's right, son," Rusty said.

"But she's not sick, right Daddy? She's still gonna be around for a while still, right?"

"That's right, son," Rusty said, the conversation as familiar as a nightly lullaby. "She's still got a few good years left in her."

"Okay," Jacob said. He twisted the fingers of his right hand in the death grip of his left for a few moments, and then said, "How was your walk?"

"It was fine," Rusty sighed. He leaned back in his recliner and closed his eyes, pinching the bridge of his nose to stave off the headache he could feel coming. Every night when he got home, the conversation went the exact same way. First the comments about Maggie, and then asking about his walk. And the sad thing was, Rusty knew that it was Jacob's way of trying to have a normal conversation. But if he were to try to introduce something new -

"You know, you're always welcome to join me if you want," Rusty offered.

"No thank you," Jacob said. He jumped to his feet, pushing Maggie to the floor. She whined a little before jumping back on the couch and curling up on the warm blanket Jacob had vacated, very much used to the treatment. "I'm going to my room. I go to bed at ten, you know."

- Up came the brick wall, and Jacob retreated to his solitude.

"I know, son," Rusty said. "I know. You wanna yell for your mom when you go to your room?"

5. But really, what have you got to lose?

"**H**ey Carol?" Rusty said later that night. He and Carol were lying in bed. She was out, but Rusty was hyper aware of Jacob's movements in his own room. As in all things, Jacob had a routine. He went to bed at ten, true, but that didn't mean he went to sleep. He would stay in bed for about ten minutes or so and then get up to use the bathroom. Then he'd lay back down but be up another twenty minutes later to use the bathroom again. He'd lay back down for a third time, but this time, he'd click on his radio, the only other thing aside from his dog that Rusty and Carol *knew* that he cared about and listen to his favorite rock station for a while. That would finally put him to sleep – for a couple of hours, and then the whole ritual would repeat again.

"What's up, Rusty?" Carol asked after a few moments, her voice thick with the sleep he'd interrupted. It was a talent she possessed that he'd always admired, almost envied. As soon as she hit the pillow, consciousness fled from her, while he almost always tossed and turned for at least a half hour before sleep claimed him.

"Rusty," Carol said, and oops, he must have gotten lost in his thoughts. She sounded perturbed. "You need something, or did you just call my name for the hell of it?"

"Yeah, sorry," Rusty said. "I was just wondering something. You ever think about what it would have been like if Jacob had been normal?"

The heavy blanket that Carol had cocooned herself in rustled as she sat up in bed. "You woke me up to ask me that?" she said.

"Yeah," Rusty said, ignoring the unspoken *idiot* implied in the question, quite uncharacteristic for a man who had taken the idiom *happy wife, happy life* to heart. "Yeah, yeah I did. I'm serious. You ever given it any serious thought?"

Carol sighed. She knew how Rusty was around this time of year and decided to indulge him. "Of course I've thought about it," she said. "Especially after what happened with Katie, how could I not?"

Rusty winced. Katie was the name they'd given their stillborn daughter, and just hearing it was enough for him to momentarily lose his train of thought. He shook his head, willing the depressing distraction away. "But what would it have been like, do you think?"

"If Jacob had been born normal?" Carol asked. "I don't...I don't actually know. He's twenty-one now, so I suppose he'd be off at college, hopefully. His, what, third year?" She chuckled. "We'd have probably had to deal with more than one romantic entanglement, I suppose. Without the drama that resulted from your particular entanglement, with any luck."

"That's a rather polite way of saying you hope he wouldn't have knocked up some girl," Rusty said, not without a little bitterness.

Carol didn't seem to hear him. "I think he would have gone into radio," she said, her voice far away. "Lord knows how much he loves to listen to his rock stations, even being the way he is. And don't forget, when he was younger, he used to make those fake YouTube videos on his iPad. Maybe he would have gone into streaming. Making Let's Play videos or something. Whichever. It doesn't matter. I think, though...I think he would have done something creative." She chuckled again, a chuckle that turned into a quickly aborted but heart-breakingly sharp sob.

Rusty realized that this was a well-worn fantasy, thumbed through as often as one of her scrapbooks. He was surprised to feel a spike of jealousy. He'd never known that she'd thought about what might have been in such detail.

Carol cleared her throat, and when she spoke again, the uncharacteristic show of emotion had disappeared. "Why, though? What brought this on?"

Rusty had never been one to hide things from his wife, but something deep inside kept him from sharing his encounter with the fast-talking Matthew. "Not sure," he said. "I guess, with Katie's eighteenth just around the corner, and given how Jacob just turned twenty-one, I was thinking about roads not taken, that sort of thing."

Carol snorted and lay back down. "Well, keep those sorts of thoughts locked up until tomorrow night," she said. "I've got one more day of riding roughshod over a bunch of freshmen to look forward to before the weekend, and the last thing I need to be thinking about is how my autistic, retarded son is more well-behaved than they are."

"I don't see how what I asked has anything to do with that," Rusty protested.

Carol smacked his shoulder. "Just go to sleep, Russ. In case you've forgotten, you've got work in the morning, too."

Rusty propped himself up on his elbow, leaned over, and kissed his wife on the forehead. "Love you, baby," he said, but the only response he received was a soft, open-mouthed snore.

6. Is it a lie if it doesn't hurt anybody?

For the first time in over five years, Rusty took a sick day. He told himself that it was because he wanted a mental health day, but he'd never been very good at lying to himself. And he didn't even bother to lie to Carol when she woke up at 6:30 and found him in the kitchen still in a pair of shapeless "workout" shorts and a graphic tee.

Carol quirked an eyebrow at him as she walked over to the Keurig machine and slipped in a pod of Espresso Roast. But she didn't say anything until she'd taken the first sip of her blessed caffeinated elixir.

"Shouldn't you be at work?"

Rusty shrugged. "Called in."

"You. Rusty Jenkins. Mr. I'm dying but I still need to put in my forty hours. You called in."

"Yeah." He squirmed a bit under her considering gaze before blurting out "What? Not like I've never called in before."

"That's true," Carol agreed. "If I recall correctly, the last time you called in sick was in 2019. Jacob had pneumonia. You and him spent all night in the hospital. So tell me, do I need to worry?"

Okay, that was different. Where was the censure, the disapproval?

Something of the question must have shown in his face because Carol uttered an exasperated sigh. "For the love of God, Rusty. I'm your wife, not your mother. As long as we can afford it, and I don't know why we couldn't, I don't care if you take a day off or not. Just, you know, don't make a habit of it. Not that I think you would, but…I don't like to think about you in the house by yourself so close to Katie's birthday." Unspoken was the fact that he wouldn't exactly be alone, but then again, Jacob didn't exactly count.

"No habit," Rusty assured her. "I just thought that maybe I could get Jacob out of the house for a bit."

"Really? How were you going to manage that? The park doesn't do anything for him anymore, he hates to shop, and he has no more school."

The lie slipped through his lips with no hesitation, as though it had just been waiting to spring forth fully formed at his command. "He might go out to look at cars, don't you think?"

"Huh," Carol said, sipping the last of her coffee. They both knew driving was out of the question for Jacob, thanks to the great go-cart debacle of his sixteenth birthday, but their son still loved to *look* at cars, and they also knew that he had several dealers' websites saved on his iPad. "General Lee or Bumblebee?"

"Bumblebee," Rusty said, even as he sneered at Michael Bay's ridiculous re-imagining of the yellow robot instead of the Volkswagen Beetle he and Carol had grown up with. "I read somewhere that Chevy's discontinuing the Camaro. Thought it might be a special treat for him to see a new one for the last time."

"That might work," Carol said as she rinsed out her coffee mug before placing it in the upper rack of the dishwasher. It was almost pathological with her — she couldn't stand to leave a dirty dish in the sink. It was one of the flaws she'd worked hardest to rid him of; he was more than content to let the dishes build up before deigning to wash them. She grabbed her purse from the counter, and gave him a quick embrace and a quicker kiss before heading out through the garage door. "But you know, you could have just taken a half day."

7. BREAKING FROM THE ROUTINE, ONE CAUTIOUS ATTEMPT AT A TIME.

It turned out for once, Carol was wrong. Almost as soon as the garage door had closed Rusty heard sounds of life coming from Jacob's bedroom. Before his bedroom door opened, Rusty had frozen waffles, the same breakfast that Jacob had consumed for over three years, in the toaster and had pulled maple syrup from the refrigerator.

Jacob shambled into the kitchen as the waffles popped up from the toaster. His hair was a disheveled mess, and the patchy growth of beard on his chin and cheeks attested to the fact that Rusty hadn't shaved him in at least a month. He was wearing a wrinkled polo shirt (the only type of shirt he would wear) and a pair of grungy jockey shorts that had once been white but could now only be considered washed-out grey. Rusty, used to the sight, still couldn't hold back a smile, especially at the little bundle of mottled brown and white fur that trotted along at Jacob's feet.

Jacob sat down at the comfy little table where the Jenkins family took most of their meals while Maggie slipped through the doggie door Rusty had installed in the kitchen door, heading out into the backyard to relieve herself and possibly chase a few birds while Jacob ate. Rusty topped the waffles with a dab of syrup and slid the plate onto the table.

"I need a fork, Daddy," Jacob said, his voice still thick with the remnants of drugged sleep. "I can't eat my waffles without a fork."

"Of course, son," Rusty said, taking a fork from the utensil drawer and handing it over to Jacob. Then, breaking protocols established years earlier, he sat down at the table with his son.

Jacob eyed him warily for several long seconds, and then, certain that there would be no unwanted physical contact, dug into his waffles. Rusty was content to let his son eat in peace. The upcoming "conversation" would be difficult enough without beginning before his son had had the chance to feed himself.

Jacob finished his food in short order, and brought his dish and fork over to the sink. He didn't bother to rinse off the sticky residue, of course. Rusty and Carol had given that up as a lost cause a long time ago. Maggie came in from the yard and nuzzled her master's ankle, impatient for her breakfast now that Jacob had finished his. Jacob grabbed her food bowl, plodding over to the pantry where they kept her food. Then, a dim light bulb flashed inside Jacob's mind, and he turned back to his father. "Daddy, you work today! It's Friday! You work Monday through Friday, 6:00 AM to 4:00 PM. Why aren't you at work?"

"Well, son," Rusty said. "Why don't you feed your puppy, and we'll talk about it?"

8. Hope costs nothing, but does priceless always equal worthless?

"How long are we gonna be gone, Daddy?" Jacob asked from the passenger seat of Rusty's Ford Focus. "Maggie's not happy when she's in her crate, right?"

"No, she's not," Rusty said as he surreptitiously glanced once again at the address that Matthew had given him right before they'd parted. *Parted, shit*, Rusty mentally corrected himself. *You stormed out, and you know it, and what the hell are you doing tracking him down after the bullshit he spewed, anyway?* "But you know that she'll tear the house apart if we leave her to her own devices.

"I know," Jacob said. "But we won't be gone long, right? And we're only going the one place, right Daddy?"

"Maybe two," Rusty said, suppressing the twinge of guilt he felt at the lie. "I told you, before we go look at cars, I've got someplace I want to stop first. Now, why don't you turn on the radio?"

"You don't like the radio, do you Daddy?" Jacob said even as he stabbed the button to turn on the radio. Almost instantly, the overpowering sounds of heavy metal filled the car before Jacob twisted the knob, and the loud roar was subdued to a volume that Rusty could barely make out. Jacob loved listening to the radio, true, but he couldn't stand loud noises at all. The two facts clashed to an unnerving degree, but despite the inherent contradiction, Jacob refused to listen to anything but Rock. Rusty and Carol had tried to get Jacob interested in other types of music over the years, but every single time the boy had refused to take the bait.

"You know that I don't, son," Rusty said, unable, or perhaps after all this time, unwilling to stop the exasperation that crept into his tone.

"That's right," Jacob said as though it was only the second time they'd had this exact same conversation, with these exact same words, instead of the hundredth or the thousandth. "You like listening to your own music from your phone, 'cause the radio doesn't play your music."

"Mmm-hmm," Rusty answered automatically. Following the GPS to the address listed on the business card Matthew had slipped him during their ill-fated first meeting had led Rusty to a part of town that he hadn't visited in years. They were off Kishwaukee Street on Airport Road. There wasn't much out this way with the exception of the UPS facility, still going strong despite Rockford's depressed economy, and a few derelict factories, including the building that had once housed the first "grown-up" job Rusty had ever had. He'd gotten the job, leaving a Mcjob that he'd actually loved, when he'd impregnated his girlfriend and had suddenly needed insurance that wasn't provided by his father. Even though they'd broken up, Rusty had found that he enjoyed factory work, in spite of his parents' warnings, and had worked in manufacturing ever since.

Rusty was almost to the point of giving up on the mysterious address as a lost cause and taking his son to the Chevy dealership, turning a guilty lie into the unvarnished truth, when his GPS pinged, announcing their arrival. And yet, even as he pulled into the parking lot of a nondescript one-story office building, Rusty couldn't help the large course of doubt that ran through him. The building was the very definition of anonymous, more an overly large trailer than anything else. There was no sign announcing the name of the people headquartered in the building, and aside from his own, there were only a few other cars parked in the lot. But even as he pulled into a slot and turned off his vehicle, Matthew stepped out of the building's main entrance. He looked like a realtor or a car salesman, wearing simple black slacks, a red polo shirt, and a cream-colored blazer.

"What are we doing here, Daddy?" Jacob asked, and even through the haze of disbelief that he was actually going to take Matthew up on what was undoubtedly a pie-in-the-sky promise, Rusty heard the trepidation in his son's tone. The man-boy didn't like dealing with people other than his parents at the best of times, and meeting a stranger without proper preparation had the potential to turn disastrous.

"Daddy just has to talk to this man for a few minutes," Rusty reassured his son. "He's a doctor, see, and he has some medicine that might help with a few things."

"Help who, Daddy?" Jacob asked in that penetrating way that he occasionally had about him. "You or Mommy aren't bad sick, are you?"

"No, son," Rusty said, but he was spared any further dissembling when Matthew walked up to Rusty's car. He halted a few feet from Rusty's front bumper, standing with the gait of a man who, now that he had what he wanted, could wait patiently for things to run their inevitable course. A sour lance of dislike speared Rusty right through the stomach, and he wondered again just what the hell he thought he was doing here, entertaining the man's bullshit, but then he glanced over at Jacob, who was twisting the fingers of one hand in the tight, surely painful grip of the other, and he shook off the thought.

Matthew had been right about one thing. Conventional medicine and therapy had done nothing for Jacob. Maybe sometimes, every once in a great while, far-fetched thinking could be justified. With a sigh, Rusty got out of his car, and prepared to see if the man who had promised the moon could deliver even cosmic dust.

9. Could it be over before it begins?

"**I** thought you might come by," Matthew said as soon as Rusty's feet touched the tar-black pavement of the parking lot. "I know things didn't end so well the last time we talked, but I had a feeling nevertheless."

"Did you?" Rusty said. "Well, that makes one of us."

Matthew shrugged. "And yet here you are," he said, his smile growing even larger. "It takes a smart man, a *brave* man, to try to change his circumstances even though everybody else says it's impossible."

"Not my circumstances I'm trying to change," Rusty said.

"Very true," Matthew said. "I assume that the charming young man in the car is your son?"

"Yeah. Yeah," Rusty said. "Gimme a minute, would ya?" Rusty circled over to the passenger side door and opened it. Jacob shrank away from him, an action that Rusty was all too familiar with, and Rusty leaned in to speak to him in low, soothing tones. "C'mon out, son. We won't be here for too long, but I want you to talk with this man for a few minutes."

Jacob shook his head. He was clenching the bottom hem of his shirt in both hands, twisting the fabric in knots, and his eyes were wide with something that Rusty didn't recognize, but almost thought was revulsion. And that was very out-of-character for his simple-minded son. Oh sure, distrust was a regular occurrence when Jacob was confronted with people he didn't know, but outright…what? Hatred? Could that possibly be true? No, Rusty was imagining things. He had to be.

"It'll be alright, son," Rusty said, offering a helpful, prodding hand to Jacob. "Just a little bit of time, and then we can go look at cars."

"Don't want to," Jacob said. "Let's go home, Daddy. I want my puppy. And it's almost time for my lunch."

"Jacob, it's not even 9:30," Rusty said. "We've got plenty of time before lunch. Like I said, a half hour, no more, and then we're outta here. What do you say?"

"I said no!" Jacob snapped. He reached for the door handle suddenly, violently wrenching the door shut heedless of the fact that Rusty's arm was resting on top of it. The upper corner of the door sliced through Rusty's flesh. Blood almost immediately welled up, little drops of crimson pattering to the ground, but Rusty barely felt the pain through his shock. Despite the fits, despite the fact that he'd once hurt his mother, Jacob had never before attacked Rusty, even inadvertently.

"Holy shit," Rusty whispered to himself. He turned to face Matthew, who'd at least had the decency to drop the cheesy grin. But he didn't look disturbed, either. In fact, the briefest look of satisfaction crossed his features before they rearranged themselves into a more appropriate expression of sympathy.

"Sorry, man," Rusty said, and was surprised to find himself meaning the words. "I don't think this is gonna happen today. I thought if I sprung it on him, he wouldn't have time to object, but I guess I should have known better. Lord knows it's never worked before."

"I understand completely," Matthew said. "Believe it or not, this isn't the first time I've seen this sort of reaction, and if you want to try again some other time, that's perfectly fine. But…"

"But what?" Rusty said, taking the bait.

"It's just, you're already here. I'm betting it was a chore getting him to come out in the first place, and it probably won't be any easier to get him out here a second time, right?"

"Probably not," Rusty said. "But seriously? Welcome to my fuckin' life. Give it a week or so, and he'll forget all about this. Another week of preparing him for the visit, and you'll see a different kid."

"No doubt. No doubt," Matthew said. "But, before you surrender completely, at least let us give your arm some medical attention. I know we don't look like much," he said, gesturing to the building, "but we've got some top-notch supplies in there."

"I don't know," Rusty said. He lifted his arm over his head, glancing up at the exposed underside. "Looks like the bleeding's almost stopped, and if Jacob is really that uncomfortable here, I don't think I like the idea of leaving him in the car by himself."

"You mind if I talk to him for a second?"

Before Rusty had a chance to disagree, Matthew brushed by him, opening the passenger door and leaning in to speak to Jacob. Then, after few moments of hushed conversation, Matthew offered a hand to

Rusty's recalcitrant son. Before Rusty's disbelieving eyes, Jacob took it and got out of the car.

10. Second thoughts are natural.

"What the hell did you say to him?" Rusty demanded as soon as the pneumatic doors of the building hushed to a close behind the trio.

Jacob walked slightly ahead of the other two men. Unlike others of his age, his eyes didn't waver from path he walked, not that he was missing all that much. The inside of the building was just as non-descript as the outside. Aside from the set of double doors at the other end of the building to which they were heading, the inside was starkly bare, divided into a dozen or so unoccupied cubicles. If Rusty's first thought on seeing the outside of the building was that of an overly large trailer, the inner view had done nothing to change his mind. Except for the doors that their path seemingly led to – there was something ominous about them. They were like the swinging doors that one would see on the way to surgery, and Rusty didn't like the look of them at all.

"You know," Matthew said, apropos of nothing, "you may find this hard to believe, but your son cares for you very much."

"Say what?"

"You asked what I said to him," Matthew elaborated. "And I'm telling you, your son cares for you a great deal. I'm guessing he has trouble expressing that feeling, but all I had to do was tell him that you were hurt and that we were going to fix you up, and he was more than willing to come inside with us."

"Huh," Rusty said. "I gotta admit, I didn't see that one coming."

Matthew chuckled. "You'd be surprised how many times I've heard that since we began this program," he said. "Excuse me for a moment, will you?"

The trio had reached the double doors, and as they drew close, Rusty saw a number pad set in the wall just to the right of the doors with a small lens above the keypad. Matthew bent forward slightly. The pad hummed momentarily, and then beeped, a light to the left of the lens turning green. He keyed in a six number combination, and then stepped back. Rusty heard a deep *chunk*, and the doors swung silently open.

Beyond the doors – their final destination, Rusty guessed – was a seemingly normal looking examination room. There was a bench in the middle of the room with the standard paper tissue covering. Two visitors' chairs were set by the exam table, one on each side. There was a desk off to the side of the exam table with a laptop upon it, an office chair in front of the desk. The expected accoutrement of a doctor's office was visible – blood pressure monitor, thermometer attached to a spiraling black plastic encased wire, the whatever it was called that doctors used to look into ears and noses. All very normal. Very ordinary.

But then, there was the chair.

Rusty supposed that one could call it a chair, at any rate. It reminded him of nothing more than the seat he had been directed to on the few occasions he'd given blood, but with a few added features. Features such as thick padding on the back and armrests. An extendable headrest rising from the top of the chair, also thickly padded. And oh, let's not forget the heavy straps anchored to the chair at five points – two at the feet of the chair (*one for each ankle*, Rusty's mind prompted him), two at the armrests (*again, one for each wrist*, Rusty's mind gleefully supplied), and then a final one attached to the armrest.

To go around the forehead, Rusty thought, but doubtfully. *Maybe around the neck? And does it really matter? Those aren't* straps, *they're* restraints, *and just what the hell have you gotten your son into, anyway?* Speaking of Jacob, Rusty saw to his horror that his boy had wandered over to the chair and looked ready to sit down.

"Don't!" Rusty snapped, and when Jacob turned his dully inquisitive gaze in his father's direction, Rusty continued in a slightly calmer voice, "That's for patients, son. Why don't you sit in one of the chairs by the table instead?"

"Rusty. Rusty," Matthew said, and was that disappointment Rusty heard in the man's voice? "We got him through the door by telling him it was for you, but there's no further need for subterfuge, don't you think?"

"What I think," Rusty spat, uneasy eyes resting on that monstrosity of a chair, "is that me and my kid are out of here."

"Every single time," Matthew muttered, more to himself than the other two people in the room. He looked up at Rusty, and for the first time, Rusty saw not a huckster, not a glad-handling used car salesman, but a fanatic. He stepped in front of the doors that the trio had just come though, reaching into the blazer he wore, and Rusty wasn't too terribly surprised to see his hand re-emerge with a pistol in his grip. He was turned away from Jacob so the man-child couldn't quite see the weapon he was holding, but Rusty saw. Rusty saw all too well.

"Just once, I'd like to do *this*," he motioned toward the chair, "without resorting to *this*," he gave the gun a little wave, "but it never works out that way. But listen, Rusty. I'm not going to hurt your son. I told you; I'm going to help him. Look, your part's done. You got him here. Let us do the rest, yeah?"

"Under the threat of a gun? In what world do you think that's gonna happen?"

"Fine," Matthew sighed. "The gun very rarely works, anyway. It takes a certain sort of person to raise kids like your son, and cowardice is an uncommon trait, indeed." He slipped the pistol back inside his blazer, and stepped to the side, leaving the path to the double doors wide open.

Rusty stared at him for a few brief moments as though to ascertain his sincerity, and then took Jacob by the hand. "Let's go, son," he said.

"But Daddy, what about your arm," Jacob said, and under other circumstances, Rusty would have been touched, but right then, all he wanted to do was leave.

"I'm okay," Rusty said. "Let's just get out of here, and I'll put something on it when we get home."

"We're not gonna look at cars?" Jacob asked, and in spite of the tension, Rusty almost groaned at his son's one-track mind.

"After I get some bandages on my arm," Rusty said.

"Okay," Jacob said. "But that's it, right? We're not going anywhere else?"

"No, son," Rusty said. "Now let's get outta here."

"Rusty," Matthew said, and Rusty paused. Damning himself all the while, but still, he paused. "Are you sure you want to do things this way? We've helped others like your son, and we can help him, too."

"The kind of help that comes with a chair like that, I think we can do without," Rusty said, and pulled his son back through the double doors.

11. BUT IT'S TOO LATE TO CHANGE YOUR MIND.

Four men stood beyond the doors. All four were big and burly, at least six feet tall, with identical buzz cuts, identically clean-shaven faces, and practically identical expressions of bored malevolence.

"Gentlemen, would you mind bringing our friends back inside?" Matthew called out, and the four men split off into two pairs. Two of the men grabbed Rusty firmly but painlessly, one at each arm, while the other two men took Jacob by the hands and led him back into the room.

Matthew swiveled in the office chair once Rusty and Jacob came back into view, and as the two men holding him by the arms led him to one of the visitor's chairs by the exam table, Rusty saw that the pistol was back in his right hand. Not quite pointed in Rusty's direction, but ready to be aimed if things came down to it.

The other two men led Jacob to the chair with the straps. Jacob, who had been uncharacteristically quiescent up to that point, perhaps remembered his father's panic when he had first tried to sit in the chair and went completely berserk. "NO!" he shrieked, and with a strength that made a lie of his normal slothfulness, he windmilled his arms out of the grips of the men who held him. "Don't want to sit in that chair, Daddy! Want to go home! I want my puppy! Where's Maggie? I need to see my puppy!"

A lump rose in Rusty's throat, one born not of sorrow but of fury. Fury at the way things had gone sideways so completely, fury at his own stupidity, but most of all, fury at the way that this glad-handling prick Matthew had taken any semblance of choice away from him. He struggled to get to his feet, but one of the men who had escorted him to the visitor's chair clamped beefy hands down harshly on his shoulders, forcing Rusty to remain seated. The other man went to help the two restrain Jacob, and no matter how hard his son struggled, the three men, all larger than Jacob, forced him in the ominous looking chair, and quickly buckled the heavy straps around his ankles and wrists. The fifth strap, the one attached to the headrest, was left dangling free.

"Let him go!" Rusty demanded, regardless of the helplessness of his situation. "Let him go right now, or I swear to God I'll kill you all!"

Matthew stood, slipping the pistol once more back into his blazer. He walked over to a small refrigerator in the corner of the room, opened it, and took out a syringe. At the sight of the needle, Jacob went still. He'd always had a fear of shots, a fear that froze him quicker than any threat from his parents ever could.

"No," he whimpered, but all the volume was gone from his voice. He turned to Rusty. "Daddy, don't want a shot. Please, don't want a shot, Daddy."

"Look," Rusty said to Matthew, his heart breaking for his son. "Just…don't, man. Let us outta here, and that'll be the end of it. I swear."

Matthew shook his head, a look of pity in his eyes. He walked over to Rusty's imprisoned son, nodding his head at one of the men attending to Jacob. The man to whom he nodded returned the gesture with a nod of his own, gripped Jacob's jaw, and forced his mouth open. One of the other men wound the final strap around Jacob's mouth, securing it to the other side of the headrest. Jacob whimpered against the strap, fearful tears falling from his eyes.

Not only a restraint, but a very effective gag, Rusty realized with horror and once again struggled to get to his feet. The solitary man still guarding Rusty, with no change in expression (not that Rusty would have seen since the man stood behind him), slammed an elbow onto the top of Rusty's head. Dazed, vision blurred from the sudden blow, Rusty could only watch helplessly as Matthew injected the syringe directly into Jacob's neck.

Almost immediately, Jacob's fearful whimpers turned to tortured screams. He heaved against his restraints as though galvanized by a powerful current of electricity, and the cords on his neck stood in stark relief to the paleness of his skin. His fists clenched spasmodically, and his feet drummed a rhythmless beat against the laminated tiles of the floor. Then, after a torturous, eternal minute, he fell still.

"You can let him go now," Matthew said. "The hard part's over."

In response, the man standing behind Rusty let him go, and Rusty surged to his feet. "What did you do? What the fuck did you do?" he demanded, the blow to his head forgotten as he stalked over to Matthew and grabbed him by the lapels of his blazer.

Although the pistol was still in his hand, Matthew made no move to defend himself. He simply tore himself out of Rusty's grasp, stepping over to Jacob and placing two fingers against Jacob's throat. Nodding in apparent satisfaction, he looked over to Rusty. "Helped your boy, just as I promised," he said mildly.

"I don't know what the fuck that was, but it sure as fuck didn't look like *help*," Rusty hissed.

Shrugging, Matthew flipped the pistol in his grip, and offered it to Rusty, butt first. "Five minutes, Rusty," he said. "Give it five minutes, and if things haven't changed dramatically, then you do what you have to do."

Numb with shock and yet shaking with rage, Rusty took the offered pistol. He cocked the hammer, aiming it directly at Matthew's chest. Matthew shrugged again, cocking his head slightly. It seemed to be an unspoken command that the other four men in the room recognized, and they turned as one at the gesture and left. And for four of the five minutes, silence reigned.

Until, at the end of the fourth minute, Jacob's eyes shot open and he took a deep, heaving gasp.

Rusty started toward his son, but Matthew shook his head. "Just wait a bit," he said. "It's almost over, but this last bit can get a little rough."

Jacob seized, tremors running through his body. Runners of drool drained from around the strap holding his mouth open, and once again his feet tapped against the floor tile. Then, he went still again. He blinked once, twice, and then his gaze concentrated on his father's familiar form. His eyes were unusually focused, and smothered words emerged from behind the gag. Rusty moved again toward his son, but hesitated, looking at Matthew for permission.

"Go ahead," Matthew said, sounding as though he'd been through this same scenario many times before. "It's all over."

Rusty walked to his son, gingerly undoing first the gag around Jacob's mouth and then the restraints around his wrists and ankles. Almost absentmindedly, Jacob reached up and wiped the remnants of drool from his mouth, and then turned an inquiring eye to Rusty.

"Dad," he said, and his voice was deeper, somehow. No. Not deeper. More mature. "What are we doing here?"

And with a fatherly instinct, Rusty knew — *he knew* — that somehow, he'd just witnessed a miracle.

12. DEALING WITH THE AFTERMATH OF DOUBT.

"It never gets any easier," Matthew said.

"Say again?" Rusty said, barely paying attention as he watched his son step out of the building into the sunlight. There was purpose in Jacob's stride that he'd never seen before, and he wanted to drink in the sight. They'd take him to doctors, Rusty knew that much, psychologists or psychiatrists or whatever, but there was already no doubt in his mind. Matthew had kept his promise and cured his son. Or made him normal. Or however you wanted to phrase it. He didn't know how; he didn't know how one simple injection could overwrite a lifetime of disability, and he didn't care. It was possible he would in the future, but for now, the only question he had was how he could express his gratitude.

"This whole…process," Matthew elaborated. "It's like it follows a script. First comes the angry denials that we can do what I say. Then comes the – hell, I don't know, the first gasp of hope? Like, can they really do what they say even though everybody says it's impossible? Then they show up, supposedly on a whim. And it's always just one parent. Never two. Then the changing of the mind. Then the threats of violence, both from us and the parent." He chuckled. "And then the moment of truth."

"The miracle," Rusty said.

"It's not a miracle," Matthew protested. "It's the result of literally years of medical research. Hell, pardon my French, the research is still ongoing. You and your boy, you're part of that research, now."

Rusty frowned, those last few words burning through the haze of unreality in which he had found himself. "So, you don't *know* that it works."

Matthew snorted. "Look at your boy," he said, and for the first time, Rusty felt that he was hearing the real man. "I'm sure you'll take him to whatever specialists you feel necessary, but what do you think? What's your gut feeling, right here, right now?"

Rusty shook his head, not willing to put his gut feeling into words. Besides, he thought that Matthew knew what he was thinking regardless. "But then why the gun? The thugs? And goddamn, that chair, man. That chair is hideous."

"The gun is for protection," Matthew said. "Several parents, and not all of them fathers, got a lot more violent than you did. Those *thugs*, as you put it, are fully trained medical professionals. RNs, just in case things go sideways, not that they ever have. And the chair?" Matthew shook his head. "Quick story, before you leave. And on that note, don't forget that we'll be visiting soon to check on Jacob's progress."

"Yeah, I remember," Rusty said. "But the chair?"

"It's simple," Matthew said. "You saw the tremors, right? It looked like he was having an epileptic seizure. Well, with the first patient, we didn't really know what to expect. What I mean is, according to all of our simulations, this was going to work, but we couldn't exactly do animal experimentation. After all, who's ever heard of retarded lab rat?"

That didn't sound exactly right to Rusty, but he merely nodded.

"So anyway, we just had the first boy lay on the exam table while we administered the shot. He shook so hard he fell off the table. He ended up cracking his skull on the floor. There was blood everywhere. Shit — again, forgive my language — everything was almost over before it began. I thought that kid was dead. But he must not have hit his head as hard as I thought, because in five minutes, he was up and walking. More importantly, he was talking. Something to keep in mind, Rusty: as bad as your son may have been, at least he was verbal."

"I know," Rusty said, and then something occurred to him. "So, how many times have you done this?"

"Enough times to know that it works," Matthew said. "Now, why don't you take your boy home. I bet your wife will be thrilled to meet the son she should have always had."

13. The more things change, the more they change.

For the first week after the shot, the changes in Jacob were more subtle than overt. He still spent most of his time in his room, really only coming out to let Maggie into the backyard or to feed her breakfast and dinner. The limited conversations he and Carol had with their boy were still as stilted and one-dimensional as ever, and if Jacob seemed more present, more aware, than he ever had before, Carol didn't comment on it, and Rusty dismissed the thought as a trick of an overly hopeful imagination.

Until.

Until one night, heading into the second week from the shot, Carol made an offhanded remark as they were finishing dinner. As was his habit Jacob had eaten quickly and headed back to his room to listen to the radio, and so it was just Rusty and Carol sitting at the table, Maggie noisily slurping water from the bowl they kept near her kennel.

"You want to hear something funny?" Carol asked after she swallowed the last forkful of spaghetti Rusty had made for dinner.

"What's that," Rusty asked, glancing up from his tablet. His mom and dad had always told him that reading during meals was rudeness personified. Then again, they'd told him a lot of things that he'd since found to be complete bullshit, and he and Carol rarely took meals without their tablets at their sides.

"So, it was Amy's turn to drive us to school and bring us home," Carol said, "but she was running a little behind this afternoon. So I called up Jacob. He answered just like always, but he sounded a little funny, you know?"

"Funny how?"

"Funny like he was blowing into his phone," Carol said. "So I asked him if he was okay, and he said he was fine, just out for a walk. With Maggie!"

It's strange, the things that can short-circuit a person's way of thinking. Rusty froze in the act of mopping the last of the sauce in his bowl with a bit of garlic bread. He was sure his wife had spoken relatively common words in the English language, but the concept behind the words eluded him.

"Close your mouth," Carol said, and Rusty did so with an audible clack. "But yeah, that's how I reacted as well."

"Jacob. Went for a walk. I'm sorry, let me rephrase. Jacob went for a walk around the neighborhood. Something he hasn't done in forever. Not only that, he harnessed his dog, his dog he loves but has never walked before, and took her with him?"

"Yeah," Carol said with a slightly hysterical giggle. "Isn't that something?"

"Did you ask him about it?"

"Ask him what? Ask him why, after three years of self-imposed isolation, he decided to up and change his routine? Well, yes, Rusty, yes I did. And you know what he told me?"

"What?"

"He told me he was bored and wanted to get out of the house for a bit. Told me, in fact, that he'd been feeling restless since you took him out to look at cars a week ago. Those were his exact words. 'Feeling restless'." Carol paused, staring at him intently. "Except, it wasn't looking at cars he said you two did a week ago. He said you guys went somewhere else instead."

Rusty shifted uncomfortably. He recognized that stare, the look in her eyes. He hadn't really thought he would be able to hide the visit he and Jacob had made to Matthew's "clinic". But to finally be confronted with actual, physical proof of what that one shot had done had frozen his useless tongue in his sealed mouth, and the reasonable explanations he'd rehearsed in his thoughts at work and at home fled from him, leaving him a blank canvas of pitiful excuses.

Carol reached across the dining room table and took one of Rusty's hands in her own. "Rusty," she said, her voice level. "What did you do?"

14. The truth will set you free.

So let me see if I've got this right," Carol finally said.

In a way, Rusty was relieved. Carol had sat in silence for nearly ten minutes after his hushed, somewhat guilty explanation, her gaze distant and distracted. She hadn't let go of his hand when he'd told her what he'd done, though her grip had tightened painfully as he'd recollected the four thugs that had entered the room and shoved Jacob into the chair and forcefully strapped him in. And then, when the words had died in his throat, and he waited for her judgement, she'd given him nothing but disconcerting peace that he suspected was the calm before her storm.

In that, Rusty was to be proven absolutely correct.

"You took our son, our autistic, intellectually challenged son, to somewhere you'd never been before. You let him be poked and prodded by a stranger, and then you let this same stranger give our son an injection that you knew nothing about? That could have, in fact, been nothing but poison?"

And yep, here came the storm. Rusty, in his own inimitable way, tried to ward off Carol's anger but failed spectacularly.

"I mean, in all fairness," he said, "I tried to back out, but Matthew had a gun. He had those guys with him, too. And they were bigger than me."

"Really," Carol drawled. "That's the best you can do?" Her voice rose into a mocking falsetto. "*They were bigger than me, Carol. What else was I supposed to do?*"

"Well, yeah," Rusty said. "What else *was* I supposed to do?"

"You were supposed to be smart enough not to bring our son into that sort of situation in the first place!" Carol snapped, slamming her fist down onto the table.

Rusty flinched. Had he thought Carol was merely angry at him? Maybe, but as the impact of her fist rattled the dishes that they'd pushed off to the side of the kitchen table as he'd told her what he'd done, he realized that anger was too mild a word. No, she was furious with him.

"What the *fuck* were you thinking? For God's sake, you know that what's wrong with Jacob can't be cured with a simple vaccination. Hell, autism can't be cured at all, you know that! Couple that with his intellectual disabilities, and the result is a man-child that'll be living with us for the rest of his life! Nothing's going to change that. Nothing!"

"So you're saying that you haven't seen some differences in him?" Rusty challenged. "Hell, this whole conversation started because you noticed something off about him."

"Granted," Carol said. "But just because he took his dog for a walk, that doesn't mean this so-called cure worked. It's just not possible."

Rusty shrugged. "I know that," he said. "But what if it *is* possible? What if, no matter how it happened, Matthew gave us some hope when we've never had it before?"

"And that's the other goddamn thing," Carol snarled, barreling through his weak protestations as though he hadn't spoken them. "You never met this fucker before. You don't know who he is, you don't know who he works for, you don't know anybody else they've 'treated', but you were willing to let them touch our son? Were you fucking crazy, or just fucking stupid?"

Rusty's hackles rose, and he felt his temper begin to rise as well. In the entire length of their marriage, Carol had never before spoken to him with such contempt. It was as though the decades' worth of trust and love they'd built up between them had never existed.

"Number one, don't talk to me like I'm one of your fucking students," Rusty said, raising his index finger in the air. Up came finger number two as he said, "Second, I'm not crazy and I'm not stupid. I was depressed. Not blue, not down in the dumps, but depressed. It would have been Katie's eighteenth, and maybe I was feeling a little desperate, but that's hardly the same thing as being stupid. And three, how was this any different than you thinking, when Jacob was younger, that if you put him on *this* diet or tried *that* exercise, he'd…how did you put it? Snap out of it?"

"Oh, that is just complete bullshit!" Carol cried. "*Number one,*" she sneered, "Jacob was two. The doctors couldn't even get their diagnoses straight. If you can't see the difference between trying a few home remedies and the incredibly reckless, incredibly dangerous thing you did, then maybe you really are…"

Carol's voice trailed off into nothingness, her eyes widening and her lower lip quivering, shock plainly written on her face. Rusty, as his accustomed seat at the kitchen table faced away from the kitchen doorway, turned to see what had so surprised her, and found himself struck speechless at the sight that greeted him.

Jacob stood at the kitchen entrance. Maggie, in her walking harness, was tippy tapping at his feet, her little nails scratching on the linoleum. She wagged her tail wildly, her leash trailing from Jacob's right hand. He was wearing a Simpsons t-shirt; a shirt Rusty had bought him once upon a time in a vain attempt to get him to wear something other than his customary polo shirts. He was also in jeans and sneakers, and it was obvious he was planning on…going out, maybe? To take Maggie for a walk?

"Hey Dad," Jacob said. "I thought that me and Maggie could come with you downtown when you go walking. But I gotta know – just what the hell are you and Mom fighting about?"

It was the most intelligent question he had ever put to his mother and father, and Carol, after digesting the casual way in which he asked it, promptly burst into tears.

15. Lulling you into a sense of security doesn't count if it's real security.

Downtown Rockford at dusk. The Sinnissippi bike path. It was a trail that Rusty had walked for years, but tonight, it felt new somehow. Part of it was the fact that for the first time, Carol and Jacob were walking with him. But that wasn't all of it. Not in the slightest.

"Look at him," Carol said for the thousandth time that evening. Her grip on Rusty's hand tightened as she pulled him closer to her. Almost subconsciously, Rusty wrapped an arm around her waist. He staggered a bit as he turned his head to press his lips against her hair. They both stumbled, giggling and punch drunk, before righting themselves and continuing onward.

"I appreciate the thought," Carol said. "But I don't think either of us are coordinated enough for that, Rusty."

"Probably not," Rusty agreed.

"Still, just look at him, Rusty!" Carol insisted. "God almighty, look at him!"

"I am, hon. I am."

And Rusty was, indeed, watching his son very closely. At first glance (aside from the fact that the boy was out with them in the first place) Jacob wasn't behaving any differently than any other boy – man – his age. He held Maggie's leash loosely in his hand, stopping every so often to let the pup smell the scents only a dog could detect. But watch closer, and Rusty could tell that this was a different Jacob than the one that he and Carol had raised for just over two decades. His stride was more…aware…than it had ever been before. As he passed others on the path, he acknowledged them with a wave of a hand or a jaunty tip of his head. Hell, several times, Rusty saw his son turn his head to watch as a particularly attractive girl passed him by, and in turn, one or two those girls gave him an appreciative glance in return. He was, after all, a good-looking boy just starting the prime of his life.

And wasn't that an interesting thought, unthinkable just weeks earlier? A normal Jacob could have a normal life, and might that not include a family of his own? But then again, that was putting the cart before the horse. They needed, he and Carol, to think about Jacob's whole future. And yes, a family was a part of that, if Jacob wanted, but they needed to make certain that he could be self -sufficient. He'd gone to school, true, and had actually graduated with decent grades, but that had been in the limited scope of the special education classes he'd attended. How, exactly, would that translate into the real world? Hell, was his diploma a real thing, or just a formality? Would any college accept –

Carol smacked the back of his head lightly, startling Rusty out of his thoughts.

"What the hell was that for!" Rusty demanded.

"You're thinking too hard," Carol said. "I can tell, and you need to stop."

"But Carol," Rusty said, "we've got so many decisions to make. I mean, this is great, it really is, but what happens now?"

"What happens now, Rusty Jenkins, is we wait. We watch."

"But Carol!"

"No, Rusty," Carol said. Her tone was that of a loving wife who had watched her husband jump impulsively into certain decisions over the years but who had to pull him back every once in a while before he did something catastrophically short-sighted. "Listen to me. I don't know why you decided to go through with this 'treatment', but that doesn't matter now. We don't know how long this is going to last. So we wait, and we watch. And if it seems permanent, then we very cautiously help – *help*, Rusty – Jacob plan for his future."

Rusty started to protest once more but bit his tongue. There was something in what Carol had said that he hadn't considered. If Jacob was cured, as impossible as it seemed, then it wasn't their job to plan out his life for him anymore. God, if he was normal, then the mistakes and triumphs of life would be Jacob's alone to earn. And suddenly, Rusty was almost more frightened for his son then he had been when he'd once contemplated the boy's future when he and Carol were gone. They'd thought he'd have to rely on the generosity of family, or failing that, a state home for disadvantaged adults. Why those options were suddenly less terrifying than Jacob deciding his own future was a question that Rusty couldn't answer.

Rusty was once again shaken from his thoughts as a man approached Jacob on the walking trail. Even though Jacob was about twenty feet in front of them, Rusty saw his son tense on the man's approach, shortening Maggie's leash and then gathering the Basenji in his arms. Rusty shared a concerned glance with Carol and hurried to catch up to their son.

But they needn't have worried, it seemed. The man who had come up to Jacob was none other than Matthew, the person who had set everything in motion. Though, Rusty reflected, he could certainly understand why Jacob had been wary. The last time the two had met things hadn't gone well at all.

Matthew smiled as Rusty and Carol approached them, and just as he had been when he'd first encountered the man, Rusty detected a bit of the huckster in the man's grin, a thought he chided himself for immediately. That was unfair; the man had helped, even if that help had come at the barrel of a gun.

"Rusty," Matthew said, holding his hand out. Rusty shook it.

"Matthew," Rusty said. "You spying on us?" He meant it as a joke, but the smile on his face faded when Matthew nodded.

"Little bit," Matthew said. "I told you we'd be seeing you soon." He shook his head. "Observation. That's the key. Got to make sure things stick."

"So you don't know if this is permanent or not?" Carol said. "What the hell gives you the right to play God if you don't know that you can really deliver?"

Matthew blinked as though surprised at the question. He shot a look at Rusty, frowning a slightly perplexed frown.

"You…didn't really tell her a whole lot, did you," Matthew said. It wasn't a question.

Rusty shook his head with an embarrassed blush. "She didn't find out anything about the trip until today," he admitted.

"Wow," Matthew said, a bit of admiration in his tone. "You know, I'm not married, but I imagine that if I'd been making this kind of decision that I'd want to consult my significant other. Maybe I've got the wrong idea about what marriage is supposed to be."

"You don't, and Rusty should have talked to me," Carol said. "But what's done is done. So, why don't you fill in the gaps that Rusty left out. In detail. Starting with, 'experimental'? What exactly does that mean?"

16. THE EXAM WITH NO WRONG ANSWERS.

Matthew, claiming confidentiality, asked to go somewhere a bit more private, but Carol was reluctant to let a man she didn't know into her home. Therefore, the four (and one puppy) slipped into the greenhouse considered to be the centerpiece of Sinnissippi Gardens. Given the time of year, most of the plants were dead, and the place was practically deserted. A scant few visitors wandered in and out in the half hour that the group discussed things, but for the most part they had the place to themselves.

"Alright, spill," Carol demanded of Matthew as soon as they were relatively alone, asking the questions that Rusty knew he should have asked before succumbing to temptation. "What exactly did you do to my son? How long do we have before he goes back to the way he was? Or is this permanent?"

Matthew shook his head, and instead of addressing Carol's questions turned his attention to Jacob. "Hello, Jacob," he said. "My name's Matthew. Do you remember me?"

Jacob, who had let Maggie out of his arms to frolic among the dead greenery, nodded slowly. "Yeah," he said. "Vaguely. Dad took me out to see you a few weeks ago."

"That's right," Matthew said. He slipped a hand into his windbreaker. Rusty tensed, remembering the pistol the man had pulled the last time he and Jacob had seen him, but Matthew merely withdrew a palm-sized notepad and a pen. "And do you know why your dad took you to see us?"

"Not really," Jacob said. "I mean, I think it's because I've been sick for a long time, and you thought you could help make me better, but I'm not sure."

Matthew chuckled as Carol and Rusty marveled at the sheer coherence of their son's answer. It was like listening to an entirely different boy than the one they'd lived with for almost twenty-one years.

"That's exactly right," Matthew said, scribbling a few notes onto his pad. "And what do you think? Have you been feeling better?"

"I…think so," Jacob said. "It's kind of hard to explain."

"I'm sure it is," Matthew said. "But you think you can try?"

Jacob shrugged. He reeled Maggie in close to him, picking her up as he had when he'd first encountered Matthew on the bike path. She nestled in his arms, letting out an adorable little whine as he began to stroke her head.

"I know for the longest time, I couldn't think real clear," Jacob said, and Rusty drew in a breath, understanding that Jacob wasn't struggling with language as he would have in the past, but with the concept he was trying to articulate. At his side, Carol let out a sharp exhale of her own, seeming to conclude the same thing her husband had.

"Things are better now," Jacob continued. "I feel like I can think things through, and that's not something I could do before."

"Mm-hmm," Matthew muttered, continuing to write in his notepad.

"It's like, my brain's been in cotton for as long as I can remember," Jacob said at last. "But that shot you gave me…I don't know, set the cotton on fire? Something like that, I guess. I don't feel like I'm punching through a pillow every time I want to talk to Mom and Dad."

Matthew scribbled down one last note and snapped the pad shut, slipping it back into his windbreaker. When he looked back up, his smile was the most genuine that Rusty had ever seen in his short acquaintance with the man.

"That's great, Jacob," Matthew said. "Everything I wanted to hear, and everything I thought I would hear." He looked down at the puppy in Jacob's arms, and if anything, his smile grew even wider. "You really love that cutie, huh?"

"She's my best friend," Jacob said simply, and Rusty swallowed back the sudden lump that materialized in his throat. He and Carol had always hoped that getting Maggie would help their son, but to hear Jacob acknowledge the fulfillment of that wish was almost more than he could bear.

"Well, she's been a good girl while I've talked to you, but she looks a little restless," Matthew said. "You want to let her burn off a little steam while I talk to your mom and dad?"

"In other words, get lost so you can talk to my parents?" Jacob suggested. "You can just say that, you know. I'm not stupid." He paused, arching his eyebrows so high they seemed to disappear into his hairline. "Huh," Jacob said. "I'm…not…stupid. That's…different."

A shock of laughter that was almost a sob escaped from Carol's lips. She reached out to Jacob, gently touching his arm. "We never – Jacob, you were never stupid," she said.

Jacob shrugged, the gesture so heartbreakingly normal that the lump in Rusty's throat grew twice its size. "It's okay, Mom," he said. "I know what I was. But I think I'm getting better."

And leaving his parents wide-eyed at the blunt appraisal, he let Maggie out of his arms and walked out of the greenhouse, leaving his parents alone with Matthew.

17. CAUTIOUS HOPE AND EVASIVE ANSWERS.

"How long do we have?" Carol asked after Jacob left. The hostility was gone from her tone. All that was left was a sense of helpless wonder – wonder at the miracle that Matthew had facilitated, but helplessness in the face of her suspicion that the miracle would only be temporary.

"As I explained to Rusty when I first approached him, and as I said to you both when I found you today, we don't know, not exactly. The treatment is still experimental." Matthew paused, and lowered his voice in what he might have thought was a comforting tone, but Carol seemed top regard as somewhat sinister. "I'll tell you this, though. We've treated over two dozen patients just like Jacob, going back about two years, and not one has relapsed. Not one."

"But you don't know," Carol insisted. "It might not be permanent."

Matthew shook his head. "Nothing's guaranteed, Carol. Not when it comes to breaking new medical ground. That's why we monitor things. And that's why we touch base on a regular basis but don't make traditional appointments. It's a spur of the moment thing. No preparation. I know it's different than the way other medical professionals do things, but we want unbiased, untainted observations. The way we figure it is, once the parents – not just you two, but the parents of the other children we've treated – have seen the first signs, you might start seeing improvements that don't actually exist."

"That's a little unorthodox," Carol said. "I can't speak for any of the other parents, but I know we wouldn't lie."

"Like I said, we're not worried about lies," Matthew said. "More about false signs. You'll find that that's why when we come to visit, we don't really talk to you at all until we've talked to Jacob."

Rusty had been hanging back, letting Carol take the lead in the conversation. He figured that he owed her that much since he'd basically gone behind her back to get Jacob to the initial visit to Matthew's nondescript "clinic". But something about the man's explanation had been tickling at his mind; had, in fact, been bothering him since he'd first met the man.

"You keep saying 'we'," Rusty said at last. "But aside from your bully-boys when I took Jacob to see you, I've only ever seen you."

"That's true," Matthew agreed readily enough. "That's how we do things. The person who makes first contact stays on as the…oh, let's say family handler…if and when the treatment is complete."

" 'Handler'," Carol repeated. "That doesn't exactly make you sound like you're on the up and up."

Matthew chuckled. "Well, we're not FDA approved," he snorted. "Let's face it, we're facilitating miracles, here. Again, as I told Rusty, we've skipped directly to human trials. That's sort of frowned upon in the scientific community. I've got no doubt that we'll be vindicated in the end, but until that blessed time comes, it's best if there's some sort of basic anonymity. Like, for instance, if you two decided to sic the authorities on me, then I'm the only one truly at risk. One phone call is all it would take, and our entire clinic would be shut down in a day, moved elsewhere. We're very mobile."

"But who are you?" Rusty asked again. He wouldn't have gone so far as to say that he was desperate for the answer, but he was more than slightly curious. Despite the secrecy, despite the odd way in which things had begun, the treatment had worked, and Rusty wanted to know to whom he should direct his gratitude, if nothing else.

"Now we come to the sticking point," Matthew said. "Because I can't tell you a whole lot about us. What I can tell you is this. Our group is composed of dozens of highly intelligent people – doctors, surgeons, research scientists – who came together with the idea that we could change the world. We've had the most success in treating people like your son – younger men and women with mental deficiencies. But once we've perfected our treatment, we're looking at branching out. We firmly believe that mankind was meant for more than the things that we've already achieved, and we're trying to help things along as best we can."

"Those are some lofty goals," Rusty said, only half-kidding. He was suddenly exhausted, as much from his desperate explanations (or excuses) to Carol as from Matthew's half-answers and evasions.

"Lofty goals indeed," Matthew said. "But can you honestly look at Jacob and say that we're not achieving them?"

18. Charting a new course.

The Jenkins family enjoyed six months of a new normal after their meeting with Matthew at Sinnissippi Gardens. It was remarkable just how quickly Rusty and Carol got used to the improved version of their son.

The three began to tentatively plan out Jacob's future. Perhaps unsurprisingly, Jacob decided that he didn't want to pursue the path to higher learning. No, for him, college seemed like a waste of time. "We all know," he said at one point during a particularly intense conversation, "that my diploma isn't worth the paper it's printed on. That was for a different kid." When Rusty tried to argue that college would open up all sorts of doors for Jacob that a paltry high school diploma couldn't compete with, Jacob shut him down with a simple rebuttal.

"You've done pretty well for yourself with no college education," Jacob said before storming off to his room, ending the debate. And Rusty had to admit, he couldn't argue with that.

Instead, Rusty used his limited influence to nab Jacob a job at the same factory in which he was employed. And he had to admit, he felt a distinct jolt of pride on that first day, when he and Jacob left the house together to go to work. It was a secret little fantasy he had nurtured in his heart for the longest time, and to have it realized choked him up just the tiniest bit. And though she moaned that Jacob was wasting his second chance, even Carol had to admit that the sight of father and son leaving for work together was something special.

Very few of Jacob's personal habits changed. He made a few work friends and went out with them every once in a while, and he continued to take Maggie for her nightly walks, but for the most part, he stayed a homebody…right up until he met a girl at work.

Her name was Erica, and she was the niece or daughter or friend of a friend of one of the factory bigwigs, the kind of bigwig who might show up on the floor of the plant once every few months to complain about how things were running before vanishing back into his office to count the money his badly run factory was making him. Erica was his secretary/ aide, and Rusty had noticed her a few times previous before dismissing her as unimportant. But Jacob…

He saw her for the first time about a month after starting at the factory and was instantly smitten, though he tried to hide it under a poor facsimile of aloofness. Rusty wasn't sure why he bothered. Because of his former condition, he had no practice in hiding his emotions. He needn't have worried, in any case. Erica, upon spotting Jacob on the floor, was just as smitten and walked out on the plant floor alone the very next day.

Rusty was a fixture at the factory, the longest tenured associate by almost a decade. As Erica told him later, she reasoned that someone who had worked at the factory for as long as Rusty had would know just about everybody. If she'd known that Jacob was his son, she'd told Rusty, blushing in embarrassment, she wouldn't have asked for an introduction to the newest hunk on the floor. But in all reality, Rusty hadn't minded her brazen request. He'd found it charming.

Soon enough, Erica became a regular fixture at the Jenkin's home. She took dinner with them almost every night and afterwards walked the time away with Jacob and Maggie (who, as it turned out, was a very patient puppy. She endured this intrusion into her time with her buddy with an aplomb that was almost human). And if, after they'd walked Maggie, Erica and Jacob spent most of their time in Jacob's room, well, Rusty and Carol were willing to give them a few liberties.

In all the ways that mattered, it was a fantasy come true for Rusty and Carol. A few of the particulars weren't what they'd imagined, but all in all, things were good. Happy, even. And every time Matthew came by for an unannounced visit with Jacob, he merely affirmed what they knew in their hearts. This new Jacob was here to stay.

In short, they grew complacent. Rusty, although he never would have admitted it, had been blinded by hope from the very first. Carol, despite the hostility with which she had first met Matthew, had allowed her defenses to fall without even realizing it.

But to be fair, when things went wrong, they went wrong so quickly that nothing could have stopped them.

19. THE COURSE DERAILS.

The pattering of little puppy feet was the harbinger of a welcome change in the Jenkins' home. It was only fitting, then, that the pattering of little puppy feet was the harbinger of the end.

Six months to the day of Jacob's one and only treatment, Rusty and Carol were sitting in the living room watching the nightly news. Jacob and Erica were in his room. When Maggie came rushing down the hallway, whimpering a high-pitched Basenji whine that she rarely unleashed before leaping into Rusty's lap and burrowing under the blanket he was using to fight off the chill of the late winter air, Rusty was only momentarily distracted from the television.

"Hey Jacob," he absentmindedly called out while briefly stroking the top of Maggie's head. "I think your puppy needs to go out."

"Eh, leave the kids alone," Carol said. "It won't kill you to let Maggie out yourself."

"It might," Rusty grumbled. "It's cold out there, and I'm comfortable right where I am."

"Oh, don't be such a baby," Carol teased. "The way she is, she'll only be out back for a few minutes. Little princesses don't like being out in the cold any more than big strong adults."

"Fine. Fine," Rusty said. He pushed the blanket off his lap and made to stand, expecting Maggie to jump off his chair and make her way to the back door. Instead, Maggie stayed huddled at his side. It was only then that Rusty noticed that she hadn't ceased her whining. She was, in fact, trembling so intensely it seemed her whole body might just shake apart.

"Maggie? You okay, girl?" Rusty asked. It might have seemed strange to outsiders the way he talked to her, but he'd always treated her as more human than animal. And sometimes, though he would have denied thinking so to his dying day, he thought she understood everything he said. "You not feeling good?" he continued, and then glanced down at her.

He recoiled at the sight that greeted him. Maggie's short fur was matted and covered in red, as though someone had dyed a tubful of water crimson and then soaked her in the resulting combination. There was a distinct, copperish odor coming from the little dog. And most disturbing of all, a ragged chunk of flesh had been torn from her side, a chunk big enough to expose the muscle beneath her skin.

"Jesus Christ!" Rusty exclaimed, drawing Carol's attention from the television and over to him. When she saw what had so shocked Rusty, she was out of her own chair in a flash.

"What the hell happened?" Carol said.

"Hell if I know," Rusty said. He gathered Maggie in his arms, wincing as her whining intensified at the sudden movement. "Jacob!" he called out even as he started toward his son's room. "What on earth happened to your dog!"

There was no answer from Jacob. Only, right at the edge of Rusty's hearing, a low-pitched growl that sounded more animal than human.

"I'm calling the vet ER," Carol said, grabbing her cell phone from her end table. "Get your son out here, and let's get Maggie to the vet before something worse happens."

Rusty waved her comment away even as she spoke. Of course they'd get Maggie to the vet right away. That went without saying. But of more concern was the fact that Jacob hadn't rushed out of room with her. There was no way, even before he'd been "cured", that Jacob would have ignored how badly his best buddy was hurt. And the silence from his room was…disconcerting.

As if in answer to his last thought, a sudden, savage thump vibrated the wall Jacob's bedroom shared with the living room, followed closely by a glass-shatteringly high-pitched scream. Without hesitation, Rusty handed Maggie to Carol. She fumbled the phone out of her suddenly blood slicked grasp, but didn't have the time to utter a protest before she was looking at Rusty's back as he dashed to Jacob's room.

Jacob's door was open. That was good, well within the bounds of even Rusty's relatively loose sense of decorum. But everything else that Rusty's gaze fell upon when reaching Jacob's room was decidedly wrong.

Erica was sprawled face up on Jacob's twin-sized mattress, her already glazing eyes wide with shock. Jacob straddled her body, one knee on either side of her chest, and as Rusty watched in horror, Jacob dipped his head down to her neck and tore a large chunk of flesh from her throat. He chewed, swallowing convulsively, and then dipped his head to her throat again, tearing out another chunk of flesh. He growled deeply as he ate; his fingers clenched into claws that dug deep furrows into Erica's sides, and as nausea threatened to overwhelm him, Rusty realized that Jacob was tearing into her body as though she were a savory roast.

Rusty didn't pause for thought. Thought would come later. He rushed into Jacob's room, grabbing his son by the shoulders and throwing him off Erica's body. Jacob hit the bedroom floor with a sickening thud, but almost immediately scrabbled back to his feet. Shoving Rusty roughly to the side, he leapt back onto Erica's body, not going for the throat this time but settling for her exposed belly. He nuzzled against her in an absurd parody of affection, broken only by the sickening sound of his teeth grinding together as he ripped a chunk of meat from her.

"Jacob, stop!" Rusty yelled, and pulled Jacob off Erica again.

The boy that turned toward Rusty as he rose unsteadily to his feet for a second time may have worn his son's face but could not have been Jacob. His eyes were feral and bloodshot. The snarl he wore on his gore-stained lips was an expression that Rusty had never seen before on Jacob's face, no matter how deep into one of his fits he might have been.

With a guttural roar, Jacob rushed at Rusty. Acting only on instinct, Rusty side stepped to the right. As Jacob lunged past him, but before he could turn around, Rusty clenched Jacob in a bearhug. Immediately Jacob began to struggle loose from his father's grip, wildly whipsawing his head in an attempt to slam his skull into Rusty even as he dug his fingernails into Rusty's arms, pulling this way and that to get Rusty to let him go. He growled and snorted, drool running from his bloodstained lips, more a rabid animal than a man.

"Jacob, stop!" Rusty pleaded once again. "Stop, for God's sake. Look at what you've done!"

Rusty wasn't expecting a verbal response, not the way that Jacob was acting, but what passed his son's lips froze him to the core.

"HUNGRY!" Jacob screamed. "PUPPY! ERICA! MOMMY! DADDY! FOOD!"

"jesus christ," Rusty whimpered even as Jacob continued to squirm violently in his grasp. Those words, the way Jacob had said them. It was as though the last six months had only been a pleasant dream. The old Jacob was back, a boy driven by a two-year old's understanding of the world in the body of a grown man, a grown man whose frame had now been tempered by the physicality of factory work. Whereas Rusty, while also a factory man, was almost fifty years old, with the body that resulted from thirty-plus years of heavy labor and thirty-plus years of drinking. In the end, the outcome would have been predictable, save for divine intervention.

Except…

"Rusty, let him go!" a voice called out. Instinctively, Rusty loosened his grip. Howling madly, Jacob leapt back toward Erica's corpse. Simultaneously, Rusty heard something that sounded like a padded fist striking a heavy punching bag, and Jacob dropped bonelessly to the floor.

Rusty stood still for a moment, his body paradoxically trembling from the strain of trying to subdue his feral son. His heart thudded wildly in his chest, and for the briefest moment of time, his world greyed. With effort, he calmed himself, blinking away the spots in his vision and letting his heart resume a somewhat normal rhythm. By the time he turned to Jacob's bedroom door to face his somewhat unsurprising savior, he was almost under control.

A control that shattered when he saw a very familiar pistol in Matthew's right hand. A small plume of smoke rose from the silencer attached to the barrel of the gun, the acrid smell of gunpowder filling Jacob's bedroom. Just behind Matthew stood two men in pseudo military garb. Carol was slung over one of the men's shoulders, her arms bound behind her back. There was a bloody gash on her forehead, and her eyes were closed.

Matthew followed Rusty's gaze and shook his head ruefully. "We didn't kill her," Matthew said. "But when we came in, Carol tried to stop us. We couldn't have that. So we had to subdue her."

"Before you killed my boy," Rusty said. The accusation was surprisingly devoid of anger. Given what Jacob had done to Erica, what he'd done to poor little Maggie…

But Matthew shook his head. "Oh, it's not quite that simple, I'm afraid." He sighed heavily, and then raised the pistol, pointing it at Rusty. "Last time, I gave you a choice. This time, unfortunately, I don't have that luxury. You need to come with us."

20. THE PRICE OF PROGRESS.

Once more, Rusty Jenkins found himself on Airport Road only this time he wasn't driving, and the man who was, bypassed the nondescript building that served as the clinic where Rusty had taken Jacob once upon a time in favor of the derelict factory that had housed Rusty's first grown up job.

Although, Rusty mused disjointedly as the driver pulled up to the large overhead door that had once served as a loading dock, *maybe not as abandoned as I thought.*

The driver pressed a button on a small black box hanging on the sun visor of the car, and the overhead door trundled open almost soundlessly. The nameless man drove through the door, and the overhead door shut behind them, leaving the car's occupants in temporary darkness. Listlessly, Rusty considered the notion of escape before dismissing it out of hand. Given the neat, almost bloodless hole in the middle of his son's forehead, the result of the single gunshot Matthew had fired, what did escape matter? Either way, Jacob was dead and Carol would most likely never forgive him. Not that he would ever deserve forgiveness. But he might finally, finally, get some answers.

In the inky darkness of the abandoned factory, Rusty heard the car's back door open, and Matthew, who had been sitting beside him, got out. His footsteps trailed off into the distance, and then, seconds later, the factory was flooded with light. Before Rusty could take in his surroundings, the door on his side opened, and someone roughly pulled him out of the car.

"This is where the real work is done." Matthew's voice echoed in the cavernous factory, and Rusty blinked his eyes at the scene the sudden light revealed.

Nearly two dozen solidly built cages lined the factory floor. A solitary figure was inside nearly each cage, all naked. While some (prisoners? Patients?) paced their cells, growling savagely, reaching out from between heavy metal bars to futilely clutch at the various lab coat clad men and women bustling between the cages who dodged their hungry grips with an ease born from familiarity, still others were strapped to the bunks that were the only furnishings of the cells. At the perimeter of the rows of cages several armed men, dressed in the same pseudo military fatigues as the men who had accompanied Matthew, prowled relentlessly.

Behind him, Rusty heard someone open the trunk of the car, and then the sound of vinyl rustling as Jacob's body was removed. He supposed he should have demanded to know what they were going to do with his boy, but again, what did it matter? Jacob would be dead regardless.

But then, why was the fatigue garbed man taking the body bag containing Jacob's remains to one of the only empty cages?

At a signal that Rusty couldn't see, one of the labcoats rushed over to the empty cage and opened the door. The man carrying Jacob's remains practically threw his son inside the cage, and the labcoat slammed the door closed. Just in time, as it happened, for almost as soon as the body bag touched the floor, it began to pulsate, the heavy vinyl groaning in protest.

"What?" Rusty whimpered.

"Yeah, it's hard to watch, even after all this time," Matthew said, materializing at Rusty's side as though by magic. "But on the plus side, this is the quickest I've ever seen it happen. I thought we had another hour or so."

"Seen what happen?" Rusty demanded weakly.

Jacob tore out of the body bag, shredding through the thick vinyl as though it were nothing more than wet tissue paper. His glazed eyes were wild but unfocussed, and the throaty roar he delivered as he threw himself at the bars composing his cage was inhuman. Again and again he attacked the solid metal bars, slamming his body against his prison with reckless abandon.

"I'd love to say he'll calm down," Matthew said, wrapping an arm around Rusty's shoulders almost companionly, "but the truth is, he'll be like that until we strap him down and run our first series of tests. That usually takes something out of them, but not for very long. They're surprisingly resilient. You know. For walking corpses."

"What…the hell…did you do to my son?" Rusty said, his voice hitching. He wasn't weeping yet, the horror just beginning to penetrate the shroud he'd been in since watching Jacob try to devour Erica, but the tears were close, so close, to the surface.

Matthew cocked his head to the side, and then nodded. "I suppose you deserve to know. C'mon. I've got something to show you."

21. The end of the lie.

Matthew led Rusty to an area of the factory that had once served as the office of the factory manager. The door leading to the office, once a cheap pressboard thing that barely deserved the name, had been replaced with something a bit more durable, a heavy lock just above the door handle. Matthew fished inside the front pocket of his black slacks for a moment before withdrawing a gleaming silver key.

"The thing always hides in my pocket," Matthew said ruefully as he slid the key into the lock. "I should get a key ring, but it's the only key I carry when I'm working, so…" Matthew shrugged, trailing off. He opened the door to the former office, and prodded Rusty inside.

The room was well lit and empty except for the *thing* lying in the middle of the room. It might have been human, once, but now was a completely desiccated shell to which, perversely, several IV bags had been attached. Slowly, impossibly, each bag filled with a rusty liquid. Four thick chains were bolted directly to each of the figure's hands and feet and staked to the floor.

"We found him, oh, about twenty years ago," Matthew said. "His name was," Matthew paused, and then shook his head, "you know, I don't remember. Doesn't matter, I suppose. Point is, his ex-wife reported him missing after he missed an alimony check. The police did a wellness check on him. He was in his easy chair. They figure he'd been dead for at least a week, given the state of decomposition he was in."

The figure on the floor let out a shuddering gasp and opened its eyes. They were black, pupilless, malevolent voids. Slowly, as though it were under water, the figure began to tremble, and Rusty realized that it was trying to rise.

"Ouch," Matthew said. "He only gets like that when we've drained him dry. He gets feisty."

"That?" Rusty said, pointing at the IV bags, the answer coming to him in a leap of sickening logic. "That's what you put in my son? That's what you thought would cure him?"

"Yep," Matthew said. "It makes sense, if you think about it. Somehow, this fellow reanimated himself. Scared the hell out of the coroner when he got off the table. Killed a couple of people, too, but progress is rarely painless. When we got ahold of him, someone put forth the notion that his blood might be able to resurrect dead and corrupted synapses as well."

"In what fucking world does that make any sort of sense at all?"

"But it worked, didn't it?"

"For a while, before Jacob went crazy and ate his girlfriend!" Rusty spat.

"Yeah. That's how it goes. The patients get better for a while, but eventually…well, you saw what happened to Jacob. That's what happened with all the rest, as well. But we'll figure it out. It'll just take some time."

"And you think I'll keep quiet? After what you did to Jacob? After what you turned him into?"

Matthew chuckled. Before Rusty could react, Matthew pulled the pistol from his sport coat and pulled the trigger. Rusty's midsection exploded in a universe of pain, and he crumpled to the floor. Dispassionately, Matthew grabbed ahold of Rusty's wrists and dragged him closer to the figure bolted to the floor. The figure turned its decaying head in Rusty's direction, mouth yawning wide. A bit of drool trailed from its mouth, pooling on the floor, hissing as though it were acid.

"You'll keep quiet," Matthew said as he walked to the door. "Well, you won't be talking, at any rate. But don't worry. I'll be sure to put you in a cage right next to Jacob. Oh, and before you ask? I'll make sure that Carol keeps you two well fed."

THE FELLOWSHIP OF ETERNAL RESURRECTION

R. C. MULHARE

Dedicated to the memory of David Lynch
1946-2025
Rest in Peculiarity. Because of your Dale Cooper, my Blake and Dante exist.

A late September Sunday morning Mass, and I'd just risen from the pew my family occupied to assist in taking up the collection when a zombie shuffled and moaned out of the vestibule of St. Mary Magdalen in Houlton, Massachusetts. Not a young, otherwise healthy person who'd had a rough night partying, or some weird public art performance, but an elderly woman in a flannel nightgown, who looked like she'd crawled off her deathbed or a mortician's slab.

Kathleen, my wife, looked past our three teenagers at the intruder. Other people in the congregation peered about, whispering among themselves. Brigid, our youngest, boggled at the intruder, taking her phone from her tote bag.

Special Agent Blake Matherton, my partner sitting in the pew behind ours, glared over his shoulder and over the metal rims of his eyeglasses. "My first time back at Mass in ten years and work shows up."

A second figure, a slightly middle-aged white man in a navy polo over khakis, as middle-class as you can imagine, had risen up (pun intended) behind the shuffler, crying out: "People of St. Mary Magdalen! The fullness of eternal life, the true resurrection stands before you! God has revealed His power through science!"

One old woman in a pew at the back stood, snapping back, "Jesus gives us eternal life through the Eucharist!" A middle-aged woman, likely her daughter, pulled her back down attempting to shush her, wide-eyed as she stared at the figures in the aisle.

The other three ushers looked at me as if awaiting orders. Bianca, our oldest, took her phone from her purse, looking at me. I nodded to her and went to assist the ushers, hearing Bianca tapping her phone. Blake followed me, his eye on the shambler and her companion.

I approached the man in blue. "Sir, you're going to need to sit down quietly. Is your friend all right? She looks pale."

Emitting a wheezing moan, the zombie shuffled toward Blake, reaching for him. He shucked his leather duster, tossing it over the zombie's head. The being wobbled then fell on her face.

The ranter glared at me. "You're stifling the good news!"

"You're stifling this congregation's ability to worship peacefully," I said.

"And what right do you have to tell me what I can and cannot do?" the ranter sneered.

I reached into my breast pocket taking out my billfold with my FBI badge and credentials and displaying them, Blake doing the same.

The ranter eyed them, scoffing. "Now you're infringing on my First Amendment right to spread the true Gospel of Life."

"We're protecting the rights of this parish to be secure in their persons," Blake added. "You're free to go about your business, just not inside this building."

By now Father Hoffbauer, the celebrant, had grown aware of the commotion. Sighing, he left the altar, going to the pulpit. "Could the gentleman in the back of the center aisle please leave the premises? Your sermon contradicts the Gospel. We can't say for certain what the Resurrection will look like, but I doubt it involves …what looks like a zombie."

"You would deny these people the chance to discover what *could be* the fullness of the Gospel!" the ranter called, taking a step toward the altar.

"Sir, kindly leave, unless you intend to sit down quietly and pray quietly," Father Hoffbauer ordered.

"Priest, I will not!" the ranter insisted.

In a single stride, I reached the ranter, grabbing his wrists in one hand, and putting my free hand on his shoulder. "Let's take this outside nicely, shall we?"

At first he slumped under my touch, but he quickly straightened, recovering his voice. "I'm being detained against my will! This is police brutality!"

"Agent Stamos was the captain of his high school wrestling team," Bill Padgett, one of the ushers, said, joining us. "If he was brutalizing you, you'd know it."

The ranter let out the middle-aged male version of an angry toddler yell, flinging himself forward. My much-higher center of gravity got the better of me and before I could let him go, he'd pulled me down. I managed to somewhat recover with a stumble onto my knees. I pinned him gently.

Blake knelt beside us, producing a pair of handcuffs from his belt and snapped them onto the ranter's wrists.

"I don't want to know why you have a pair of handcuffs on you in church."

"Dante, outside my usual preparedness, you really don't want to know," he said. We rose.

The parish nurse approached to examine the shambler. The zombie lifted her head, snapping at the nurse, who backed away. "Ma'am? You are not going to bite me."

The zombie awkwardly pulled herself onto her knees and clamped her jaws on the nurse's nose.

An emergency medical crew and several police officers entered. One of the officers, Jake Miller, whom I'd met elsewhere, stared at the ranter on the floor with a "We're doing this again?" lineface, while his partner, a young woman likely fresh from the police academy looked from me to the still-yelling ranter, to the nurse trying to remove the zombie from her face with the assistance of the EMTs.

"George, are you intruding again? And who's this woman biting someone?" Officer Miller asked.

"This is my Aunt Grace, who's discovered the fullness of eternal life, thanks to the Vital Elixir," George replied with the pride I'd expect from someone whose aunt had been declared a saint.

The paramedics finally pried Aunt Grace from the nurse's face, one examining the nurse, the other holding Aunt Grace and examining her. My heart skipped in my chest; I looked at Blake. "Is this what I think it is?"

Blake let out a sigh that sounded like a growl. "And we just had the training about it."

"What's the Vital Elixir?" Bill asked innocently.

"If it's what we think it is, I'd say you're better off not knowing, but considering what went down here, you're owed an explanation," Officer Miller said, as he helped George off the floor and guided him outside.

"It's a research chemical at best, at worse it's unsafe because it's unproven—" one of the paramedics started to say.

"What more proof do you need?" George cried over his shoulder. "Grace died two nights ago, but our Fellowship prayed over her as we administered the Vital—"

"And this is why I should inform you that you have the right to remain silent and that anything you say may be used against you in a court of law," Officer Miller said.

"And I have the right to practice my own belief system and use it to comfort my loved ones!" George snapped, as Officer Miller and a police supervisor guided him into the back seat of a patrol car.

"If this patient died, why is she still acting like she's alive?" the nurse asked.

"Yeah, much less acting like something that wandered out of *The Walking Dead*," a younger paramedic said, as she and her partner managed to get Aunt Grace onto a gurney, preparatory to bringing her to the ambulance below.

"You didn't get the memo on zombie juice?" her partner, a seasoned veteran, asked. To the parish nurse, he added, "You better come with us and get that bite looked at."

"I really should finish praying at Mass," the nurse insisted.

"Suit yourself, but you know the risks," the paramedic said.

"Well, that got exciting," I mused, heading back to the pew.

"That's the last time I go to Mass with you," Blake muttered, trailing me.

***

One thing stayed the same, namely, Kathleen and I joining her brother Ronan and his wife Collette for lunch at their home.

"Heard through the grapevine something exciting went down at St, Maggie's," Ronan said.

"If you mean a ranter with a zombie in tow, yeah, work kind of followed me there."

"Was someone under the influence?" Collette asked, innocently.

I took a sip of the homemade sangria I'd brought. "Under the influence of zombie-juice, specifically"

"All right, enough codenames: what's zombie-juice?" Kathleen asked.

"New experimental chemical. It was supposed to stay in the lab while the white coats figure out how safe it is, but this one escaped, because it appears to bring dead tissue back to life. There's talk it could be used to extend the lifespan on transplant organs, but then someone decided to test it on some cadavers intended for Miskatonic Medical School."

"Oh, that mess on the news last October that was straight out of a horror movie?" Ronan asked.

"That's it in a nutshell." My work phone vibrated against my hip. I took it out, finding a text from our director:

Special alert – All agents report to HQ immediately. Priority assignment, former Lady Eagle.

"Work followed me to Mass, now it's following me to brunch."

"Can't it wait?" Collette asked

"From that expression, it looks like it can't," Kathleen said, rising with me as I took my leave.

At the door, she turned me aside gently. "From your frown, I thought someone had died."

"No, but it's top priority: can't say more."

I took the car to Manuxet, to the field office in the rear of a converted brick mill building at the confluence of the Manuxet River, the Miskatonic River, and the Cabot Canal. My Sunday suit would have to suffice.

To no surprise, I found the place surrounded by more than the usual number of black Suburbans with darker than Bureau-standard tinted windows. When I entered, I found Blake in the vestibule–getting a thorough pat-down from the agent in a black polo shirt and khakis. Blake kept his gaze averted: I could fairly hear him calculating square roots to keep from glowering at the Secret Service agent as they scrutinized the boot knife they found on him.

"You're clear," the agent said turning to do the same to me, finding my off-duty Walther before turning us loose. We headed for the elevator.

A pair of Secret Service agents met us as the doors opened, running the same gauntlet.

"We're all batting for the same team here," Blake said. Even still, one of them confiscated the knife before they escorted us to the conference room.

Half the agents in the field office had gathered in the conference room, while the other half stood outside the doors peering in. Our director Locke stood by the head of the table to the left of the woman who occupied the chair there, Candace Kincade, former First Lady and widow of the late but not lamented Clifton Kincade, who'd had the dubious designation of being the first U.S. President to have to concede losing reelection before being eaten by an eldritch entity. I always had to check myself to keep from staring at her for how much she looked like a regular citizen. She still wore a black cardigan over a black A-line skirt, still mourning her husband, yet today she wore a navy-blue floral blouse with a gold quill pen broach at the throat. Blake stood a little straighter as we approached the table. I hung back but on instinct stood at attention.

She smiled at us, grateful and even a little relieved. "At ease, Agent Stamos." She gestured toward the two empty chairs closest to her. Blake sat down carefully in one, while I pulled out the other and settled onto it.

"This needs to stay out of the media, but my son has gone missing and my security team has uncovered strong evidence that Colton was taken by a cult," Candace informed us.

"We're sorry to hear that, Madame," I said. After the former president's demise at the protoplasmic protrusions of a shoggoth following the last election, Colton had slipped into some troubling behavior. Watching an eldritch abomination eat your father would knock anyone's psyche on its ass. Colton had since flunked his first year of college, and his father's family had debated sending Colton straight to boot camp to "adjust his attitude". Candace, with her gentle heart, had turned that down in a confrontation which a household worker had leaked onto YouTube.

Blake went still, his pale eyes colder than usual. "How do you suspect he was taken by a cult?" he asked, not standing on formality. I doubted he would, after the shoggoth-wrangling had brought him and a now-widowed Candace into close proximity, the kind of proximity that formed the stuff of the romance novels she wrote.

"My security team searched his computer and phone. He'd been contacting members of some fringe belief systems in recent months. He's suffered a crisis of faith. It's not unusual for a young person at his age, and after what happened to his father, he's struggling."

"You don't have to polish the matter for us, Madame. We're the last to judge your situation." I darted a smirk at Blake. "Well, Agent Matherton might frown at his choice of a faith community." Blake glared back at me around the hinge of his glasses.

She managed a tiny, amused smile, her face turning serious again very quickly. "Before he vanished, Colton tried to wipe his search history. One of our technicians managed to find some communications between him and a group calling itself 'the Fellowship of Eternal Resurrection'."

"Oh God dammit," Blake murmured. Locke side-eyed him.

Candace perked up, hopeful. "You know about this group?"

"A contact in the DEA warned us about them. Seems they may be involved in making something known as the Resurrectional Reagent, otherwise known as West's formula, or 'come-back-to-life-juice'. Or Zombie Juice."

"That's the weird drug that's turned up on the Deep Web, the one linked to some people acting like horror movie zombies, isn't it?" Candace asked.

"The Dark Web, rather," Blake said. "But you're correct: We've been trying to crack down on its distribution, as it's largely untested."

"At worst, a big-enough dose will kill you and bring you back as a non-transmittable zombie."

"So this cult or whatever it is, how does that involve the zombie juice?" one of her security detail asked.

"There's any number of groups who think they hold the key to eternal life, but this has to be one of the first which claimed chemical assistance, rather than taking the trust-fall of faith," Blake said. "This group in particular appears to assure resurrection even before the Second Coming comes around."

I had to pinch myself discreetly to keep from humming a few bars of "When the Man Comes Around."

Blake continued, with a hesitance born of quelling his annoyance at yet another Christian In Name Only group, after dealing with one which had literally left their mark on him. "They claim to be Christian, and their literature uses language consistent with some of the less familiar Christian entities. But if they're actually Christian, that's anyone's guess. And we aren't in the habit of deciding how Christian a group is."

"They'd be within their First Amendment rights, even for the substance use, considering cases involving Native American Shamen using nature-based psychoactives in specific ceremonies," Locke said. "However, we may have a case, considering the use of a suspiciously manufactured substance and for taking your son. The latter case might be harder to stick."

"Can you still get him back?" Candace asked.

"We'd have to find him and ask. He's an adult, albeit a young one, and it sounds as though he went with them of his own volition, or are we mistaken?" Locke said.

Candace looked to one of her agents. "Show them the footage."

The agent took a flash drive from her breast pocket and approached a smart screen on the wall. Locke found the remote and handed it to Candace. She tapped several buttons, opening a folder and selecting a .vid file and opening it.

The window showed a high angle view of the interior of a parking garage, a few sedans and SUVs visible.

A nondescript gray minivan pulled into an empty space. The driver's side door opened and a woman in a long gray cardigan and a nearly ground-length A-line skirt, a kerchief covering her hair, emerged, walking to the back of the van. She opened the rear hatch and fumbled in the back.

A shadow moved between the parked cars. Colton Kincade, a gangly young man who looked like a male-presenting version of Candace, approached, clad in a baggy sweatshirt, aviator sunglasses hiding his eyes and a trucker's cap with his late father's campaign slogan shading his face. Kerchief Woman approached him; he stood up straighter. No audio, but the two spoke cordially, Colton peering around, as if looking for eavesdroppers. Kerchief Woman laid a reassuring hand on Colton's shoulder, at which he relaxed.

A robust figure lunged from the rear of the van, grabbing Colton by the shoulder. Colton jolted and stiffened, throwing his hands up as if to fend off the attack. The figure hauled Colton inside, the young man flailing his legs as he vanished. Kerchief Woman slammed the hatch shut before hastening to the front seat. The rear lights lit up and she drove away at a normal pace, not rushing, not speeding.

"That was dramatic."

"That doesn't look the most willing," Blake said.

Candace looked away, breathing hard. Blake shifted as if he might offer her a comforting shoulder to lean on.

"Are you taking the case?" Candace asked, her voice brittle.

Locke looked to Blake and I and the rest of the FBI agents behind us. "Yes, we are," I said.

"With all due respect to the Bureau and its function, why aren't we going in immediately to extract the First Son?" one of the Secret Service agents asked.

"Seconded," one of our Agents in Training spoke up.

Because this isn't **Resident Evil 4** *and none of us is Leon S. Kennedy,* I thought.

"Because a group like this could argue that we infringed on their or the First Son's First Amendment rights," Locke said. "Especially in this day and age, we have to approach this with care. We can't afford to repeat the mistakes made in similar cases in the past. And because if we went off half-cocked, we could end up harming Colton."

Candace breathed easier. "Good." She looked at Blake and I. "May I have a word with Agents Stamos and Matherton?"

Locke raised an eyebrow. "You may, Mrs. Kincade." She rose and beckoning to our colleagues, went out, the rest following her, a few of the Secret Service agents following them.

Candace turned to us, smiling, relieved. "I'm glad you're on this case."

"Considering *our* relationship, Dante and I may be on the back end," Blake said.

She blinked. "There's a lot of roles in handling a case, and not all of them in the field," I said.

"So you're going to send someone else into the field to find him?" she asked.

"We've got young agents who need to learn the ropes of cult infiltration," Blake said. With care, he added, "And considering… the connection between you and I, there's… a conflict of interest."

Her face fell. "Yet they say you're the expert in infiltration."

"That's true, but after what happened between you and I in November, there's plenty of folk who might talk. There's already been whispers around the office," Blake said.

She smirked. "There's been whispers in the tabloids about a short blond man in a dark suit or a black leather trench coat."

"It's a black leather duster, dammit."

"If I'm not mistaken, your two recent novels added some fuel to that cozy fire," I added.

She peered past Blake to me. "Do you read my books?"

"My wife's sister-in-law does: asked me if the recent one's accurate. I appreciate your effort making a fictional FBI agent more like a real one. "

Her cheeks colored. "I may have some insights."

"I had to tell her *Love Not For Sale* was a little awkward, though accurate as to how we handle trafficking cases. I might've read *Freed from the Circle of Darkness*, since it hit close to home."

Candace's saddened eyes warmed with appreciation. "I hope you enjoyed either of them?"

"*Freed* was more fun."

"If a bit Satanic Panic-heavy," Blake added. "Not to say we haven't seen things that would put verbs in the panickers' sentences."

I side-eyed Blake, who had rolled his eyes toward the acoustic tiles. "You been helping her?"

"In an unofficial capacity and not via my official lines of contact," Blake replied.

"I'd shown him some manuscripts and notes," Candace said.

"It's not like I've suddenly found time in my busy life to read her work cover to cover," Blake added

"I'd wonder if he'd been replaced by a doppelganger if he did."

Candace reached out, laying her hand on Blake's wrist, her fingertips resting between the cuff of his glove and the cuff of his shirt sleeve. His hand flexed as if he would return the gesture. "Thank you, Agent Matherton." She released him and rose. Her detail stepped closer to her, forming a hollow square about the former FlotUS as she departed the conference room. I caught Blake angling his head slightly as if to catch a glimpse of her between the agents as they stepped into the hallway and headed for the elevators.

"Get your eyes back in your skull," I ordered.

"I wasn't thinking what you think I'm thinking. I'm processing what happened and why I agreed to it, Blake said.

"I never know what to expect from you whenever a case involves a powerful woman. You probably agreed because you got your wrist patted by an attractive woman you have history with that could make or break your career."

"An attractive woman who writes treacly Christian romance novels and has poor taste in men. And I haven't run deep cover on a cult since the debacle in Seabrook when I nearly got taken by the sea."

"So this time, I'll go in. I've done deep cover with the Providence Mob."

"I would think a cult and an organized crime cell would be different beasts."

"They're both groups of people looking for community, and they're both high-control structures existing outside of social norms as most people understand them."

Blake looked up at me, eyebrows raised, nodding slowly. "Well said."

"Does this have something to do with what went down when we couldn't save Clifton Kincade? Are you agreeing to this to make good on how that fell out?"

He sighed audibly as he left the conference room and lead the way back to our office. "Are you referring to the incident with the shoggoth or the incident with Clifton's doppelganger?"

I trailed him and for once, despite the literal foot of height difference we share, I had to lengthen my stride to keep up. "Both, because we failed to save him twice and I distinctly remember the both of us nearly losing our guns, badges, and security clearance over it. At least this time, the factors are more quantifiable—"

"You needn't use the word 'more' to modify 'quantifiable'; something is either quantifiable or it isn't." By this time, we reached the elevator bank; he hit the up button.

"At least with this, we're only dealing with a group of humans."

"Humans who think they've discovered a cure for the common death."

***

"Looks like you had a long afternoon," Kathleen said as I entered our townhouse that evening and hung my coat on our coat-tree.

"One of those cases where I can't tell you the particulars, but where we have some ironclad evidence of a cult breaking the law in a major way."

Bridget, our fourteen-year-old, leaned down the stairs, eyeing me. "As long as you aren't stepping on their First Amendment rights."

"We got nothing against what they believe, but when they've kidnapped someone and their practices are linked to the improper handling of the deceased and illegal substances, that's where we have to intervene."

Kathleen dug me in the ribs, grinning. "I thought you said you couldn't give out specifics?"

I returned the dig gently. "Didn't name names, doesn't count."

***

INTERLUDE

ARKHAM *EXAMINER*, NOVEMBER 12TH 2015

Dead Walk at North Shore Medical Center – In a scene straight from the dark creative minds of Stephen King or H.P. Lovecraft, a group of bodies rose up from their mortuary slabs in Peabody's North Shore Medical Center, after students from nearby Miskatonic University Medical School appear to have tampered with them.

Around eleven pm. November 11th, NSMC security guards Michael Vuong and Paul Sutton reported hearing shouts and banging in the hospital mortuary. A nurse who wishes to remain anonymous emerged, running and calling for help. Vuong and Sutton ran to the nurse's assistance, finding the mortuary doors open and a group of unclothed figures, all displaying signs of injuries and physical trauma had emerged into the hallway. Security attempted to contain the patients but found themselves overwhelmed. An unidentified nurse pulled a fire alarm, evacuating the building and summoning emergency services. Police arrived to find medical staff escorting patients and visitors to safety. Vuong and Sutton had attempted to block off the mortuary with file cabinets and gurneys, intending to contain the formerly deceased patients. The group managed to force through the barricades, attempting to attack the guards and any people nearby.

"If it weren't for the footage in the hallway cameras and my partner's bodycams, you'd think we'd watched too many episodes of *The Walking Dead*," says Officer Connor Abbott, an Arkham officer on scene. Police were required to shoot the formerly deceased patients to prevent them from attacking the living, which seemed only to enrage them, unless, true to most modern zombie lore, they were shot through the head.

Medical examiners are currently examining the bodies of the strangely resurrected, but initial reports suggest an unknown chemical agent is involved. The public need not be concerned of the dead rising en masse. Security footage suggests two medical students working in the mortuary may be involved.

SALEM *NEWS* NOVEMBER 20ᵀᴴ 2015

Mystery Chemical Linked to Mortuary Chaos in North Shore Medical Center – Like something from H.P. Lovecraft's *Herbert West: ReAnimator*, a formula has resurfaced, which has been linked to the bizarre resurrection at the North Shore Medical Center.

Essex County coroners examining the bodies from that incident discovered they were tainted with a bizarre chemical compound found in Brazilian amphibians known for their ability to quickly regenerate injured limbs.

Miskatonic Medical School student Danielle Kanawa came forward to campus police to admit that she and fellow student Han-sook Kim had, while helping their professor Avery Halsey sort through some files in the school archives, discovered a notebook dated from the 1920s, which had wedged itself in the back of a wooden file cabinet, its pages containing, among other things, several chemical formulae, including one which, according to the compiler, Danforth Kaine, would resurrect laboratory animals, albeit with side effects. Kanawa and Kim, students of biochemistry, decided to replicate the serum and test it on human subjects. "We knew a guy who works in the mortuary at North Shore Medical Center, Philip Barry. He offered to test the serum for us," Ms. Kanawa admitted to reporters.

Police investigated Barry and another mortuary worker, Emily Olney, who confessed to tampering with several bodies. "We injected two bodies with the serum, with no effect. So we injected another two," Barry confessed. "Still no effect. So we treated another pair. That's when the first two came back to life."

EAST MANUXET *TOWN CRIER*, FEBRUARY 12ᵀᴴ, 2016

Alleged Meth Lab Proven Zombie Juice Operation – A call regarding a strange smell coming from the end of

Patton Road ended in a scene lifted from Resident Evil. The occupants, identified as Scott Palmer and Peter Badden, had a known involvement in a local floating methamphetamine manufacturing operation. Officers, however, found the pair in the basement, where they had taken refuge on top of a metal cabinet, after a third member of the operation, Radley Bond, had tried to attack them and was now shuffling about the basement laboratory, knocking over glassware and spilling chemicals. Bond had, according to Palmer and Badden, died in a mishap with a snowthrower the night before, but now appeared very much alive, albeit displaying horrific injuries. Officers were obliged to use deadly force to stop Bond from attacking them and biting them.

Badden and Palmer admitted to concocting "some kind of resurrection zombie juice. We found the recipe on the Dark Web." Palmer added, "We thought he'd heal up when we dosed him with the stuff. He healed up a little too well."

Besides the production of illegal substances with the intent to distribute, the pair are also charged with mishandling of a decedent.

The Boston *Globe* June 12, 2016

FBI, DEA Report Emergence of "Zombie Juice" — Boston (AP). FBI Regional Director Manuel Tillinghast reports a concerning number of persons injured in various accidents as well as "elderly and terminally ill patients [have been] awakening after otherwise confirmed clinical death" and displaying "unusually aggressive behavior".

These previously deceased persons have shared one thing in common: tests on their tissues have revealed a chemical concoction similar to the solution found in the bodies which resurrected in the North Shore Medical Center [,,]

The compound has not been formally added to the schedule of controlled substances, however medical professionals have been advising legal control of the compound commonly known as "zombie juice". "The compound is at best untested, due to the fact that it is being manufactured by amateur chemists in unregulated labs," says Dr. Dana Serras, Dean of Miskatonic School of Medicine. "To say nothing of the way people who've received doses of the compound. It's untested on the living, but so far, the effects on the deceased make it difficult to recommend as a viable treatment."

COLLINSVILLE CT *HERALD* AUGUST 15TH

Zombie Juice Claims First Living Victim – Collinsville – A quarrel between a couple on a bridge over the Farmington River near the Collinsville Museum turned deadly before it turned violent. Maggie Coltrane and Reggie Jackford had gotten into an altercation over Jackford's substance use, when Jackford tripped on a crushed can and tumbled over the railing into the water.

Emergency services managed to recover Jackford's body. He was pronounced dead at UConn John Dempsey Hospital. However, a moment later, Jackford resuscitated and proceeded to attempt to attack the attending staff, who managed to subdue and sedate him. A toxicology screening he had a substantial amount of the compound known as "zombie juice" in his system.

***

The following evening, as Matherton parked in the electric vehicle section in the condominium complex where he lived and got out to plug in his car, an unmarked black SUV pulled up, boxing him in. He let his hand stray toward his sidearm.

The front passenger door opened and a member of Candace's security team emerged. "Agent Matherton?"

He sighed. "She better have a good reason for the social call."

"She wants an update on the investigation."

"So does my section chief. We're still very much in the preliminary stage." He turned on his heel.

"She misses you," the agent replied.

He sighed, harsher this time. "All right, as Milady wishes." He allowed them to pat him down and usher him into the rear of the SUV. *This is what you signed up for when you accepted the role of queen's lover,* he thought as he settled back in the corner.

They took a circuitous route to a hotel in Haverhill, entering via the loading dock and a freight elevator. The agents led him to the honeymoon suite, one opening the door and ushering him in.

Candace sat at the desk in the front room, making a pretext of writing in a bound journal, her pen sat slack in her hand. As Matherton approached, she set the journal aside, the pen marking her place. "Is there any news?" she asked, rising and putting her hands on his shoulder.

He put one hand on her waist, letting her draw close and kiss his cheek. "There's nothing that couldn't be relayed via secure email."

She looked into his eyes. "Still in the preliminary stage?"

He held her off slightly. "These things take time and care. But I can say we're forming a plan that involves sending in one of our best agents"

"You?"

"No. Stamos. He's had twelve years of experience infiltrating the Mob, before they switched him over to Unusual Cases."

"I see."

"And as I said, I have a conflict of interest, due to our involvement."

She relaxed her hold on him, sliding her hands down to the hollows of his elbows. "Do you… would you prefer if we stayed apart for the time being?"

"It would keep tongues from wagging. I know your people are discreet, but there's always that one person who sees something and can't help saying something."

She released him, folding her arms loosely on her chest. "I figured that. Do you think your team can get him back?"

"I can't make any guarantees, but he'll need deprogramming afterward, if they don't shock him so much he decides their philosophy isn't for him."

She managed a brave smile, then held out her hands to him, palms up. "It's probably messed up for me to say this, but I hope something does happen to make him change his mind and come home."

He removed his black gloves before he laid his hands atop hers. *"If they let him go. Groups of this nature can be highly exclusive and possessive of their members."*

She gently clasped his fingers. "You don't think they'll...do something to him?"

"If they truly value him, given his status, they may treat him better than the average rank and file member."

She leaned in, burying her face in the side of his neck, at the edge of his shirt collar. "I hope they do. I hope they're different from the other groups you've taken down."

He pulled her close, even though he knew their proximity would lead to an enmeshment...

"...Better than dealing with paperwork?" she asked softly against Blake's shoulder, one of the few unmarked areas on his skin.

"Hm. Far better. Though I should be going over transcripts from a private Discord server. If you don't know, it's a surface Web microblogging and chat site -"

"Yeah, my publisher wants my social media manager to set up a server, though I'll have to figure out how it works. You think I should go on theirs and see if I can't convince him to come home?"

"I wouldn't advise that. They could turn it around and try convincing you to come find him. It's not unusual for cults to sequester their new recruits as part of the process of breaking them down and separating them from their life and everything that matters to them. You said he'd been short-tempered with you?"

"He's been moodier than usual since we lost his father. I think he blames me for not being more firm with Clifton, for not keeping him from giving that concession speech on the beach when we'd been warned about something weird in the water. But I think part of him also blames himself for surviving all that."

"Has he been in counseling?"

"He went a few times. I'd made it clear he had to do something to help himself. But it's hard. Clifton always scoffed at psychology." A minor scandal had erupted when a hot mike had caught Clifton joking about bringing back mental asylums (his words) to handle the mental health crisis.

"Trust only in Jesus to cure your diseases?" Blake mused.

Candace shoved him playfully and turned over onto her back. "I'd forgotten that stupid line he'd quoted so many times."

"So instead of seeking help from your pastor, Colton went seeking a different pasture?" Blake sat up and rummaged on the floor beside the bed for his shorts, stepping into them and taking his eyeglasses from the bedside table. Candace stopped herself from staring at the scar-crossed full tattoo of Baphomet covering his back.

"You're making terrible puns. You do that when you're nervous."

"I've every reason for feeling nervous: sending someone to infiltrate a cult to observe illegal activity is one thing. Sending someone in to extract a member who already had a high profile is a whole other book I've never cracked the cover of."

"For someone who's talked about living on the razor's edge, you can get pernickety about exercising caution."

He eyed her over his glasses, barely breaking eye contact as he found his undershirt by touch and pulled it on. "For now. For the sake of the investigation. It's the definition of 'delicate'. Especially since we're dealing with a fringe group who plays with syringes of a suspect chemical."

"Understood. Do you want to stay the night?"

"I was about to leave and find some dinner. I've had a long day."

She playfully sprawled on her back, folding her arms behind her head. "Oh, who needs supper when you could have another round with me?" she asked, her eyes snapping mischievously.

He laughed, one of his rare genuine chuckles of pleased amusement. "Wasn't that a line from one of your books?"

She sat up, reaching for her robe. "One of the rare spicy Regency novellas: 'The Earl and the Tavern Wench'. It's an old shame for how badly it's written. And I don't mean the spicy parts. The whole thing is just wretched. But I had bills to pay." She reached for the bedside phone. "Let me order room service for you: the grill has a Portobello burger to die for."

"Is my vegetarianism rubbing off on you, along with my adventurousness? And will the goon squad fetch it?"

She punched a number. "Naturally."

A half hour later, Candace had resumed jotting while Blake ate. "I have to ask," she said, looking up. "If you were granted a chance at immortality, would you take it?"

He stopped chewing and blinked before swallowing. "I have PTSD and anxiety as well as an increased risk of several debilitating health conditions. I've accepted my mortality. I've also been in situations where

I've calmly handed my life into God's hands, even though on most days I have little to say to Him beyond reporting for duty."

"Is that a no?"

"In so many words. What about you? Would you accept the chance for immortality if it was offered to you?" He took the last bite of his sandwich before wiping his fingers on a paper napkin.

"I believe that I'm going to be resurrected someday, so I suppose I have no use for immortality in the 'not dying at all' sense."

"So becoming a vampire or a werewolf is out of the question?"

She raised both her eyebrows. "Those exist?"

"Yes, they do. Remember the biker gang who were in the feel-good news in Cherryfield, Maine?"

"The ones who keep an eye on girls in the local bars so guys don't harm them? The story I thought would make a good Hallmark Christmas movie? They're actual howl-at-the-full-moon-and-shift werewolves?"

"Oh yes." He adjusted his glasses. "On a somewhat related note, what would you do in the event of a zombie outbreak?"

"I'm not sure. I'm a romance novelist and a stay-at-home mom. I suppose I have the skills to help rebuild society. Nothing like you have. I mean, you'd keep your head in a zombie outbreak."

"I could, though there's more to dealing with zombies than shooting your way through them. Going by what we know about these particular zombies, they're resilient but they're as easy to take down as a living person of the same height and build. They don't spread the plague since their condition is caused by a chemical solution."

"Does anyone know what happens to someone who takes the stuff while they're alive?"

"That's unknown. If I had to hypothesize, the chemical causes heightened tissue regrowth, which could potentially speed up your healing process. Or it could induce cancer, due to rogue cells being formed during that heightened regrowth."

She blinked. "I see. I guess Captain America's healing ability might not hold up in real life?"

"It might not. But I'm the last person to be 'That Scientist' when it comes to fictional universes."

The room phone rang. She eyed it. "Shall I answer that?"

"It's your room. Were you expecting a call?" he replied around a sweet potato waffle fry.

She picked up the phone, putting it on speaker. "Hello?"

"Mrs. Kincade? This is the front desk. There's a Clare down here who wants to speak to you. She's not on the list of people you want us to put through to your room, but she says she's a fan of your work."

Candace muted the phone looking to Roarke, one of her security detail, who looked like Central Casting's idea of an old-school Irish beat cop. Blake pushed his plate aside slowly and reached for his holster, laying on the table, slipping it around his shoulders and securing it. "Ask them how they know you're here."

Candace unmuted the phone. "It's nice to hear from a fan, but how did she know that I'm staying at this hotel?" Roarke went out, heading for the front room. The hall door opened and closed.

The line rustled. *"Oh, I'm a friend of Colton's. He told me you were staying here at this hotel,"* Clare replied, innocently.

"I'm sorry, but I'm busy writing at the moment. I'm afraid I can't come down."

"But Colton promised you were here and you always make time for your fans."

"That's true, but it applies to my public appearances. I do need space to write, and right now, I'm working in my home away from home."

"Please? Just a minute? He wanted me to see you and tell you he's just fine. He hopes you can come see the place where he's staying."

Blake pointed at the mute button. Candace hit it. "Standard cult talk and tactics: ask them where he is, but keep it light."

"I figured." She hit the mute button again. "If he's well, may I ask how come he's not with you? I haven't heard from him in a few days and it's got me worried."

A long silence on the other end. *"He's busy getting settled. You know how it is when you're in a new place and you're starting a new life. You need time to get used to your new surroundings. I should go."* The line cut out.

"Dammit," Blake muttered. "Sorry."

"Apology accepted it. It's tense."

"Much as I wouldn't mind staying, now that I'm here, I'd better go and notify Locke."

The phone rang again. Candace snatched it up, hitting the speaker button.

"Roark here." his voice replied. *"She ran off. Security pursued her, but she took off with a partner on a motorcycle. We're moving you to another hotel."*

"I'd better start packing." She hung up the phone.

"I'd better pack up in a different way," Blake said.

***

The moment he left Candace's room, Blake called the situation in. "Locke, we need to advance the timeline on the infiltration."

No sound came from the other end of the line. Then she spoke, *"How do you mean?"*

"A member of the Fellowship of Eternal Resurrection tried to approach Candace and I."

"Is the First Lady safe?"

"Yes, her detail is taking her to a secure location which I certainly don't know the address or coordinates for. I have a feeling she's likely to contact you shortly, thus I made the executive decision to inform you first."

"Understood. I'll see about expediting the necessary documents for your cover— Wait. Did you say you were **with** *the First Lady?"*

"Affirmative."

A harassed sigh rattled on the other end of the line. *"Do I have to ask if this was a social call?"*

"No, she sent the goon squad to pick me up for a personal debriefing."

"At least Agent-in-Training Johnson isn't here with his puns."

"He might not be, but it sounds like his idea of humor infected you."

***

"We might have an in on the Fellowship of Eternal Resurrection," McLosky, the tech analyst, pulled up the Facebook page for the town of Newell, New Hampshire, a picturesque town not far from a ski area in the White Mountains. "They're selling their organic produce and homemade jam and baked goods at the community farmers' and crafters' market."

Blake eyed the post, his eyes going cooler and thoughtful. "It's a good way in. And Locke's aware of our need to expedite some matters."

"All right, just let me tell Kathleen I got a business trip I can't tell her about. Please tell me there aren't any weird sex things involved?"

"They don't seem especially big on sex," Blake said.

"From what I saw on their private Discord server, they discourage it. Something about Christ saying that the resurrected would be like angels in heaven," McCloskey said.

"I suppose that excludes the Watcher angels," Blake mused.

"Not something I remember from Catechism class, but then again, it wasn't exactly the 18+ crowd."

"Good to hear there's a cult that *doesn't* do weird sex things," McCloskey said.

"Extra good. I wasn't looking forward to the paperwork to deputize Kathleen."

Between waiting for my cover documents (ID, Social Security card, etc.) and preparing myself physically (showering only every other day), a few days passed before I could go into deep cover. On paper, I'd take the name and identity of Dante Petrucci, a forty-eight-year-old divorced combat veteran who'd worked on and off for several construction companies till his wife left him over his frequent job changes and his prison sentence due to accidentally killing a man in a bar fight gone wrong. I didn't particularly care for the persona, but it added a certain self-loathing that added to his personality.

"I didn't particularly care for some of my covers either," Blake said, with an air of understanding.

Once I found a beater pickup truck from a used car dealer who worked out of his backyard, I headed north, going slightly off grid for a couple of days before meandering to Newell, checking in with Kathleen and the kids on my personal phone and Locke on my work phone.

On the third day, I settled into a motel near the highway on the edge of town, not quite a fleabag but north of one, then spent the first day making myself visible around town but not conspicuous (not easy when you're the tallest person in the room). I applied for entry-level jobs at a gas station and a landscaping company.

The following day I went to the Farmers' Market where I chatted up several folks at their booths, asking who needed an extra hand for the harvest or as a general farmyard worker. Most turned me down, especially when I mentioned paying off my debt to society. One grizzled older man nearly drove me off.

"Better if I tell you up front: I need one day out of the week to check in with my parole officer. I'm recently released from prison after I served my time for accidental homicide," I said to one woman with a booth of herbs, some dried in packets others suspended in olive oil.

"Do I want to know about the accidental part?" she asked.

"Bar fight got out of hand. Guy shoved me; I shoved him back. And when you're my size, shit gets real, really fast. I plead out and did my time. But it's tough finding work afterward."

A sandy-haired woman in a tan cardigan over a peasant blouse and an autumn-colored A-line skirt approached from a neighboring booth selling freshly made soup and jars of preserves and honey. "I should start by apologizing for eavesdropping."

I recognized Kerchief Woman from the security footage. "Apology accepted. My voice carries even when I try to keep it down."

"I bet it does. So you're looking for work? Our farm could use another pair of hands maintaining the place and helping with the harvest. I hope you don't mind working for a faith-based initiative."

I shrugged. "Not at all. Grew up Catholic. Been doing some exploring since I went in and got out."

"Back to fish on Friday or away from it?"

"Got introduced to a lot of different belief systems when I went in, so I might be taking a walk around the world as far as faith and enlightenment go." I smirked slightly. "I'm Dante Petrucci."

She smiled, offering her hand. "I'm Sister Alice Aldridge. Are you new in town?"

"Staying in a room in the Bentley Motel."

She wrinkled her nose. "Not bad, but I bet you wish you had a better roof over your head and better meals."

"Wouldn't mind either."

"You can stay with us if you like. We're in the habit of helping folk who could use a hand."

"Sure thing. You cool, though, with someone who has to check in with their parole officer twice a week?"

"That's fine: we've had people in similar straits work with us. But twice a week? Sounds a bit strict."

"I had friends in the Mob. The law's keeping me on a short leash."

She rolled her eyes. "Gotta love the Feds."

"Mind if I buy a jar of fig preserves to send home to my mother?"

She approached the booth, taking a jar and a brown paper bag to wrap it up. "Consider it on the house."

"Nah, Dad taught me to pay my debts."

She smiled, pushing it toward me. "Consider it part of your pay for helping out."

I accepted it. "Fair enough."

I hung around the booth for the rest of the market day, chatting with Sister Alice and accepting a bowl of clam chowder from Brother Joe, the cook manning the kettle. As the sun lowered behind the trees that ringed the town green, the crowd thinned. When the vendors started packing up their booths, I helped Sister Alice and Brother Joe pack up and break down the booth. "I got my truck nearby, if you need more space. 'Cept I gotta run back to the motel and get my stuff."

"You can fetch that in the morning," Brother Joe said.

We slid one of the tables into my truck. I followed them, convoy-style, passing houses and shops, which gave way to stands of trees and farmhouses and fields. The trees thickened and closed in around the road, the branches hanging over us, the daylight fading behind them.

The woods fell back behind farmland on the left. We passed orchards marching over the hillsides, dairy barns and a farm with a paddock of alpacas, before we passed a stretch of cornfields cut back this late in the season.

I'm not sure what I expected a cult compound to look like, probably something like Jonestown's rough-constructed shacks and huts or Spahn Ranch's repurposed Western movie town, though that's not exactly typical for the Northeast. The truck ahead pulled into the mouth of a long drive between rough-made rock walls, passing a stand of apple trees and blueberry bushes, majestic old maples lining the road.

We pulled into what looked like a cross between a traditional farm and a New England old money estate, a main house to one side, several barns and outbuildings to the other. We pulled up before the house, a well-maintained Colonial with Victorian additions, electric candles in the windows. To the left of the house, behind a hedgerow, stood a pergola festooned with vines and white string lights already lit. A breeze carried the scent of wood smoke from a nearby fire pit. The truck before me stopped in the shade of a porte-cochere. I slowed to a stop behind them.

A handful of people emerged from the side door, led by an average-looking white guy in his fifties, clad in a fleece vest over a quilted flannel shirt, who approached my truck while the others unloaded the truck ahead of me. I rolled down the passenger window. "Welcome! I'm Brother Spencer. Sister Alice called ahead and told us we'd have a new guest by our fireside."

"Nice to meet you. I'm Dante, not yet a Brother."

He chuckled. "She tells me you're looking for a place to do some soul-searching."

"Just looking for good work, maybe a place to rest while I work through some things,"

"She tells me you're looking for a second chance. Fortunate for you, we're firm believers in those."

"Guess I've come to the right place." I parked alongside the farm truck and locked it up. Sister Alice beckoned me to follow her into the house.

Voices chatted in the direction where you'd expect a kitchen and down the hallway we traversed. They'd gone for a minimalist approach. They'd repainted the wainscoting and covered the wallpaper in neutral shades, though some vintage ornate designs had ghosted through. Framed canvas and shadow box-style mottoes decorated the walls, things in the style of those *"Live Love Laugh"* mottoes, but with sayings like *"Life Will Endure"* and *"Death Cannot Conquer You"*, alongside artistic skulls and skeletons draped in flowers or with plants growing through them and engravings of skeletons and flayed human figures in pensive poses.

We entered the dining room where two long tables stood; several young women set out soup plates and utensils. On one wall hung a tapestry depicting the Resurrection of the Dead in an early 20th century churchyard: graves and tombs opening, people of all walks of life emerging, some stepping out, some levitating. To one side a couple of skeletons emerged, their skulls downcast. Outside of a radiance in the sky in the shape of a cross and another cross atop the steeple, the All Mighty seemed oddly absent.

More people gathered in twos and threes, some entering from the doors to the foyer, other entering via a set of French doors opening onto the porch.

A girl's voice spoke behind me. "You like our artwork? It's Brother Spencer's favorite inspiration for the fellowship."

Another girl added, "Yeah, though they're not exactly metal-heads or something." I turned to find two girls setting a smaller table. One wore a white blouse under a cardigan and a black skirt, the other, her eyes averted from the tapestry, clad in an over-sized red hoodie over worn, baggy black jeans.

"It's certainly different," I said. "Think I've seen stuff like it in the rectory of my old parish."

"It's a vision Brother Spencer hopes to make possible in spirit and principle, if not literally," the girl in the skirt said. "I'm Sister Clara." She nodded toward the girl in red. "This is Martine, not a Sister."

"So you're the new guy Alice called about?" Martine asked.

"Yeah, got hired to help around your farm. I'm Dante."

Sister Clara chuckled. "Like in the *Divine Comedy*?"

"Or *Devil May Cry*?" Martine asked.

I snerked. "Yeah, either one."

The porch door opened and a group of young men entered, laughing and playfully nudging each other, Colton among them, looking worn. I glanced his way, barely registering his presence. Sister Clara looked toward them warmly, Martine rolled her eyes.

"Is that...?" I pretended to just know Colton from news blips.

Clara brightened, while Martine sighed irritably. "Colton Kincade?" Clara asked. "Yes, though he's soon to be Brother Colton once he finishes his Quest."

"Small world. I voted for his dad the first time around."

"Hopefully he can get his mom on board and she can help us spread the word," Clara said.

"If she's not too busy writing or promoting her next silly romance novel," Martine said.

"Maybe she can write a novel about literally undying love," Clara said. "Or she could help people find a way to avoid being parted like her family was, so no one will know that fearsome thing we all dread."

"And that is?"

"Death," Clara replied.

By then, Brother Spencer and Sister Alice had guided the rest of the fellowship into the dining room, where they took their place along the rustic tables, pulling up mismatched chairs. Sister Alice beckoned me to approach and sit at an angle to her and Brother Spencer at the head of the table. I smiled, taking my place.

Colton and the other two young men sat down at the smaller table under the tapestry. Getting close looked like a tough act, but I filed that away as something to discuss with the team the first chance I got.

A group of older men and women entered carrying baskets of bread which they set along the tables and large kettles of thick lentil soup which they set at the head and foot of each table.

"We have a new face among us," Brother Spencer looked my way. "But I won't belabor that news, as you're all probably ravenous." A few people chuckled. Brother Spencer raised his eyes toward the ceiling. "Provider of Life, we bless you and thank you for this food and for all the means of sustaining our selves and our lives, which you have given us. Bless the Provider!"

"Praise and exalt the Provider, above all forever!" the fellowship responded.

We sat down to eat. People passed their soup plates to the ends of the tables to be filled, chatting among themselves. Colton looked my way, his brow furrowed as if he was trying to place me. I gave him a similarly puzzled look back. An older man, seated at the smaller table, nudged him, shaking his head. Colton looked away, fixing his gaze on his plate.

The people closest to me introduced themselves: no last names, so I nixed mine.

"So, what, you go on a spirit quest?" I asked.

"Something like that," Clara said. "Brother Spencer or Sister Alice will explain it during the conferences after supper."

"Makes sense. Mind if I ask what's the recipe for this stew?" I asked. "It's delicious." Not entirely true: my tongue detected something brackish, but not strong enough to overpower the dish.

She smirked. "You'll have to ask Sister Millie the cook. She rules the kitchen. You cook?"

"I'm Italian. It's what we do."

Once the fellowship had eaten and the servers cleared the tables, the gathering filed out to the pergola with the fire pit where they settled onto benches and random chairs. Sister Clara seated herself on the end of one bench, patting the middle of it. I perched myself on it, giving her space as best as I could.

At length, Brother Spencer emerged, the kitchen help following him and settling among the fellowship. I didn't detect a hierarchy outside of the older men who stood behind the young men with Colton, to one side of the fire pit, separated from the rest of the fellowship.

"I had a different talk in mind, but we have a newcomer who's expressed some curiosity about our fellowship and our mission. So tonight, I'll start with a hopefully brief elevator pitch," Brother Spencer said. A few of the fellowship chuckled. "We could all use a refresher."

I rubbed my hands, then tucked them inside the pockets of my jacket, hitting the button on the hidden recorder there.

"We are the Fellowship of Eternal Resurrection. We are, at the risk of sounding like a bunch of woo-woo optimists, working toward a brighter future, where no one need fear the pain of death. I know, I know: sounds like something you might hear from 'g-g-g-gasp, a cult!'" he said, with a comical chirp of fear and widening his eyes.

The fellowship chuckled. Resuming his composed cheerful demeanor, he continued, "But this is the furthest from who and what we are. We aren't going to harm or exploit you or anyone else. We aren't going to tell you how to dress. We aren't going to tell you what to believe or not to believe, other than to believe humanity can find the secret to perfectibility. We aren't going to tell you what God or Goddess to pray to or how to pray to Them, though we do believe in the Great Intelligence and Provider which exists beyond this universe as we know it. Whether you believe in God or the Goddess or Wisdom or Allah or Jehovah or nothing at all is up to you. But we believe the Provider, the source of all life has planted in us the desire to live forever, to break free of the constraints of death and illness and old age.

"And we found the means to this end – and beginning – in a chemical formula that had been, for a time, lost to humanity in the cluttered files of Miskatonic University, but which some enterprising soul rediscovered—"

"In a folder that fell behind a file cabinet!" one questulant called out. The fellowship chuckled. Colton sighed.

"Hey, Questulant Dennis isn't wrong," Brother Spencer said. He reached into the pocket of his vest and took out a small glass vial containing an orange fluid that seemed to glow with its own inner light, though the firelight could have glinted through it. The gathering murmured respectfully. The questulants nudged each other, except for Colton, who looked from the vial to me and back again.

"You came here freely. You came here for a reason. You've sought to better yourself. You want to take a step sideways from the world, to find a fresh start to a life without end. No one here will pressure you in any way, shape or form. You won't be pressured into relationships you don't welcome – I certainly won't pressure you."

A few women and one man in the gathering let out a disappointed "Awww!"

"That said, the only lines we will cross with you occurs when you assume your quest." With a dangerous grin, he added, "We shut you up in an iron cage for your own good." A few of the fellowship laughed while others gasped. Colton boggled, appalled, but his fellow questulants laughed, playfully slugging him.

"I'm messing with you. But in all seriousness, as with many cultures and belief systems, we have our questulants take a step away from the day to day to consider if they really want this, to clear their minds and souls before they start the rest of their forever. Later tonight, they're going into the hills to an old hunting camp. Ten days from now, when they've made their decisions, they'll return and be even bigger pains in the neck than they were before but maybe even better."

"Ruuuuude," Dennis called out.

"I'm still messing with you lads. They're good boys, full of life and fire, hopefully they'll stay that way."

The fellowship murmured in approval.

"Now, opening up the floor," Sister Alice said. "Does anyone have something they'd like to share?"

A few people in the gathering rose and asked questions or shared observations. Brother Joe got up and described someone at the farmers' market calling them "kooks" and grilling them about the weird incident at Sankt Maria Magdalen.

I raised my hand. "I heard about that in the news before I came to town. 'zit all right if I ask what went on there?"

Brother Spencer sighed tiredly. "One of our ex-members decided to make a show of what we hope to achieve, thinking this would boost our reach. He and two other members also made the mistake giving his elderly aunt a dose of the elixir as she lay dying and after she had changed her mind. He made a complete mockery of our philosophy and mission. We'd warned him not to do something so foolish. After he was jailed and bailed out, he came back to us. We dealt with him. We fed him to the zombies." A beat and he chuckled. "No seriously, we removed him from our group and told him never to come back and we've told the fellowship to give him a wide berth. The last we knew, his aunt has been placed in a secure care home, but we're trying to have her removed so we can better take care of her."

After more questions and answers, the gathering dispersed, some heading toward the farmyard, others returning to the house. Sister Alice rose. "How about I show you to your room, unless you'd rather see the farmyard first?"

"Sounds too much like work. Kinda had a long day, so I'd rather see my room and bunk down." I rose, following her inside and up to the second floor.

I expected something like barracks, but instead I found a long hallway lined with doors to small rooms. We passed by several bearing small name placards. She opened one minus a placard. "This used to be

George's, you might be curious to know since you asked about that incident at that church," she said, opening the door.

I made a show of wariness. "Uh oh, is it haunted? This isn't some kind of hazing, is it?"

She chuckled. "No, we cleaned out his things when we let him go. If there's any ghosts, you let us know." I stepped into a small but tidy room with moss green walls and simple, natural wood furniture.

"Nice space, 'specially after I've had to stare at white cement block walls at night. Permission to go back to the motel and fetch my stuff?"

"Other than needing to be in your room before midnight and that we need you to keep it down if you come in later than that, we won't tell you where you can or can't go," she said.

"Sounds better than home growing up."

"Trust me, we have one guy working second shift in a retail warehouse. We won't hold it against you."

I returned to the motel, gathered my stuff, and checked out. I dropped a message to Locke, giving her the basics before I returned to the compound.

Sister Clara let me in at the side door. I found my way back to my room, unpacked and settled in. Footsteps passed my door. I continued shuffling around, training my hearing toward the door.

"I swear I've seen that new guy before. He's a cop or with the FBI," I heard Colton say.

"He's the opposite of a cop: he's recently released from prison. He's looking for a chance to start over," I heard Brother Joe reply. "You're probably paranoid that your mother sent someone to drag you back to your old life. It happens. You're not second-guessing yourself. Everyone has their hesitations."

"I suppose," Colton's voice replied. Footsteps passed on. I slipped out my phone and jotted some notes on what just happened.

***

I woke up later in the morning to someone tapping at the door. "Rise and shine, Dante!" Sister Clara's voice called out.

"On m'way," I murmured, taking my phone from under my pillow and getting up to find my pants.

After breakfast, Brother Spencer gave me a tour of the grounds, showing me around their working farmyard: a firewood kiln, a cider house, an open machinery shelter covering several four wheelers, ride-on mowers and a forklift, with several farm trucks parked alongside it. "You used to farm work?" he asked.

"I'm used to hard work, but this is new territory for me." I glanced around the yard to what looked like a warehouse or a cow barn across the access road from the vehicle shelter. "Barn full of cows over there?"

"No, just a warehouse where we store the odds and ends," he said a little too quickly. "I inherited the farm from my uncle who'd made his fortune in technology and retired a gentleman dairy farmer. I'd made my fortune in pharmaceuticals. I've seen too much death in my life."

"So returning to a simpler life and making sure people can live long to enjoy it?" I asked.

"A good assessment. We've converted the back pasture into a pumpkin field. Next year, we're considering taking a page from Wampanaak farming practices and mixing the corn and squash plants together." I followed him along the road, pretending I hadn't noticed his gaffe. I may have grown up in Providence, Rhode Island, but even I know a cow barn turned into a warehouse didn't have the vaguely sickly-sour reek of rot, unless they'd left a dead cow in there.

We reached the pumpkin field to find a group of fellowship members gathering pumpkins and piling them at the end of each row. A few of the crew looked up and waved to us.

"Want to give it a try?" Spencer asked.

"About time I earned my keep." I stepped into the field, picking my way around the vines. One woman on the crew offered me a folding knife and showed me how to cut the stems.

I worked slower than the rest of the crew, taking care around the gourds, chatting with the others and getting the feel of the group.

By sundown, we trouped back to the main house for supper and another pep talk from Brother Spencer, who updated us on the questulants, that they'd settled in peacefully but he couldn't say more.

The gathering split up for the night when my phone pinged. I pulled up a message from Locke, posing as my parole officer:

Meeting tomorrow. 9 a.m. Newell Dunkin Donuts. Don't be late. This is not negotiable.

Next morning, I left a note on my door and headed out. I kept peeking into the rearview more often than usual, expecting to see a vehicle pretending not to follow me. My agent instincts kicked in as soon as I pulled into the lot of the Dunkins close to the highway, across from the Bentley Motel: doesn't get more New England LEO than that. I walked in, and ordered my usual espresso and roved the dining area, finding Blake, Roarke, and Obanhein in plain clothes gathered about a table in the far corner.

"Dante Colasanto?" Blake said as if he'd never seen me or said the name before.

"In the flesh," I replied.

"Take a seat." Roarke gestured toward a fourth chair at the table. "So how's it been?"

"Found a job as a handyman-general fix-it and farm-it type for a commune of some kind. I've got an in but not much of one."

We chatted a bit, exchanging the narrative we'd invented for my persona, all the better for the clerks behind the counter and any passing customers to overlook us. Our dumb luck, one of the Fellowship worked here and had their marching orders to keep an eye on me, but the counter clerks gave us no mind, from what I could tell.

"You keeping your nose clean? No contact with the Massimos?" Blake asked.

"They're in Maine, not New Hampshire. Think they decided I'm too much of a hothead."

"And now, they suspect you've turned informant," Roarke suggested. "Did you get eyes on the package?"

"They got the package sorted somewhere else."

Blake sighed, looking at Roarke, who tightened his jaw. "Shit just got real," Obanhein murmured.

"Do we want to know how sequestered the package is?"

"It's quest-level sequestered."

"Damn," Roarke muttered.

"Oh, Christ, help us," Blake murmured. "Is there any way you can possibly get closer?"

"Not unless I commit to the group. Doubt they'd take me this soon. Got the feeling they process their packages in batches. Doubt they'd grandfather me in."

"You think you can lean on them?" Roarke asked.

"In my extensive experience, if you lean on leadership in these kind of organizations, it spooks them and they shut you out," Blake said.

"Yeah, I would: this group keeps their cards close to their collective chest. They got this whole shtick of 'We're not a cult' to a level that has me thinking if they gotta insist they're not a cult, they're probably a cult, even if they aren't a *cult*-cult."

"As in, they aren't going to coerce you into group passionate hugging or serve as the leader's...highly personal servant," Blake said. "Those are the most insidious ones and the most likely to violate boundaries."

"How close you think they're watching you?" Obanhein asked.

"Not very. Don't think they have me pegged. But I wouldn't recommend the hard intercept. Something screwy's going on." I reached into my jacket pocket, taking out the preserves and placing it on the table. "You might want to have Leiermann look at the contents."

Blake took it, bagging it. "Please tell me they aren't selling these to the public."

"That's how I got it. Outside that, they seem harmless. They preach a good gospel, real inclusive and welcoming. Too welcoming, if you get my drift. I'm concerned they're cutting the food with that stuff."

"You ready for a drug test?" Obanhein asked.

"If you got the necessary." Blake dug in a backpack at his feet and taking out a specimen bag containing a labeled plastic jar with a screw-top, handed them to me without looking my way. I headed for the men's room, Obanhein following me.

For all the drug tests I've done, I will never get used to them or having an LEO standing outside the door waiting to collect it. I suppose if I ever do, it's time I found another line of work. After that necessary indignity, we went out to the parking lot.

"They about admitted they got zombies on the premises, in one way or another," I said.

"Similar to the one which that guy dragged to the church?" Blake asked.

"The very one, though we'll need proof they're hiding them somewhere. There is a weird warehouse on the property: I don't see a lot of activity about it, no one but the older members go near it."

"That does seem a little odd," Obanhein said. "I take it we need to have a look?"

"We don't have probable cause," Blake said. "But the samples may give us one."

We stepped into a spot out of the range of the security cameras on the building. "How're Kathleen and the kids holding up?" I asked

"From the little I've seen, Kathleen's holding up well: she's checked in, asking if you're all right. Brigid's a bit geeked from your sudden disappearance."

"Kind of expected it: Brigid gave me the usual worried talk she does before I leave on a work trip. She's still not used to it: I was always home for dinner when I was infiltrating Massimo's crew, even if I ended up having to go out afterward for my Donnie Brasco routine."

I glanced to the SUV with darker than normal tinting and official license plates parked alongside Obanhein's patrol car. "How is She doing?"

Blake drew in a long breath. "Not well. This is… very hard for her. This has made her more protective of him. He's her only son whom she had a difficult time carrying. She's holding her own, but she's had moments."

"And you've been offering her consolation?" I asked, softly.

Blake focused his attention on a viburnum on the edge of the lot. "That's between her and I."

Not surprisingly when I got back to the compound, Sister Alice met me at the door. "Parole hearing so soon?" she asked.

"Since I started a new job, I had to check in."

"Fair enough. A bunch of us are picking apples in the orchard and we could use someone to handle the upper branches."

"Time for me to earn my keep." I headed for the apple barn.

***

"Is there any way you can get a search warrant immediately?" Candace asked from across Locke's desk.

"I wouldn't advise it. We need the proverbial solid evidence," Locke replied calmly. "We're waiting on the toxicology report on the jar of preservers Agent Stamos received."

"Meanwhile, my son is sequestered away, with that cult doing God only knows what to him," Candace said, clearly trying not to snap.

Locke met her gaze unwaveringly, "Mrs. Kincade, the wheels of investigation need to turn at a speed that won't derail the process. I want Colton returned as soon as possible. But I know from experience that we can't send anyone else in without the risk of the investigation exploding in our faces."

"Is there any way to speed up the lab work?" Candace begged.

"The lab work can only proceed at the speed of science. Dr. Leiermann already fast tracked the analysis," Blake said. "We don't yet have the technology for instantaneous results."

***

"'The speed of science'? Candace said, over supper in her hotel room.

"Leiermann, our forensics lead, promised she'd call me the moment she got the results," Blake replied.

"I'm sorry if I sound like a Karen. I'm just... I'm worried sick for Colton."

"I give you my word: you'll be the next to know the results. And a Karen? You?"

"Colton's half-sister Margot uses the term, though she'd be the first to say everyone we know with the name Karen doesn't act anything like the meme," Candace said.

Blake's work phone vibrated in his trouser pocket. He snatched it out. Leiermann's lab number showed on the lock screen. He answered, putting it on speaker. "Blake Matherton here, Mrs. Kincade is listening."

"I've got good news and bad news," Leiermann's husky alto spoke.

"Just give us the news, good or not," Candace said.

"The news is, the preserves tested positive for the reagent."

"Oh, hell," Blake murmured.

"God help us," Candace prayed. "And is there any evidence that my son is...consuming this drug?"

"Dante indicated the food tasted odd, not bad, but as if they'd laced it with something," Blake said.

"I've got that urine sample from Agent Stamos. It's currently processing," Leiermann said. *"I'll get the results to you after I forward them to Agent Stamos."*

"Is my son going to end up like that... thing which showed up at the church?" Candace asked.

"Let's take it one step at a time," Leiermann said.

* * *

I waited until after lights out, feeling like I'd slipped back to junior high school camp and plotted to TP the least-liked counselor's cabin. My time in the military had taught me how to half sleep with one ear open.

As soon as the house settled down, I crept out of bed and finding my boots, tied the laces together and slung them around my neck. I moved as quickly and quietly along the hallway as I could, heading for the rear stairs. I found the side door and slipped out into the night, pulling my boots on. I stalked across the grass, avoiding the gravel paths as much as possible as I approached the warehouse. Once I reached it, I crept along the side, seeking an unblocked window or an unlocked door.

Hearing footsteps, I pressed against the wall, going still and holding my breath.

Lanterns bobbed along the path. Sister Alice and Brother Joe appeared, carrying large brown paper bundles. They headed for the front door, rattling it open. A strip of wan fluorescent light spilled across the grass. Still hugging the wall, I crept close, taking out my phone, opening the camera and hitting record.

What I took for a warehouse had clearly served as a dairy barn. Metal stalls and stanchions lined the walls and ran down the middle of the building, but I didn't see a single cow. Instead, a dozen people lay chained in the middle stalls, some lying inert, others flailing and snarling at the ends of their chains. A few stood silent, staring into space.

Sister Alice and Brother Joe approached each person – I wasn't sure if I could call them zombies in this context. They unwrapped the bundles uncovering pieces of raw meat, carefully laying a piece in a bowl in a corner of each stall.

"Easy, easy, be at peace," Sister Alice said to the more aggressive figures. They quieted down, but only just that. Some picked up the meat and munched on it, others tore into their meal.

I'd seen enough. I pulled away from the door and hastened back to the house. I had more than enough to share with the team.

The next morning, I got a moment to call "my girlfriend", as well as the privacy a call like that needed.

I went out to a far corner of the orchard, the trees already picked clean and shedding leaves and, called Locke. "We got heavy evidence."

"How heavy?" Locke asked.

"I'm sending a video."

When the file loaded, I could hear Locke breathing more audibly on the other end of the line. *"Zombies."*

"Maybe, though they're more like Ganados."

"What?"

"The spawn in *Resident Evil 4*. I don't think they're truly zombies, since some of them seem to have some level of sapience. Some calmed down when Sister Alice spoke to them."

"...I see. I might be able to send in an agriculture inspector along with one of ours. We already have a case on them for the jam. And your urinalysis."

"Leiermann do her magic?"

"Yes. How much have you eaten?"

"They serve it at breakfast and dinner. I had some at breakfast, but I try and turn it down at supper. They might be cutting the soup with it."

"That makes sense, given the level they found."

"That explains the energy I've had since I got here, and it explains the energy of this lot: they're working morning to night without showing much fatigue. But we're not talking about the usual cult members pushing themselves to the breaking point. I've been going the whole day without tiring: they got me harvesting their apple crop. Hate to say it, but this elixir, this zombie juice works."

"At what cost?"

"No argument there." I ended the call. I spotted Martine, the pale girl who looked like Sister Alice's younger sister or cousin peering at me from among the trees. I smiled and approached her. "Yah know, it's rude to eavesdrop on someone's phone call. You might hear things unfit for your virgin ears."

She looked at me with a blasé expression. "Considering the stuff I put up with between my dad and his whore girlfriend, and my mom and her revolving door of boyfriends, it wouldn't be anything I haven't heard. It's why my aunt Alice had custody of me."

"You're with better people." Messed-up world when a zombie cult does better by a kid than her own family.

She shrugged. "They're okay, if you can handle the happy shiny people holding hands shit. Call me Mart. None of this Brother-Sister shit, okay?"

"Okay by me. It's a bit weird to me anyway: I grew up Catholic. Only time I called someone Brother or Sister was when I was talking to the nun or the friar who taught my class or the deacon in my parish."

"Oooh, used to getting your knuckles whacked with a ruler if you lost your homework?"

"They don't do that anymore, the Church doesn't allow it."

"Least they did something right. You think this crowd is as weird as I do?"

"They're a little too nice for me to trust them. But the work is good."

"Fair enough, if you like farm work."

"I'm guessing you're bearing with being here."

"Better than the alternative, and I don't have the brains for college." A flicker went through her eyes. "Hey, maybe I could do the Instagram tradwife thing, only with a zombie cult instead of Mormonism."

I chuckled. "Go for it. I think there's a corner of ex-cult members on YouTube. Someone might find it interesting."

"One can hope."

Later that day, a truck from the state Department of Agriculture showed up. I kept my head down as I helped load freshly cut firewood into the kiln. But I noticed Brother Spencer giving the inspectors the grand tour. One looked alarmingly like Leiermann, who carried herself like she tromped around farms all the time.

Later, the dinner table conversation seemed muted, though I overheard several members talking to Brother Spencer regarding the unexpected visitors. This led to a conversation about needing to push back, while others speculated what government would look like in a world without death.

The next day, my "parole officers" messaged me, on account of my drug test results. I kept an eye on my rearview mirror expecting someone to follow me.

Locke herself showed up to the meeting, which we held in a van. "We're pulling you out, given your test results."

Officer Obanhein looked ready to go toe with the fellowship. "I don't care how someone worships. People can wear colanders on their heads to keep demon aliens from reading their minds. But drugging people and turning them into literal zombies is a bridge too far. At least they're keeping them confined so this doesn't turn into *Night of the Living Dead*."

"We can't just barge in without a warrant," Locke said. "We couldn't even get the inspectors inside that warehouse."

"Which raised the suspicions of the inspector," Blake said. "Which brings us to the burning question: Where is Colton?"

"I'm not entirely sure where they took him, but I'm gonna slip out tonight and find the hunting camp they're hiding him at. I might have help: a girl in the group who's at best displeased with, at worst indifferent to the group, Sister Alice's foster daughter Martine."

Blake typed on his laptop. "Might be the 'Mart' who showed up on the Discord server...Hm. There's a record of a guardianship granted to an Alice Aldridge dated to four years ago."

"That tracks: Martine looks like she's fourteen, but she talks like she's maybe twenty."

"Yeah, I know her. She aged out of foster care, but she'd rather stay with her aunt till she figures out something better," Obanhein said. "She's moody, but that's most teenagers."

"We'd better move soon," Locke said. "Let's wire you up."

"Tonight. We can pull this off tonight. You got a shaving kit?"

Blake adjusted his glasses and reaching into the backpack at his feet, took out a CVS bag with a bulge shaped like a can of shaving foam. I drew in the proverbial breath and peeled off my fleece jacket.

Once wired up I drove back from the meeting, finding no evidence I'd been followed. When I arrived at the farm, Brother Spencer set me to work, picking sugar pumpkins and loading them into large crates for delivery to a local farm co-op. I worked alongside Mart, her carrying two pumpkins at a time, me carrying one at a time. "You can pick 'em up by the base of the stems," she said.

"You sure?"

"They're tougher than they look. I mean, you can't bonk 'em around hard, but they aren't made of tissue paper."

At lunch break Mart stuck by me but eyed me sidewise as we ate, sitting on the edge of the gathering.

"You're not just some drifter who joined up for a fresh start, are you?" she asked in a low voice, averting her eyes to make our conversation less obvious.

Gad, she had sharp senses. "Okay, if I'm not a drifter, who or what am I?"

"If you really are, you turned informer, or you're a cop in disguise."

"You're good, though I'm higher on the food chain than a cop."

"CIA? NSA? Secret Service? Homeland Security? Some shadow three-or-four letter abbreviation the Feds won't tell us about?"

"FBI."

She looked up at me. "I knew it. I knew they'd send in heavy artillery after Sister Alice reached for the fruit at the top of the tree. I almost called the cops myself when they dragged the dead president's kid in through the Discord server I helped them set up. And then they locked me out."

"That's gotta hurt." I eyed the rest of the crowd to see if they'd taken notice of us. "So what do you know about the hunting camp they took the questulants to?"

"Tell you? I could take you there. They got me going once a day to bring them food and bring the dishes back."

"Once a day?"

"Yeah, it's supposed to keep them focused on other things, like meditating on what they're choosing. I personally think it's a dumb way to prepare, but it's not like I got a vote."

"Back in the medieval times, squires would fast the night before they were made knights. And there's a passage in the Gospel where Christ says some things can be solved only by prayer and fasting, but there's a limit to what He likely had in mind."

"Weird way to do it: only thing fasting does is make me hangry."

"'S why some priests recommend fasting from other things besides food."

"Smart priests." She rose as Brother Spencer approached.

"You two look like you're getting friendly," he said.

"We both had rough times as youngsters," I replied.

"Fair enough. Ready to get back to work?" Brother Spencer asked.

"Ready when you are," Mart replied. He moved on to the next cluster of workers. Mart let out a whuff of relief. "Never trust a guy who's that nice or friendly. C'mon, tough guy from Providence, let's go gather more gourds."

***

The ceramic heater in the rear of the surveillance van just took the edge off the October chill. Blake adjusted his fleece jacket and shifted his can of G-Fuel from the console to the floor between his feet.

"May I sit closer?" Candace asked. "We could keep warm easier that way."

He moved the can from his feet to between his knees. "I would let you, but I'm working."

"Welcome to the drama and action that is surveillance," Agent McLosky, at the other end of the console, said.

"Asking as an author, is it always like this?" Candace asked.

"Cramped and cold with just a small heater?" Blake asked.

"Yes, more or less."

"Gotta keep the server and the transmitter cool," McLosky said.

"In the immortal words of my uncle Badger, when the window of his pick-up truck got stuck open in the dead of a Maine winter, 'Put on anuthuh sweatuh!'" Blake said, mimicking Badger's Down-East accent and baritone growl.

Candace chuckled. "Badger sounds like a character."

"He was. Imagine Central Casting's idea of the townie lobstah fisherman, that was him. I put myself through MIT working summers on his boat," Blake replied.

"Best listen up, Agent Stamos's transmitter just went hot," McLosky said.

Blake pulled on his headset, tilting one earpiece so Candace could listen in.

"All units be advised: we have ears on the location," Locke ordered.

***

Later that night, as I pretended to sleep, someone crept into my room and shook my shoulder. I slid out of bed, dropping to the floor.

"Hey, tough guy," Mart whispered, leaning over me. "Wanna go TP the boys' cabin?"

I reached under my tee shirt to the small of my back and switched on my transmitter. "I'm on it." Hearing her move away in the shadows and slip from the room, I found my pants on a chair and pulled them on. I followed her down the hallway and downstairs to the side door, which she held open for me. Before I stepped outside, I slipped my boots on.

"You been creeping around here before?" She lit an LED lantern and held it up as we walked the trail to the machine shelter.

"Slipped out to peek into the warehouse. Local cops had their suspicions over what's going on."

"Those Ag inspectors weren't just Ag inspectors, were they? Huh, local fuzz doing something for a change. Usually they're too busy chasing teens drinking in the woods to bother us." She started up a four-wheeler. "Get on." she ordered. I obliged, holding onto the back as we bumped along the farm road, past a disused horse pasture (I wondered if horses could zombify if you fed them the elixir). We passed under the shadows of the trees.

"You got a weapon?" she asked. "Spencer's got one of his goons watching the cabin 24/7."

"I got my training: FBI and Army."

"And the size of you would put the fear of hell into 'em. Was your mother Bigfoot or something?"

"Nope, my parents are both short, so when I shot up like a tree, they had no idea where that came from."

The road curved up the side of a large hill, going deeper into the woods before forking off, one side continuing into the forest, the other branching toward a forested tableland with a clearing. We took the side leading to the clearing. A figure loped along the edges. Mart slowed the four-wheeler, the sentry approaching, holding up a lantern. "Who goes there?" he asked, in an adolescent voice.

She killed the motor. "It's me, Mart. The boss sent the big guy along to keep the coyotes off me."

The sentry stepped away. "Got it."

We approached a cabin at the edge of the clearing. When we stepped up onto the porch, I noticed the windows were shuttered, and there were no signs of light. Mart unlocked a pair of padlocks on hasps holding the door shut at the top and bottom. She swung it open, stepping inside and switching on a light before beckoning me.

Four beds stood against the walls inside, one occupied by another questulant and the other, the farthest from the door, by Colton, each hooked up to an IV by the head of the bed. No sign of the questulant who'd joked around the most. What looked like a dog chain was bound each to the bed with enough slack to let them reach a bathroom at the back of the cabin.

"Hey, President's kid." Mart shook Colton's shoulder.

He moaned, turning onto his side. "Huh?"

I approached the foot of the bed. "Colton?"

He blinked up at me. "….Agent Stamos?"

"Yeah, I'm here to get you out.

"Mom found out, didn't she?" he said, sounding simultaneously annoyed and relieved.

"Your security detail reported you giving them the slip. We also found your Discord messages."

He looked away, rolling his eyes.

"Should've cleared your history," Mart said.

"So she sent the goon squad?" he asked.

"Just me. Well, as the spearhead."

"She knows I'm old enough to follow my own path," Colton said.

"Didn't look like you wanted to go with Sister Alice's crew when they grabbed you in that parking garage. You really want to be here, strapped down, with an IV taped into your arm?"

Colton looked away. Mart leaned down to him. "Colton, let me show you something. Only the inner circle knows about it, but it might give you other ideas."

"All right," he muttered.

She fetched a medical kit from a shelf, unhooked him from the IV, then taped his arm. I grabbed the chain and snapped it, then helped him to his feet. The two of us lead him out into the night.

No sign of the sentry when we emerged. "Well, that isn't ominous," I murmured, helping Colton onto the back of the four-wheeler.

"Tell me first what you're showing me," Colton insisted.

"Not telling you here. You know what they say about one picture being worth a thousand words," Mart said.

"If you don't give me a good reason for going with you, I'll scream," Colton snapped.

"All right. That IV stuff they're giving you? It's got side effects," Mart said.

"Yes, I know. It's why I signed up," Colton grumbled.

"You don't know the half of it," I said, climbing on behind Colton as Mart started the four-wheeler.

We pulled up beside the dairy barn. Mart killed the motor and got off, shinnying up a drain pipe and climbing in through an uncovered window under the eave. Colton stared after her, impressed.

A moment later, the door opened, Mart looking out.

"Gymnastics?" I asked.

"Parkour," she said, stepping aside. "Get in here." I clapped a hand onto Colton's shoulder, steering him through the door.

Howls and moans greeted us along with the reek of not-quite rot. The zombies lunged against the metal stalls, snarling and reaching toward us, their glazed eyes staring.

Colton boggled, his jaw slack. "Who are these...?"

One zombie I didn't recall seeing before, but who looked like a half-revived Questulant Dennis raged in a stall closer to the door.

"What...? No...." Colton said, dismayed.

"It doesn't always work like they promise," Mart said. "The cooker who brings the stuff to us could tell you the reasons and the real percentages better than I could."

"Seems it works like they promise for only one to five percent of the folk who take it," I added. "You sure you want to play those odds, especially for your mother?"

Colton stepped back toward the door, rubbing his bandaged arm, shaking his head. "This can't be real. They've gotta be faking this. They had some bad drink or bad drugs."

"Look at their faces. Look at their eyes! That look like only a bad trip to you?" I said.

Colton said nothing but stood trembling in annoyance and disbelief, betrayal pulling the corners of his mouth.

Footsteps approached. I turned to find Brother Spencer standing there. "Who let you in here?"

"Oh shit," Mart muttered.

On instinct, I grabbed Colton, throwing him over my shoulder in a fireman sling. He yawped and kicked my chest. "Calm down, kid," I ordered. "Mart, hold still." I grabbed Mart around her waist, tucking her under my arm and bulling past Spencer before bolting toward the driveway to the main road.

The zombies snarled and shrilled behind us. Floodlights on the building snapped on, the sudden light blinding me, even from behind. Something wet that smelled like damp rust or pennies splatted my back, even as I kept running.

"Dammit, that's blood! Why are they throwing blood?" Colton snapped.

The zombie moans turned to open-mouthed snarls. *Bloodlust*, I thought, not letting this observation keep me from pelting down the driveway.

"Where are you going? That's our best convert!" Sister Alice's voice called.

"Not anymore!" Colton yelled.

Shots cracked around us, winging off the trees that lined the drive. Lights shone in the main house, but I kept running.

"Put him down!" - "He's kidnapped him" – "Come back!" - "Don't shoot! You might hit Brother Colton!" several members of the fellowship called out from a near distance. The snarls of one of the younger zombies seemed closer. But I had the advantage of being alive.

I passed the orchards, seeing headlights blazing down the country road before they swung into the drive, followed by two more vehicles pulling in behind it, walling off the outlet. The front doors opened, Blake and Obanhein emerging, a hand each on their respective sidearms.

"Hold your fire, it's me!" I yelled, reaching the nose of the van and letting Mart down first. "I've got a witness and an injured Eagle Boy. There's blood on me, but it ain't mine!"

Shots whizzed past us. Mart hit the dirt, The zombie trailing us got close, reaching for Mart. I got low and slid Colton to the ground and toward another van.

One of Candace's detail emerged from the rear guard vans. I hustled Colton toward him. "Do we want to know why you're covered in blood?"

"Blood makes the resurrected go crazy," Mart called out. "They turned 'em loose!"

"And you are?" the agent asked.

"Martine, call me Mart. I used to be with the Fellowship. They had me babysitting Eagle Boy." Obanhein hustled her after Colton, the Secret Service agent hurrying them back to the van which peeled away, the doors slamming as it disappeared toward the center of town.

I joined Blake near Obanhein's van. "I have your Walther inside, unless you've gone native and you'd prefer the shotgun?"

I found my sidearm and a couple of clips, loading it. "Figured you'd use the shotgun, Maine Boy."

"Ha. Ha. Ha. Incoming." Blake ducked behind an open door of the van.

The shooting had died back, but some of the resurrected shambled into the circle of light cast by the spotlights on the vans.

"Who the hell are these?" one of the deputies asked.

"They released the resurrected," I called back.

Another fellowship member ran up behind the resurrected, firing toward us. I aimed for his shoulder, but another shot, likely from one of the deputies, hit him in the chest. He staggered and fell back, a second shot from Blake dropping him.

I threw out a wordless mental prayer to St. Michael and aimed for the head of the nearest resurrected. The undead stopped in their tracks, then dropped. Maybe I just imagined the gasp of relief from it.

"Aim for the head!" I called.

"That's a harder target," the deputy called back.

Blake looked up from reloading. "He probably meant the resurrected."

As we spoke, the fallen fellowship member shuffled on the ground, awkwardly pulling to his feet before hobbling toward us.

"The hell did that happen?" the deputy closest to us asked.

"We're in a goddamned Romero movie," another deputy said.

I aimed at the fallen cultist's head and fired, ventilating his skull and dropping him. "That's why I said, 'aim for the head'!"

My upper forearm stung. I glanced down, finding blood running from a hole in my shirt. On instinct, I holstered my weapon and clamped my hand down on the hole.

"Agent down!" Blake yelled.

A burning, tingling sensation cut through my arm and up my shoulder as I fell back. Blake darted a glance my way. "Dante, you've stopped bleeding."

"I must've pressed harder on it than I thought."

"That's a wound in the arm. It's likely to bleed hard," the deputy beside us said.

The shouting had died down. The team had started to move in, assessing the injured and the dead... and the not-so-dead. An EMT cut off my sleeve to examine my wound or at least the angry red patch of skin surrounded by drying blood.

"You sure you were shot?" the EMT asked.

"Sure as water is wet, dust is dry, and the Pope is Catholic. My partner and Deputy Brenner can attest to it."

Locke approached, eyeing my arm. "What's going on?"

"I got shot in the arm, but it's ...healed."

Locke stared as if her gaze might burn a second hole in my arm. "Go back to the scene unit and await further instructions from me or Chief Obanhein."

"Understood." I headed back to the battle line of vans to the tech van at the back. McCloskey looked me up and down as I collapsed into a chair.

"You okay, Dan? Teacher send you to the principal's office?" he asked.

"I'm probably not allowed to say."

The scene didn't clear till sunrise when the coroner's office got a refrigerated box-truck to transport the dead and several ambulances had transported the injured. I glimpsed Sister Alice and a few others placed in the back of a van from the county sheriff's office.

Locke ordered me transported to a local hospital, one of the deputies accompanying me while a doctor assessed my condition. We found the bullet snagged in a fold of my jacket when we removed it. A CAT scan found evidence the bullet had gone through my arm, but I showed no sign of impairment.

"What's the verdict?" I asked.

"I'd say you either only got grazed, or you have a direct hotline to the Healer of All Illness Themself," the doctor said. "But the blood on your shirt and the scarring in your arm tells more of the story."

"Well, between you and me and whatever report you file with my superiors, I think I know the rest of the story."

"I'm open to hearing that, if you're at liberty to discuss it. I've seen my share of combat wounds, and I've never seen anything like this before."

"Seen my own share. May I ask where?"

"Afghanistan 2003, and you?"

"Bosnia, 1994."

"That's going back a bit. Go on."

I drew in a breath. "I was on the team infiltrating the Fellowship of Eternal Resurrection."

"I figured that group would cause some kind of trouble. You know how some people or groups seem too good to be true?"

"Yeah. And they were. They're microdosing their members and potential members with zombie-juice. Seems it really raises the dead: got into a shootout with members – cultists, I suppose. Some of them didn't stay dead. Question is, am I going to end up that way?"

"The question to resolve that, would be if this drug has a half-life in your system, if it flushes out or if it rewrites your cells. I suppose time can only tell. But don't try anything rash to test it. No motorcycling without a helmet any time soon."

"I work a high-risk job. I might find out the hard way soon enough."

The doctor cleared me to return to duty, with some reservations on Locke's part. I headed out to catch a lift to the precinct. As I passed through the hospital hallways, a crew of EMTs and nurses hustled a gurney through the hallway. On it lay a bloodied Brother Spencer, fighting against the straps that held him down. I managed to get a look at his face, noticing the vacancy in his clouded eyes. *Light's on, but is anyone home?* I thought.

I hitched a ride back to the precinct, passing through a gauntlet of other FBI agents from the Concord field office, Secret Service agents, State Police from both Massachusetts and New Hampshire, and reporters with cameras of all sizes.

I found Blake suited up and nursing a Starbucks cup, waiting outside the door to an interview room where a deputy sat with Sister Alice who leaned back in her chair with her arms folded on her chest despite the blood and dirt that spattered her clothes.

"You cleared for an interview?" Blake asked without looking at me.

"Locke gave me the go-ahead, but she's keeping me on a shorter leash than usual."

He looked up at me while sipping from his cup. "Any shorter and she'll have you completely healed."

The deputy got up and left the room, closing the door behind her, shaking her head. "You want to talk to her?"

"About time I came clean to her," I said.

"About time I had words for her," Blake added, adjusting the cuffs of his gloves before opening the door and letting me enter first.

Alice looked up at me, blinking, perplexed.

"Sister Alice? I'm Special Agent Dante Stamos of the FBI. This is my partner, Special Agent Blake Matherton."

She blinked again, her shoulders dropping. "I should have guessed. You seemed too good to be true, but I figured I was being paranoid.

"So why am I here now?"

"You're here because you're being accused of kidnapping the son of a former First Lady and holding him in questionable conditions," Blake replied.

"He came to us willingly," Alice argued.

"He didn't look the most willing when you took him from that parking garage," Blake said. "We've seen the footage."

"And you had him and three other young men shackled to beds, with IV bags of a controlled substance taped into their arms," I said.

"They came willingly!"

"He might have, but he's started to have second thoughts. Especially after one of his fellow questulants died suddenly."

"And how do you know that, besides this two-faced liar telling you that?" Alice said, looking at me from the corner of her eye while keeping her face toward Blake.

"We've identified the questulant, also a missing college student named Douglas Seward, originally from Montpelier, Vermont," Blake said. "Also, we've had a very interesting conversation with Martine, your niece."

Alice sighed, deflated. "After I gave her a place to live, she turns against me. I know she didn't always see eye to eye with us, but I didn't think she'd go that far."

"She saw through what was going on. She didn't care much for Colton, because of his father's positions, but she decided it was more important to do the right thing."

"So what do you plan to do with me?"

"We're going to ask you a few questions. We only want answers. What happens to you depends on what a federal judge and a jury of your peers decide," Blake said. "But it can go better for you if you could explain why you chose Colton specifically."

She crossed her arms on her chest. "I'm taking the Fifth Amendment. And I want a lawyer."

I stood up. "All right, that can be arranged," Blake said.

He and I started out of the room. "Dante, if we'd offered to make you a questulant, would you have taken it?" Alice asked.

I stopped, my hand on the door latch. "I would've, to get closer to Colton and complete my mission. But for myself? No."

"May I ask you one more question?" she asked.

"Of course."

"What happens to Martine?"

"We're not at liberty to answer that," Blake said.

"She's going to be fine on her own: she's strong and clever in her own way," I said as we headed out into the hallway just as a woman in a suit carrying an attaché case entered the room.

"What *is* going to happen to Mart?" I asked Blake, once the court-appointed attorney had closed the door.

"I probably shouldn't tell even you. I sat in on a conversation between Martine and the same deputy who questioned her aunt. Martine is quite willing to inform on her aunt's little circle and serve as federal witness. She's also considering ex-cult member podcasting."

"Pretty sure no one's covered a zombie cult, and I don't mean figurative zombies, as in drones with no thoughts of their own."

"I'm certain there hasn't been a cult where people willingly became zombies, or not literal shambling undead horrors."

I felt Blake's gaze on me as we walked away from the interview rooms. "So what's the verdict on your condition?"

I caught him up on the doctor's assessment. Blake stared at my arm. "I don't want to think about the implications of that. I hope it wears off."

"You sure? It could cut down on my medical bills."

"It could augment them. It could lead to cell overgrowth."

My heart dropped into my boots. I pushed aside the memory of Kathleen's mother in hospice. "Guess I'd better start lighting candles for St. Peregrine. Think I'd better have Leiermann look at me?"

"You're better off if Leiermann monitors your condition, till we figure out what's going on."

"Better to just wait it out and nick myself while shaving and see what happens. Easily done: I shave twice a day."

"It's your decision. I'd rather you didn't have Leiermann as your examining physician, if she had the license for it."

"Why, she patched you up in the past?"

"Off the books, when a sparring match got heated. She handled it as if she was analyzing data from a crime scene."

A thought crossed my mind. "What happens if this doesn't wear off, if the worst happens and I lose my self, though my body keeps going?"

He looked up, his gaze meeting mine. "If it happens in the field, and I'm present, I will do what you need me to do."

"Do I have your word? You wanna swear in the writings of Newton or Einstein or something?"

"More like Pythagoras and Aristotle, but for you, I'd swear on the proverbial stack of Bibles. You have my word."

I released the proverbial breath I didn't realize I was holding, but the next breath caught in my throat. "I'm glad it would be you, but I hope you don't have to hold yourself to that."

"For Kathleen's sake, I hope so too. I don't want to have to deal with the paperwork afterward."

***

"I told you, I wanted to join them so you wouldn't lose me like you lost Dad," Colton insisted, pacing the floor of his mother's hotel room. "I was going to ask you to join them, too."

"Your devotion and generosity are admirable. However… the elixir is untested. We barely know what it's going to do to the living," Blake argued.

"I'm not sure I'd want to find out," Candace said.

"Then get it tested! You know something about science, do something with it!" Colton snapped.

Candace looked at Blake. "It's being tested now: we've sent it up to the FDA for a full analysis. But what happens when it's found to have some…undesirable side effects?"

"All those pharmaceuticals have side effects. You never listen to those TV medication commercials?" Colton resumed in the voice of a TV commercial voiceover. "Blaxopreen is not for everyone. Side effects include bad breath, hair loss, involuntary dancing, heart attack, cancer and nausea."

Candace hid a smirk in her hand.

"You saw what happened to the dead, we're just finding out what it does to the living. Especially on you, since you were ingesting it daily, and whether or not the effects are permanent," Blake said.

"Well, I guess we're all going to find out," Colton said, stalking to his bedroom.

"Colton, don't do anything stupid," Candace pleaded.

"I don't plan to," Colton murmured, pausing without looking up before continuing on his way.

Huhn, Roarke's partner, looked at Candace, who nodded. Huhn nodded in reply and followed Colton.

"You can send the goon squad away!" Colton yelled.

Blake shook his head. "He sounds like me."

"You're a terrible influence on him," Candace said with a wavering smile.

"Would you prefer if I stayed awhile?"

"I'd prefer that. I'd like it if you stayed the night."

"Is that a proposition? Do you want me to help you block out a love scene?"

"I have one that's stuck in my head, but blocking it out isn't obligated."

"Good. Because I have reports to write up."

"We could make it a joint writing session."

They'd only gotten settled, he at his laptop with his back to a wall for security, she with her own writing, the lids of the devices just touching. Something smashed in Colton's room. Huhn barked something; Colton shouted back incoherently. Blake slammed his laptop shut, his hand going for his sidearm. He and Roarke ran to Colton's room, Candace at their heels.

They found Huhn trying to haul Colton backward from over the railing of the balcony opening off his room.

"Someone call 911," Huhn rasped. Colton kicked him in the ankle to no effect.

"Let me go," Colton snarled. Eyeing Blake, he added, "Go away!"

"I'm staying here. If I left, it would break your mother's heart," Blake said. "Besides, my team and your security detail and the locals put too many hours into trying to get your sorry ass back."

"Fuck you!" Colton shouted.

Blake snerked. "You're going to have to step up your insult game, zombie-boy."

Colton peered around Huhn's hip. "The fuck you call me?!"

"You heard me."

Sirens wailed in the near distance. "So why the fuck do you call me that?!"

"You know the reason why." Blake grew more serious. "We're only just finding out if that elixir has a half-life, if it recodes your genetics or it merely adjusts your biochemistry. Either way, I'm not letting you splat into that patio below."

By now an emergency crew had appeared in the courtyard patio, including a fire captain and several EMTs looking up at them. More emergency workers appeared, bringing a giant air mattress which they quickly inflated.

"That's a sight better than the usual 'Oh, you have your whole life ahead of you' shit or 'Oh, it's selfish for you to throw your life away' crap."

"I'll admit, my sense of humor is at best dry as dust, at worst, my jokes sound better in my head. But in lieu of platitudes, I could tell you a tale from a personal experience."

"What, how someone talked you off a ledge and how grateful you were afterward? Spare me the sob story."

"There was one case where I went in deep cover with some neo-Nazis. I suppose I should merely call them Nazis, but this is no place to debate semantics. They'd found an eldritch text and opened a portal contacting as nasty as, if not worse than the thing which killed your father."

"And so you closed the portal and saved the world. The end."

"Yes and no, there was more: The entity they had summoned reached out to me, offering me a vision of a possible future, free of pain and suffering, if I gave it one thing."

"And what was that?"

"If I would let it ride my head and use me as a vehicle to shape the world to its vision. But I couldn't do that, not at the cost of my humanity.

"The portal collapsed, and my team arrested the Nazis for illegal arms dealing and using suppressed magical texts."

"So what're you trying to tell me?"

"I'm trying to tell you to have the good sense to value what you have and use it to better your world, instead of reaching for what you don't because the price could cost you everything."

Colton eyed him, then swung his leg back over the railing. "Now get your hands off my belt. That's weird."

Blake did as requested. "It was the nearest part of you I could grab."

Candace approached, followed by a pair of EMTs accompanied by a woman leading a Golden Retriever on a harness with a vest reading "Mental Health Support Animal."

"Are you all right?" Candace asked.

"I am, now that your dumb boyfriend got done chewing me out," Colton said.

"I'm afraid you'll still need an assessment," one of the EMTs said, as the woman with the canine therapist approached, the dog looking up at Colton as the EMTs gently guided him from the room,

"He'll be all right, if he has the good sense to keep his ears and his heart open," Blake said.

"What about physically?" Candace asked.

"We'll see what Leiermann's barrage of tests reveal."

She reached out to take his hand. He went still and allowed her to do so. "If I hadn't seen your body-cam video of that fight with the cult, I'd almost be thankful he got that dose."

"From what he told us, when Obanhein's people interviewed him, he wishes he'd never touched that stuff with a thirty-nine-and-a-half-foot pole. And who let you have that footage?"

She smiled out. "I had a chat with Locke. Until I completely knew better, the part of me that fears losing him wanted to think differently about their methods."

He loosened his grip on her hands. "But at what cost?"

"I know it's a cliché, but that part of me realized there are worse things than dying."

He pressed her hands, pulling them close to his chest. "The worse fate is a life without living."

Phantom Flu

Josiah Santos

CHAPTER 1

"You make time for what's important to you," he said, flipping a burger patty on the grill. It smelled *almost* as good as it looked so far. Miguel Shoemaker wiped his hands on his apron and let the patty sizzle for a moment.

"I guess I just feel guilty about relaxing when there's a million things to do," Bud sighed.

Miguel laughed. "I know what you mean, Bud. There's *always* something to do. But I believe that in the good Lord's infinite wisdom, He created a day of rest for a reason. We're not meant to work ourselves to death, you know."

"Never been a church going man, but I'll drink to that," Bud said, raising his beer.

Miguel flipped the patty. "Listen Bud, I know things at the office aren't slowing down anytime soon but thinking about work when you're not at work is just going to make you feel like you never left work…does that make sense?"

Bud rotated his hand from side-to-side and smiled. "You've never been the best with words, but I'm picking up what you're laying down."

A baseball came speeding towards Miguel. A child shouted to watch out, but it wasn't all that necessary. Miguel had seen his two sons playing catch the whole time. The oldest, Louis, had moments ago, thrown the ball straight over his little brother's head. Luckily, Miguel's reflexes were on point, and he managed to catch it.

"Sorry Dad," Louis apologized.

"Try aiming two feet lower next time," Miguel advised as he threw the ball back.

"Hey, I'm not *that* short!" The youngest son, Ellis, shot back.

"*Jump* next time, you little goblin," Louis teased.

"Good to see the Shoemaker family still getting along," Bud laughed.

"As always," Miguel said sarcastically.

"Speaking of which, where's the missus? She still inside?" Bud asked.

Miguel nodded. "She's been working from home this week. We think she caught a bug at the office."

Bud shook his head. He'd been a friend of the Shoemakers since they first moved in. He even brought them a homemade pie and welcomed them to the neighborhood. Granted, Bud's wife made the pie and insisted they meet their new neighbors. But the Shoemakers didn't need to know that. Shortly after moving in, Bud pulled a few strings and helped the Shoemakers land a job at his office working in finance.

Miguel's wife, Sam, peered through the window to see her boys playing and her husband talking with Bud. She opened the door but stayed in the doorway.

"You boys having a nice time?" She asked the group.

Her two sons said hello to their mother and Bud asked how she felt Sam shrugged her shoulders, not really having a good answer for that yet.

"Well, I hope you get to feeling better," Bud said with a smile.

"Thanks, I'm going to take my zombified-self back inside now. You boys better be playing nice!" Sam directed that last part towards her two sons.

"We are!" They both said in unison.

"No, they're not," Miguel said, winking at his wife.

"That's what I thought," Sam mumbled as she closed the door.

"Dad, you always rat us out! Not cool!" Ellis whined. He was only in 4th grade, but sometimes he acted older than his age…sometimes. Miguel always saw Sam when he looked at Ellis. He had his mother's eyes and her gentle spirit. It was like God hit copy and paste on Sam when Ellis was born.

"I'm just here to speak the truth, son," Miguel said, placing his hand over his heart.

"Whatever. You're here to get me in trouble with mom. I know you're up to no good," Ellis said, pointing as his father.

"I know *you're* up to no good. Miguel pointed back as the two smiled at each other.

Miguel had always worried that his sons wouldn't like him. After all, Miguel's own father really wasn't much of a father, just a man who lived in their house. But Miguel wanted to be something better; he wanted to *know* his kids. Despite Ellis and Louis being little devils sometimes, he thanked God for his two greatest reasons for living.

"Hey Dad, check this out!" Louis shouted.

"Hold on!" Miguel called back. Miguel took the patty off the grill, put in on a plate, and handed it to Bud. "There's buns over there and condiments on the table."

"Thank you, sir! I trust that this is edible," Bud joked.

"If it's not, you can choke on it," Miguel shot back.

Miguel walked over to where his two sons stood and noticed that they were bent over looking at something.

"Dad, look! It's a caterpillar!" Ellis cheered in excitement.

As advertised, there was a small caterpillar crawling up one of their plants in the garden. The caterpillar was about the size of an adult's thumb and was inching its way onto one of the plant's leaves.

"You ever seen one like this?" Louis asked his father.

Miguel honestly hadn't. The caterpillar was all black and had several thin, long needlelike purple spikes on its body. Miguel shook his head, admitting he didn't know what kind of caterpillar it was, but then again, he didn't consider himself an expert on caterpillars to begin with.

"It looks so fuzzy and cute!" Ellis exclaimed.

"Don't touch it, genius," Louis instructed as he smacked his little brother's hand away. "You don't know if it's poisonous. And those aren't fuzzy hairs, they're spines."

"Like a porcupine?"

"Sure, like a porcupine."

Miguel smiled, remembering the day Ellis was born. He held him in his arms and sat down so Louis could see his new brother. "Being a big brother is a heavy responsibility. You must protect your little brother and help him grow up to be a real man. That means correcting his mistakes with love and guiding him to make smart decisions. You sure you're up to the task?"

Louis nodded and held out his arms to hold his brother. "I want to see him!"

Miguel focused his attention back to the black and purple caterpillar. "Hey, Bud, come look at this!"

When Bud walked over, hamburger in hand and still chewing another bite, and knelt to see the famous caterpillar. "Well, look at you," he said to the caterpillar.

"Dad, can we keep it as a pet? I promise I won't touch its pines," Ellis pleaded.

"Spines," Louis corrected.

"It can be your pet, but he has to stay outside. Caterpillars aren't meant to live in a cage. They want to be free; you know?" Miguel tried to compromise. He knew Sam wouldn't be thrilled with an ugly insect living in the house.

Ellis nodded. "Okay, deal!"

"He'll need a name," Louis suggested.

"How about…Kitten? Kitten the caterpillar!" Ellis announced.

Bud laughed and Louis put a hand over his face in embarrassment.

"Perfect." Louis shook his head.

With the official naming ceremony over, everyone got up and walked back to resume their activities. The boys went back to playing catch. Miguel put another meat patty on the grill and pressed it down with his spatula.

"I always wanted kids of my own. Bud frowned but then quickly slapped on a smile as not to bring the mood down.

"You and your wife—" Miguel started.

"*I'm* the problem. When we found out, I could see in my wife's eyes how much she wanted a child. Not being able to provide that for her…" Bud trailed off.

Miguel thought quickly so Bud's mind wouldn't go to such a dark place. "You know Ellis and Louis have always looked up to you guys. You made us feel like family from the moment we moved here to Louisiana. As far as I'm concerned, you *are* our family. And the boys think of you and your wife like an aunt and uncle."

Bud smiled as he watched Louis and Ellis throw the baseball to one another. "I'm glad we made time to do this," Bud said softly.

"We make time for what's important to us," Miguel reminded him with a warm smile.

CHAPTER 2

He swished around a mix of toothpaste and water in his mouth and spit into the sink. Putting the toothbrush away, he turned to see his daughter standing in the restroom doorway.

"Teeth!" The girl exclaimed, pointing to the toothbrush.

Jeremiah nodded and smiled. "That's right. Daddy was brushing his teeth."

Jeremiah Carter looked at his one-year-old daughter and his smile faded. She was a spitting image of the woman that walked out on them both. She wasn't ready for a child and neither was he; getting pregnant young and fresh out of high school was never the plan. Jeremiah knew the risks of not using a condom, but things just happened in the moment. He didn't feel like his daughter should have to pay for that. She wasn't a mistake. A surprise, sure. But he never saw her as a mistake.

She was scared and didn't want to give up her life, so she left and told Jeremiah not to follow. Not wanting to force her to stay in a relationship she wasn't happy with, he watched her leave out the door, their daughter in his arms. Amelia Carter looked up at her father and reached out her arm. Jeremiah kissed her tiny hand and told her it was going to be alright. He was young and as frightened as any new parent would be, but he told himself he wouldn't leave, *promised* himself he'd never leave.

"Teeth bush!" Amelia said, taking a few wobbly steps towards her father.

"Tooth. Brush," Jeremiah said slowly and clearly.

"Teeth bush!" Amelia repeated.

"I guess we'll work on that. Come here, you. Jeremiah picked her up and checked her diaper for any gifts she might've left him. Clean diaper. "Thank you," he told her.

After he got her dressed there was a knock at his apartment door, right on cue. He looked through the door peephole and opened it when he recognized the woman standing in the hall.

"You're right on time," Jeremiah commented and picked up Amelia.

"Church lady is always on time," she laughed.

Her real name was Karen; they had met Jeremiah at a local church where he brings Amelia for daycare. For the longest time–Jeremiah couldn't remember her name, so he always called her "church lady" silently to himself and out loud to Amelia. One day, he accidently called her–"church lady" in front of her and his whole face rivaled Rudolph's nose. Karen never let Jeremiah forget that.

"Ready to go, little one?" Karen asked Amelia, giving her a comforting smile.

Karen worked at the local daycare and offered to bring Amelia while Jeremiah went to work during the day. Since they lived in the same apartment complex, it was convenient for them both. Amelia raised her arms towards Karen as if to say, "carry me."

"Aren't you forgetting someone?" Jeremiah asked his daughter. He went over to the couch and picked up a plush dog. Despite being half the size of Amelia, she took him everywhere. The puppy plush had a pink bow tied around its neck and was all white with some dark brown spots on his long, droopy ears.

"Pup!" Amelia exclaimed, bouncing up and down in excitement. She reached out her arms to embrace him. She happily took Pup from Jeremiah and hugged the puppy real close.

"Thanks again for taking her. I know you don't have to do this," Jeremiah said in a more serious tone to express that he really did appreciate it.

"Hey, it's no problem. You know I love taking this little cutie pie," Karen smiled. And with that, she carried Amelia and Pup off.

Once at work, Jeremiah put his apron on and got on a cash register. He worked as a manager of a small mom and pop coffee shop. It wasn't anything special, but it paid well enough. The owners knew Jeremiah was a single dad living in a small apartment, so they made sure he and his daughter were financially taken care of. Jeremiah appreciated the job, but he knew that he wanted to provide something better for his daughter someday, maybe start setting aside money so she didn't have to be a high school dropout like her father.

A young man in his early twenties, Jeremiah felt like he wasn't going anywhere special in life. However, he was willing to be a nobody so his daughter could grow up to be somebody. The owners arrived a few hours after Jeremiah clocked in, just to check in on things. The owners were elderly and saw Jeremiah as their own child.

"How are you today, son?" The old man asked.

Jeremiah smiled his best and told him he was doing just fine.

"Things seem a bit slow today," the old woman asked, looking around at a rather empty store.

"Yes, ma'am. The new guys called in sick today, so it's just me and the stockers. We should be just fine though," Jeremiah replied.

"Unreliable little—" the old man started.

"Now, now, don't use your potty mouth in our store," the old woman stopped her husband. "You know that they might just be sick."

"Both of them? On the same day?"

"Yes, give people a chance."

Jeremiah laughed to himself. They argued like the old married couple that they were but he could tell they were still madly in love. For one thing, they held hands everywhere they went. And just the way the woman looked at her husband, Jeremiah wondered if his parents ever felt that way about each other, even at their best. Regardless, he enjoyed watching them operate the store together; it gave him hope that real love did exist, that not every couple was doomed to eventually hate each other and leave a broken home behind them.

"Well, you tell everyone that we made you guys a nice salad. You've all been working so hard lately," the old woman said sweetly as she went out to her car and came back with a giant bowl of salad filled with various fruits.

"Call us if it gets too busy, son," the old man instructed.

"Have a good day, sir. Jeremiah nodded as the two owners left.

The stockers ended up eating all the salad before Jeremiah got a chance to try it. Not that it mattered, he always brought his own lunch. The rest of the day went on without incident. Business picked up later in the afternoon, but other than that, it was a normal day at work. Afterwards, he drove to the daycare to pick up Amelia.

She crawled to him immediately when she saw him. Amelia could walk, but only a few steps without falling. Her quickest way to get around was still crawling. Jeremiah picked her up and asked her how her day was.

"Colors!" She shouted.

Jeremiah wasn't sure what she meant by that.

"We colored pictures of butterflies today," Karen translated, presenting the picture Amelia had colored. Purple, blue, and green colors were all over the butterfly in crayon without any rhyme or reason. Nothing stayed in the lines.

"Butters!" Amelia said proudly as she took the picture from Karen.

"You sure did color that butters, look at you!" Jeremiah complimented.

"Pup! My Pup!" Amelia said, pointing to Pup sitting in her chair where she was coloring.

Karen went over to retrieve Pup and gave it to Amelia. "See you guys tomorrow?"

Jeremiah nodded and thanked her as he carried his daughter back to the car. Placing Amelia in her car seat, Jeremiah kissed her on the forehead and told her how much he missed her.

"Kiss Pup!" Amelia requested, holding up Pup.

Jeremiah gave Pup a kiss too and brushed Amelia's hair away from her face. "I love you so much, baby. I always will."

Chapter 3

Despite working in different departments, Bud and Miguel always met up for lunch.

"You remember that odd caterpillar Ellis found the other day when I was over?" Bud asked through a mouthful of food. Always a good guy, but never well-versed in manners.

"I assume you're referring to Kitten the caterpillar?" Miguel laughed.

Bud laughed, too. "I think I found my own Kitten in my yard yesterday."

"No kidding? It looks similar?"

"Same color and everything. Anyway, I took it inside and had a little plastic cage for it. I was hoping to raise it until it becomes a butterfly, and then Ellis and I could release it together. I just figured that Kitten might become a butterfly and fly off before Ellis gets a chance to see it. You know, if it's okay with you."

"Oh yeah! Thanks Bud, I know he'll love that."

"Well, I best be getting back now. Have a good one."

"You too, Bud. Have a good rest of your day."

Later that night, Sam started to prepare dinner as the two boys sat at the table, doing their homework.

Sam picked up a broom and handed it to Louis. "Here, make yourself useful."

Louis looked at the broom and said, "no thanks."

"Nobody is too good to push a broom. Now sweep so I can get started on dinner. After all, this is *your* dirt that you track in the house."

"Fine, but don't say I don't do anything around here."

"Let me know when you start."

There was a small tv in the kitchen that Sam used to watch the evening news. The only thing newsworthy was a statement issued by the FDA recalling various fruits, vegetables, and romaine lettuce.

"Just great. Guess that means we'll be eating more pasta and chicken for now," Sam commented out loud.

Ellis turned to face the backyard window and said, "no more carrots and leaves for you, Kitten."

Sam smiled. "Kitten can eat the leaves that are outside. It just means Mommy can't buy the leaves we eat in our salad."

To Ellis, lettuce and leaves were the same thing so Sam usually humored him. After dinner, Miguel asked how Sam was feeling.

"Better actually," she replied. "I think I'm going to try and go back to work tomorrow.

"You sure? I don't want you to push it if you're not feeling a hundred percent," Miguel said.

"I'm sure, honey. It was like I woke up this morning brand new."

"Come on, Sam. You've had this flu for nearly a week and half now. You sure you just got over it all in one night?"

"I'm not lying!" She protested. "I really do feel a lot better. You have to trust me."

Miguel sighed and nodded, "alright, alright. I believe you."

"Anytime someone says, 'I believe you' like that, it means they don't."

Miguel hung his head in defeat, I really *do* believe you. You have to trust me." He kissed her and got up from his chair. "How about I make you some tea?"

"I'm not sick, but I will take some tea." She stuck her tongue out at him like she knew he was only asking because he really didn't believe her.

Bud looked in the plastic cage where the purple and black caterpillar was. He noticed some tiny particles floating inside the cage and thought for a moment. Worried that whatever it was, it would make the caterpillar sick, he lifted the plastic door on the top of the cage to release the tiny particles.

"There you go, little fella. Sorry I didn't see these floating around in your cage the other day. Must've picked them up from outside where I found you," Bud apologized.

CHAPTER 4

Miguel looked around the office the next day and noticed a few people in his department were missing. He asked a fellow coworker if they had heard from the missing people.

"All of them are out sick. Looks like we'll be shorthanded today," the coworker answered.

"You think there's a bug going around?" He asked.

"I heard on the news last night that people have been catching a flu. That's all I know."

"Yeah, tell me about it. My wife just recovered from the flu."

"Well, let's hope it doesn't spread any farther. Last thing we need right now is *more* people out sick."

Miguel nodded in agreement. During his lunchbreak, he also noticed that Bud wasn't there to meet him. In fact, the restaurant they usually ate at had more empty tables than normal.

***

Karen carried Amelia inside the daycare and set her down in the play area. She took a headcount and noticed that three children hadn't arrived yet. Asking a coworker, she discovered the children's parents had called to inform them that they wouldn't be coming today. Their children were all coming down with the flu.

***

Meanwhile, at a local farm, a CDC truck pulled into the dirt driveway, letting out a few workers wearing gas masks and plastic covers over their faces. Hugo got out of the truck and stretched. He had worked for the CDC for a few years but hadn't seen a day quite like this. He immediately took notice of the lack of noise. Not even birds chirping. He quickly took out his phone, verifying he arrived at the right farm. The air was still, and clouds blocked out any sunlight. No animals in clear eyesight or within earshot. A farmer emerged from his house and jogged over to where Hugo was standing.

"My apologies, didn't mean to keep you waiting." The farmer began.

"That's quite alright. So, where are they?" Hugo asked.

The farmer led the CDC workers over to where he kept his cows and explained the situation. "I mean, you can see for yourselves. I'm sorry I didn't give you a whole lot of detail over the phone. As you'll see, it's just better if I show you."

One CDC worker turned and held back the urge to vomit. There was a nasty pile of puke in one corner of the barn; most of the vomit was spread across the ground.

"They just can't seem to keep anything down," the farmer explained further. "It started with one of my cows, then they all got whatever sickness the first one had. Every one of my cows!"

"Look at their eyes," Hugo whispered to one of his coworkers.

The cows appeared to have some strange puss oozing from their eyes. Even their skin wasn't right. The hair on their bodies appeared to be falling off, leaving small bald patches. The hair that did remain looked almost a dark yellow color. The white and black hair was now a sickly yellow and faded black.

"How quickly did this happen?" Hugo asked while the rest of his crew took saliva samples from the cows.

The farmer thought for a minute. "When the first cow got it, she managed to recover after a few days. But this sickness came back, and it was more aggressive than ever. The other cows didn't get it until the sickness came back. That's not even the strangest part."

"What do you mean?"

The farmer motioned for Hugo to follow him, leading him out to a nearby field. He pointed at a few horses in a pen. Hugo wasn't sure what to make of it; the horses appeared to have the same symptoms the cows did, except the horses were all pacing back and forth, some walking in circles.

"They do that all day. The horses were never even near the cows when they got sick. I purposely kept my cows far away from my horses. They *still* got it!" The farmer exclaimed.

Hugo didn't want to say anything just yet. He had a few ideas of what it *might* be but didn't want to speculate in front of the farmer and further worry him.

"I have to admit, this isn't even what I wanted the CDC to come out for," the farmer revealed.

"You know, sir, the CDC really isn't for—" Hugo began.

"I know, I know. But I needed to come up with a way to get you guys out here. Please see my son. *Please*," the farmer pleaded. "He has it the worst. I'm afraid to go near him for fear that I might catch it too. His skin is all—"

"Alright, I'll see him, okay? Just stay here and show me where he is," Hugo instructed.

"He's in the attic," the farmer stood outside his house and refused to go inside.

"In the attic? What's he doing there?" Hugo questioned.

"Please just go see him!" The farmer urged.

Hugo didn't feel right about the situation, but he still went up to the attic.

CHAPTER 5

Saturday arrived after a rough work week for Miguel. He sat at home watching TV with his wife and boys when he got a call from Bud.

"Hey buddy, how are you?" Bud asked on the other end.

"*Me?* How are you? I haven't seen you at work at all this week!" Miguel sat up in his chair.

"I think I got whatever has been going around. Listen, can I ask for a favor?" Bud's voice usually wasn't this serious, and Miguel easily caught on to that.

"Of course, Bud. What's the matter?"

"My wife was involved in a car accident yesterday, so our car is totaled."

"Oh man, is she alright?"

"Yeah, she wasn't seriously injured, just a few bruises."

"Well thank God for that. What happened?"

"This driver must've been drunk or something. She said he was driving all crazy. Anyway, I scheduled a doctor visit today and I was wondering if you wouldn't mind driving me."

"Oh, of course. When is it?"

"Two hours from now. Is that okay?"

"Just fine, I'm not doing anything today. I'll be over in a few hours. See you soon, Bud."

Two hours later, Miguel walked over to Bud's house to pick him up. Miguel asked if he could see Bud's wife just to say hi and see how she was recovering.

"Well, she's resting right now, I don't want to wake her up," Bud explained.

Miguel nodded, "no, you're right. Well, you ready to head out?"

Bud nodded and headed out the door. Miguel took note of something as he followed Bud out the door: Bud said he was sick with the flu, but he wasn't visibly ill.

"This doctor visit—" Miguel began until Bud answered his question without him needing to finish it.

"Was for the flu I had. Just want to make sure it's not anything serious, you know?"

"For what it's worth, you look better already."

"Yeah," Bud smiled, "I feel better. Just want a second opinion, that's all."

Something felt off about Bud, but Miguel didn't want to make a big deal out of nothing, so he didn't press any further.

"So, are you guys going to look for a new car? You know Sam and I are happy to help any way we can," Miguel offered.

"Oh, you don't need to do that. We don't want to be a bother."

"Bud, it's really no trouble at all."

"We don't need anything."

Miguel looked at Bud for a moment, and Miguel continued to drive. He didn't have the radio on, so the car was quiet. The strange silence remained in the car until Miguel asked if everything was okay. Bud only responded by nodding. When they reached the doctor's office, they both got out and Bud checked in. They sat down in the waiting room without saying another word to each other. Miguel looked around and took notice of the full waiting room- people coughing and discernably sick.

Miguel slowly put a hand over his nose and mouth, trying to look as casual as possible. Grabbing a magazine on the small table to his right, he opened to a random page and tried to cover his face with it. After only a few minutes, a nurse came in and called Bud to the back.

"See you soon," Bud said as he got up.

"I'll be here," Miguel mumbled.

***

When the doctor came back he recognized Bud, as he had been a patient there a few times before. The doctor sat down at his computer and began pulling up Bud's medical information to see what he was working with.

"So, what brings you in today, Bud?"

"I assume you've heard of this flu going around?" Bud asked, sitting back in his chair.

The doctor immediately shook his head at the mention of the flu. "You won't believe how many people we've been getting in lately for this flu. It's crazy."

"What's the worst case you've seen so far?"

The doctor was a bit taken aback by the odd question, but he had heard worse. "I can't really talk about that, Bud. I wouldn't worry too much about this. I highly doubt this flu will be around much longer. Most of my patients have made a full recovery already. Speaking of which, you don't look nearly as sick as the people out there."

"I've already recovered from the flu," Bud said with a blank expression.

"That's great! So, what brought you in?"

Bud's deadpan tone didn't change. "My wife has it now."

"Your wife, Bud? Why didn't you bring her in?"

"She's sleeping at home."

***

Miguel looked up from his magazine to see a line forming at the front desk. All the people standing in line were coughing or wiping their eyes.

"What do you mean? I need to see the doctor *today*!" The lady at the front of the line argued.

The lady at the front desk calmly told her to look at the waiting room full of people. "We're completely booked up. I'm sorry but I can help you find a nearby location—"

"No! I want to see the doctor!"

"Ma'am, you're holding up the line. I'm telling you that our schedule is booked."

"You don't recognize me? I was here last week! The antibiotics you guys prescribed me didn't work. The flu came back!"

"Ma'am, if this is an emergency, go to the ER."

"Just let me see the doctor for a second! Just a second!" The woman began leaning over the front counter and the front desk lady jumped back.

"Ma'am, stay back!"

The people in line behind her began to pull her away from the front desk and that's when Miguel saw her face. The woman's face was completely pale, and her eyes were oozing some yellowish liquid. The people in the line didn't look in much better shape, but this lady was clearly in need of medical attention.

"Get off me!" She growled, saliva pouring out of her mouth, "get me the doctor *now*! Get me that liar!"

Miguel and the other people in the waiting room watched in silence. The door opened and Bud came back to the waiting room, not even phased by the crazed lady still making a scene.

"Ready?" Bud asked calmly.

Confused but not wanting to stay there any longer and get what this lady had, he shot up from his chair and quickly exited the hospital with Bud.

On the car ride home, Miguel asked what the doctor said.

"It's just allergies. Turns out I didn't have the flu at all. Funny, huh?" Bud responded, appearing to be his normal self.

"Right…that's good," Miguel uttered under his breath.

When Miguel dropped Bud off and went home, he gathered Sam and the boys together in the living room.

"Is everything okay? How is Bud feeling?" Sam asked.

"I don't want any of you going near Bud, okay?"

"But—" Ellis started.

"Promise me! All of you! Everywhere you go from now on, you wear a mask. Nose and mouth covered at all times, got it?"

"Honey, you're scaring me. What's going on?" Sam asked.

"*Promise*!" Miguel ordered sternly.

All three of them immediately promised.

Sam calmly put a hand on Miguel's shoulder and asked what was happening. She did her best to maintain a calm demeanor for the boys. "Miguel, you need to tell us what's going on. What happened at the doctor's office?"

"I don't think this is a flu. Sam, you tell me if you start feeling bad again. We might have to take you to the ER."

"Miguel, I'm fine," Sam grabbed Miguel's face and made him look her in the eyes, "I'm not sick anymore. What happened at the doctor's office?"

"Is Mom going to be okay?" Ellis asked.

Louis looked at his parents and then back at Ellis. "Mom's fine, Ellis. Let's go upstairs. Come on, we'll play a game," Louis gave his parents a look and nodded as he led his little brother upstairs.

"Miguel, talk to me. What's happening? Is it airborne?" Sam asked once the boys were upstairs.

"I don't know, Sam. There was this lady at the doctor's office going absolutely nuts. She was saying something about the flu coming back and she looked horrible. I don't know *what* this is, but there might be a chance it comes back worse than before," Miguel explained, turning around with his back to Sam. He shook his head and put a hand over his face. "You should've seen her Sam."

"Miguel, that was *one* lady. I'm fine. I'm going to remain fine. The boys are fine."

"Bud was acting strange today too. Not crazy like the lady. But just…*off.*"

"He's been sick, Miguel. You're just shaken up. Come on, let's go to bed. You need to rest and clear your head. I believe what you saw, but don't let it worry you. Look at me," Sam turned her husband around. "I'm okay. I feel great. Stop worrying."

Miguel nodded, "I love you, Sam. I don't want you to get worse, that's all."

"You're not going to lose me, Miguel. You're stuck with me," Sam smiled, which made Miguel smile back.

He looked at her and fought back thoughts of what life would be like without her. Without the boys. He didn't know what this flu was, but he was sure that a flu shot wasn't going to fix it. Miguel went to bed and stared up at the ceiling, unable to get that woman's face out of his head- the bloodshot eyes and oozing yellow liquid dripping down her face.

Chapter 6

Jeremiah looked around the store; he had gotten to work a little late since Karen wasn't able to take Amelia to daycare that morning. He had to drive her to daycare himself and arrived about half an hour late. Despite this, the store looked like a ghost town. The owners didn't even call him to ask why he had been late. In fact, the owners were nowhere to be seen. After a few minutes, one of the stockers came into work and immediately asked if the store was closed.

"You'd think so," Jeremiah nervously laughed, "I just got here."

"Anybody else show up?" His coworker asked.

Jeremiah shook his head and looked around with the coworker. It was a small store, so it only took a matter of seconds to realize nobody was there. The coworker asked if anyone had called in sick. Jeremiah walked behind the counter to the store phone and checked the answering machine; no messages. The coworker suggested calling the store owners.

Jeremiah picked up the phone and tried their number. After a few moments, Jeremiah shook his head and put the phone back on the receiver. "Just out of curiosity, how was your drive to work this morning?"

The coworker shrugged. "Saw maybe a few cars on the road."

"How is it normally?"

"Bumper to bumper."

"Same…go on home. You stay away from anyone that looks sick, okay? I think this flu might be worse than we thought."

The coworker nodded. "Are you sure?"

"Yeah," Jeremiah grabbed the store keys to lock up and walked to the entrance with his coworker, "I'm going to get my daughter from daycare. This doesn't feel right."

"Agreed. Stay safe."

"You too." Jeremiah and his coworker proceeded to get in their cars and drive their separate ways.

When Jeremiah made it back to the daycare, he opened the door to Amelia's room and noticed that there were only five kids. Usually there were at least twenty. Amelia was playing with Pup by herself in a corner.

Karen was shocked to see Jeremiah back already. "Back so soon?"

Jeremiah nodded and made his way over to Amelia. She smiled and cheered. "Daddy!"

"I'm here, baby. Karen, where is everyone? The streets are practically empty," Jeremiah asked quickly as he bent down to pick up Amelia and Pup.

"All out sick, can you believe that?" Karen shook her head and looked at the few kids still innocently playing.

"Actually, I can. Only one person showed up to work. I closed the store today. I just want to get Amelia home, okay?"

"Of course, go on home."

"Are you going to be okay, Karen?"

"Yeah, don't worry about me. You two be safe."

"Pup! Pup safe!" Amelia said, holding out Pup.

Karen smiled faintly. "You be safe too, Pup."

After they left, Karen kept an eye on the remaining children as she made her way over to the first aid cabinet. She pulled out a digital thermometer, put a plastic cover over it, and stuck it underneath her tongue. Meanwhile, the other kids played with each other without a care in the world. Karen had always loved this job; she never had a bad day around the kids. They didn't worry about politics, religion, or how they were going to pay this month's rent.

They didn't worry about how they were going to feed themselves; they always relied on their parents to provide meals when they got hungry. She envied that level of peace. They had no idea how serious this flu was getting. As far as she was concerned, these kids never lost sleep worrying about anything. The thermometer made a soft beeping noise and she pulled it out to read her temperature; Karen was running a fever. She quickly pressed the reset button and threw the plastic cover in the trash.

On the way home, Jeremiah stopped off at a pharmacy and looked for pediatric face masks for Amelia. Carrying her in his arms, Jeremiah walked up and down the aisle looking for a size that would fit her.

"Pretty butters!" Amelia pointed to a box of face masks with little butterflies on them.

Jeremiah couldn't hold back a smile. "Alright, baby. We'll get you these. Now Daddy needs some."

"Daddy need butters?"

Jeremiah laughed, "I don't think these will fit me. I need to get some for adults. We're both going to wear masks for a while, okay? I don't want you or Pup to get sick."

Jeremiah purchased the masks for himself and Amelia and left the store. On the drive home, every light was green. Maybe less than ten cars were on the road. Even on his way up to his apartment, he noticed just how many cars were still in the parking lot. He got inside and quickly shut the door behind him. Amelia starting crying; Jeremiah noticed that it was the early afternoon and Amelia was probably hungry by now.

He pulled out a jar of peanut butter and a jar of strawberry jam, checking the expiration dates on each. He smelled each jar as he opened them to check for any unusual smells. He took out the loaf of bread and carefully examined each slice of bread for her sandwich. Jeremiah sliced the sandwich into four halves and took one of the halves to taste it. The sandwich tasted fine.

Amelia sat down at her tiny kid's table and stopped crying once she was eating. Jeremiah leaned against a wall and watched her finish her sandwich. Overprotective, maybe, but he wasn't taking any chances when it came to his daughter. Even if he drove himself mad with paranoia, she wasn't getting sick. He closed his eyes for a minute. She wasn't getting sick. That wasn't going to happen. Not to her.

CHAPTER 7

Five patrol cars pulled into the farm and policemen began gathering their rifles out of the trunks. Armed and ready, they began with the barn. Opening the barn door, a few of the officers turned and gagged; the stench of rotting meat flew out of the barn. Dead cows were covering the ground; the men carefully stepped around each one, making it hard to stand anywhere without a corpse right up against their feet.

"What do you think happened?" One of the cops asked.

"It looks like…a rabies test was done on these cows," one cop suggested.

A few of the other officers turned towards him.

"Testing for rabies? What makes you so sure about that?" Another cop asked.

"Look at the cows' skulls. All the flesh appears stripped off. Some of the cows are even missing their heads altogether. We haven't found the CDC workers just yet, but their vans are still here, which means they have to be around somewhere. They could've been taking brain tissue samples, and from the looks of it, they were in a hurry," the cop speculated.

The others nodded in agreement, examining the dead cows.

One cop noticed something peculiar. "What do you make of this?" He asked, pointing to a few cows neatly stacked on top of one another.

"Looks like the CDC found something," another cop whispered.

After a few more moments of looking around, the police left the barn and started walking around the farm, looking for any signs of the CDC workers. They began looking around the animal pens, which were strangely empty with no signs of the animals nearby. Moving inside the fence and towards the farmhouse, a few of the police began shouting. No response. Four cops split up and began examining the perimeter of the house. The rest of the group went inside the house, again shouting for the farmer or any CDC worker.

"Stop!" One cop shouted, holding up his arm.

The cops inside came running out, and the ones looking around the house came to where the cop was shouting. Once they had all arrived behind the farmhouse, they saw them. All of the CDC workers sprawled on the ground. Some cops stayed back and drew their guns, while a few advanced to get a closer look.

"Shotgun shells did this." One cop nodded, taking out his pistol. "Fired at point blank range. I wonder if they even saw it coming."

"Stay alert! The killer could still be here!" Another cop ordered.

"What were they all doing in the back here?" Another cop mumbled. He bent down to examine one of the bodies. The face was destroyed and one of the arms was missing. "He put his arm up to protect his face," he told another cop.

"Well, a lot of good that did him," the other cop sighed, turning away from the gruesome scene. "Look at this one," he said, pointing to another body.

The back of the body was missing a large amount of flesh, exposing the lower part of the spinal cord. Several of the bodies did have something in common: parts of their legs were missing, blown off at the knee.

"You think somebody shot them to keep them from running?" A young policeman asked an older cop.

"Most of these people are lying face down. They were running from someone," the older cop responded and looked back at the farmhouse. He thought for a moment. "Were they all inside the house at one point?" He speculated out loud. "Maybe they ran out here to get away from someone in the house? I can't explain why else all the workers would be out here laying in similar positions like this…" his voice trailed off and he quickly stood straight up as if suddenly realizing something. He aimed his rifle at the house. "The farmer…he's the only one not here."

All the cops quickly drew their weapons and slowly inched their way inside the farmhouse, making sure there was a cop covering every side. Once inside, each officer carefully made their way through each room on the ground floor. Guns drawn, they would wait until their partner had the door covered, and they kicked it open, ready to fire, but each time they would find an empty room.

One of the older cops made his way over to the basement door and waited for his partner to get into position. His partner had his finger over the trigger and aimed it at the basement door, silently giving the signal to kick it down. The older cop kicked open the door and was met with a bright flash and a deafening sound.

Chapter 8

Miguel picked up his phone and called Bud's number. It rang a couple times and went to voicemail. Five days had gone by and Bud still hadn't shown up for work. It was about a two-minute walk from Miguel's department to where Sam worked. Miguel looked around; almost every office cubicle was empty. The few people that remained were typing away on their computers. The only thing that broke the silence in the air was the soft clicking of keys on their keyboards. Miguel tried calling Bud again; still got his voicemail.

Deciding to take the five-minute walk, Miguel gathered his things and headed out the door. He found Sam sitting at her desk, just getting off the phone.

"Sam, it's been five days. Where is he?" Miguel asked, finding a chair next to her.

"Look around, Miguel. More than half of our department is out sick with this flu. It's not just Bud," Sam reminded him.

"I *know*, Sam," Miguel answered, slightly annoyed. "But he wasn't right the last time I saw him. I'm thinking about leaving work to go check on him."

"Miguel, you can't just—"

"He hasn't been answering my calls. He even said his wife was sick the last time we talked. Neither of them will pick up the phone. And don't tell me not to worry, you know how bad this flu is…if it even *is* a flu."

A few of the people around them looked up from their desks at Miguel when he mentioned the flu.

One of the people got up from their desk and quickly walked over to where Sam and Miguel were. The person had on a facial mask and wore rubber gloves. "You guys are talking about this flu going around, right?"

They both nodded.

"Our friends are sick," Miguel answered.

"*Everyone's* friends are sick, buddy. Their families, their neighbors…everyone is sick," the coworker said franticly.

"Do you know what this is?" Sam asked.

"Are you kidding?" They questioned, sounding a bit agitated, "I'm not even sure if the CDC knows what this is. Last night on the news they were calling it, the "Phantom Flu". You start having symptoms similar to a flu, then it seemingly vanishes, and you feel fine, right? But then it comes back, and when it does, it's unlike any flu you've had before. The CDC were saying that you even start exhibiting behavior like someone with rabies.

"Some people are even worse. They still don't know where or how it got started. But things are getting wild out there," the coworker finished.

"Is it just us?" Miguel asked, not really wanting the answer.

"I don't know yet. Nothing on the news would give a definite number on the number of infected people yet. I heard rumors that it's nationwide. But I can't say for sure." The coworker shook his head like he couldn't believe the situation either.

"Is it airborne?" Sam asked.

"The CDC still doesn't know that either. There's no common denominator among all the cases. It doesn't seem to matter if you stay away from the sick or not, this flu is spreading and there's no clear way to avoid it!" They answered.

"Sam, we have to check on him. We shouldn't be here. The kids shouldn't be at school," Miguel said solemnly.

"Do whatever you want, man. If I were you, I'd forget about your sick friend. Get your family out of town while they're still healthy," they warned, starting to walk away.

"What about you? Why are you here?" Miguel shouted.

"I got bills to pay," they said, sounding defeated. "I can't afford to be out of the streets, that's like a death sentence. If it is airborne, there's no hope for any of us."

Sam and Miguel exchanged glances.

"Let's go," Sam said, standing up and gathering her things.

On the drive to Bud's house, Miguel and Sam noticed how frantic other cars were driving.

"This is nuts…first there's nobody on the streets. Now everyone is out," Miguel commented.

Every grocery store they passed; the line was out the door like people were preparing for a hurricane. The hardware stores were just as bad. Cars were cutting each other off and weaving between traffic; nobody cared what the speed limit was. If it wasn't a store that sold supplies or food, the parking lot was empty. Sam silently counted to herself every time she saw a police car. After ten minutes she got to twenty-four and stopped counting.

Passing through a neighborhood, Miguel and Sam were speechless; people boarding up their homes and spray-painting the words, "Sick! Stay away", on their doors. Pulling into Bud's driveway, they were both surprised to see that Bud's car was parked outside with no signs of damage.

"I thought you said he was in an accident," Sam asked.

"He told me he was. Sam, stay in the car," Miguel said sternly as he got out.

"No way, we go together!" Sam protested.

"This isn't a debate! I can't risk you getting sick again. We still don't know if you got *the* flu or if it was just a regular flu."

"You're right, this isn't a debate. We go together." Sam got out of the car and headed towards the front door, leaving Miguel behind.

Sam knocked on the door but was met with no response. Miguel gently moved her aside and he kicked the door open.

"Miguel! What are you do—" Sam stopped.

Immediately frozen at the sight before them both, Sam turned away and screamed. When the door opened, the staircase was immediately in front of them; the carpet soaked with blood and the walls going up the stairs were smeared with bloody handprints. Miguel stepped back and told Sam to cover her nose and mouth. Before she could ask why, Miguel pointed to inside the house. Tiny particles floated around in the air like dust. Miguel took another step back so that he was all the way outside and could see the tiny particles leaving the house.

"I don't know what this is, but I doubt we should be breathing it in," Miguel said, putting a hand over his mouth and nose.

Sam did the same. "Whatever it is, Bud's house is full of it. Miguel, we should call the police," Sam suggested.

"They could need our help *now*! We should at least find Bud and his wife first," Miguel fired back, slowly heading back inside.

Sam was filled with an uneasy feeling in her stomach, but nevertheless, she followed her husband inside. They walked to the kitchen area and noticed that the tiny particles were more abundant than ever. They each kept one hand over their mouths to avoid inhaling or swallowing the particles. Instead of speaking, they relied on pointing; Miguel pointed to the windowsill and Sam saw a plastic cage sitting on it. Getting a closer look, they found a caterpillar inside munching on a leaf. The caterpillar was all black with purple spines, just as Bud had described.

"It's been weeks since he first found this caterpillar. How is it not in a cocoon by now?" Miguel asked himself.

Sam pulled on Miguel's sleeve and he followed her up the stairs. Each step made a soft squishing sound; the blood-soaked carpet oozed as they made their way upstairs. Reaching the top, they found a blood trail leading to a bedroom. Sam also noted that there were significantly less particles floating in the air upstairs. The bedroom door was closed, but they could see the blood trail going underneath the door and inside the room. Miguel stepped closer to the door, Sam pulling on his shirt and furiously shaking her head.

Her eyes and facial expression both trying to say, "not a good idea!"

Miguel shook his head, pointing to the door, and bringing his finger across his neck.

"Bud could be dead," he tried to communicate nonverbally.

Sam's face protested but to no avail; Miguel kicked the door open and rushed in. Miguel stumbled back and vomited on the ground instantly. Sam turned and closed her eyes, wishing it was possible to un-see something. The rancid smell alone could bring one to vomit, but the sight was grotesque beyond words. Unrecognizable at first, Sam glanced at the sight again and realized what they had discovered.

Surrounded by gore, Bud's wife lay, on their bed, covers up to her shoulders. Like a porcupine or a hedgehog, long thin spines stuck out of her skin. The flesh that remained on her face was a reddish yellow and looked callused. Her jaw looked dislocated, elongated somehow as if stretched beyond its limits. Both eye sockets were destroyed by the puss oozing out and the long antennas that had sprouted from the sockets. Her eyes were gone, but in their place were the antennas that slowly wriggled about.

Miguel and Sam turned, unable to bear neither the smell nor the sight any longer. As they stumbled away, heading for the staircase, they heard the body fall to the floor behind them. They sprinted down the staircase and rushed out of the house, not looking back, and keeping their mouths covered.

Chapter 9

The pulldown ladder leading to the attic unfolded as Hugo slowly made his way down. He cautiously walked around, moving his head from one direction to another like a bird. A rifle laying on the ground caught his attention and he crept closer to it. A loud thump came from downstairs, and his whole body jolted as he snatched up the rifle and made his way towards the sound. The stairs creaked with each step. A few steps and the thump came again. Hugo picked up his pace. Nearly at the bottom of the steps, Hugo heard another thump. He made sure his finger was on the trigger. Another audible thump. Hugo's heart raced as he realized the sounds were coming from the basement.

One hand on the door handle and another hand holding the rifle. Two simultaneous thumps. Hugo opened the door and fired without hesitation, luckily hitting the first figure between the eyes, sending the bullet exploding out the back of the figure's head. Three more figures in police uniforms darted up the stairs with ease. Hugo shouted while firing off two more shots. Their uniforms were tattered and bloody; their glassy dead eyes were black and purple, unable to rely on sight any longer. Each policeman, now deformed and lacking human qualities, possessed grotesque features which helped them communicate with one another. Their brains were swollen, and chunks of matter were visible through the cracks in their skulls.

Their throats were severely enlarged, creating a large sac that inflated with air, causing them to exhale through their mouths, and emit an eerie croaking sound. A few cops in the back closed their mouths, allowing the air to be pushed through their nasal cavity, creating a higher pitched croak, sounding more like a chirp. Hugo jumped back, his eardrums feeling like they were going to burst at the sound of the chirping. He fired three more shots at them, only managing to hit one cop in the chest. A policeman leaped forward and shoved Hugo backwards, causing him to fall on his back and drop the rifle. The rile landed a few feet away from Hugo and he quickly rolled over on his stomach and crawled towards it. He felt a sharp pain go through the back of his leg. He screamed and pushed himself forward, grabbing the rifle. He rolled over on his back and saw the policeman standing over him.

The policeman's arms were deformed, the bones protruding out of his skin and appearing to be pointed at the end like a blade. The cop swung his arm, the bone blade coming from his arm narrowly missing Hugo's face. Hugo quickly aimed the rifle and fired, sending the cop's brains out the top of his skull onto the ceiling, causing bits of matter to drip down. The other cops croaked and split into two groups, one group on Hugo's right, and the other on his left. Hugo shouted and fired the remaining shots as he ran backwards, out of the house. Once out of ammo, he turned and ran, still hearing the loud croaking of the policemen.

***

Jeremiah held Amelia in his arms as they sat on the floor, backs against the front door. He covered her ears with his hands and rocked her back and forth, telling her everything was okay. She whimpered like a puppy and small tears dripped from her closed eyes. They furiously pounded on the front door, screaming to be let in. It had been happening all afternoon. He didn't dare look through the peephole, but he knew from the sound that they were infected. When it first started happening, he tried to tell them that he had a small daughter inside and couldn't risk it, but it didn't stop them from kicking and pounding their door.

He closed his eyes and held Amelia even tighter. That morning, they had awoken to the sound of their upstairs neighbors shouting something inaudible. He could hear pounding coming from upstairs and several voices yelling to open the door. Insisting that they weren't infected but somebody in the building was. Jeremiah heard their neighbors unbolting the door and opening it. Amelia's tears were starting to soak the front of his shirt now. The screams reverberated in his head; he'd never heard anyone scream like that before. The neighbors upstairs shouted and called out for help as loud thumping and crashing sounds were heard overhead. Once the screams stopped he heard what sounded like the apartment being ransacked. After a few hours, he heard similar pounding and requests to be let in at his door and learned from his neighbor's mistake.

They sat against the door all afternoon until the sun began to go down. The pounding on their door finally ceased, but the screams and sounds of a physical conflict were heard in the hallway. Then gunshots. No more screaming. Then a pounding at his door again, but this time it was different.

"CDC! Open the door if you're in there! CDC! We need you to open the door immediately, for your own safety!" A booming voice shouted.

Amelia leaped up from his lap and Jeremiah stood. Still hesitant to open the door, he peered through the peephole and confirmed that a few CDC workers were outside his door…along with a few military people standing behind them. He reluctantly unlocked the door and opened it halfway.

"It's okay, sir. We're just trying to evacuate the building right now. We need you to urgently grab everyone in your apartment and follow us," one of the CDC workers instructed calmly.

"I just have my daughter, give me two seconds, okay?" Jeremiah responded.

The CDC workers nodded while the military people stood motionless behind them. The CDC workers were in full hazmat suits and the military all wore gasmasks. Jeremiah ran back inside and quickly grabbed one of Amelia's child face masks they had bought and slipped it over her face. He did the same for himself. He picked her up and headed towards the door, leaving with only the clothes on their backs.

"Pup! Daddy! Pup!" Amelia was shouting and pointing.

Jeremiah quickly spun around and grabbed Pup off the couch and gave it to her. He had half a mind to leave the silly plush dog behind. But he knew that to Amelia, it would be same as if someone told him to leave Amelia behind. He raced to the door and entered the hallway with the CDC and military, who were already knocking on other people's doors. Jeremiah covered Amelia's eyes once he saw the bodies lying on the hallway floor.

"They were infected," a CDC worker explained, noticing the look on Jeremiah's face.

The corpses did look infected. Horrible and disfigured, it was more frightening to know that these people were the ones pounding on his door all afternoon.

"Just follow closely behind us. We need to make it to the ground floor and get you people out of here. If you get separated from us or come into physical contact with the infected, we'll have to leave you both here, understand?" One of the soldiers instructed.

Jeremiah nodded. "We're right behind you."

Just outside, there were five trucks left. One of the military trucks was nearly full as people were being herded into it. A few minutes later, the truck was full and immediately drove off. People from the apartment were now being led to the second truck. Jeremiah could hear fighting on the floors above them and panicked voices from below. Holding Amelia, he stuck as closely to the soldiers as he could while CDC workers pounded on the apartment doors, ordering any survivors out into the hallway or be left behind.

Only a few people remained in their rooms, others refused to come out. A handful of survivors, soldiers, and CDC workers stayed close together as they all headed down a flight of stairs leading to the third floor. A few people from below raced up the stairs towards them, eyes bloodshot and foaming at the mouth. The military opened fire as Jeremiah covered Amelia's ears. She jumped and squealed in terror at the sound of each gunshot. Jeremiah was only glad she didn't see what these people looked like.

Arriving at the third floor, Jeremiah suddenly remembered something and raced down the hallway past the soldiers and pounded on Karen's door. The soldiers and other survivors shouted for him to come back, but he shouted for Karen to come out. One of the CDC workers shoved him out of the way and told him to get back. The soldiers pulled Jeremiah behind them as more CDC workers pounded on Karen's door.

"Do you know if she's sick?" One of the workers asked him.

Jeremiah shook his head, "I hadn't heard from her in a while, but she was fine the last time I saw her. Please, don't leave her behind!"

They pounded on the door louder and shouted for anyone in there to come out immediately. "Ma'am, if you're in there, you have ten seconds to come out!"

They waited a moment. Jeremiah could hear the thumping of footsteps coming up the stairs from below. The military shouted for the CDC workers to leave her; infected were coming. A few people in other rooms came into the hallway to see what the commotion was. The second truck was full and drove off as the third began loading up people.

"CDC! Open the door, ma'am!" They shouted again.

The door did open but Jeremiah didn't believe that Karen was the one standing in the doorway. Not her anymore. The lady's lower jaw hung all the way down, dislocated. Her eyes completely bloodshot and oozing puss. Patches of her skin were missing or in the process of coming off; in their place were hardened patches of blue skin with tiny spines protruding out. Her entire spine was exposed, bloody, and dripping fluids out of her back. Her cervical vertebrae were longer than a normal person's, causing her neck to appear severely elongated. The veins in her neck were stretched, and the skin tore as a result.

Her head bobbed back and forth on the elongated neck, reaching the ceiling. Jeremiah pressed Amelia's face against his chest so she wouldn't see what everyone in the hallway was screaming at. Two soldiers grabbed Jeremiah and a few others and quickly led them down the hall, cutting down the infected running towards them. What used to be Karen, now stumbled out of the doorway, towering above the CDC workers as they stood paralyzed by fear.

"K—Karen? Is that you?" Jeremiah whispered.

"She's infected! Open fire! Open fire!" One of the soldiers barked.

Karen screeched and vomited stomach acid all over one of the CDC workers, dissolving his hazmat suit which melted into his skin as he screamed.

The other CDC workers ran in two different directions in a panic while the military opened fire on her again. Karen stumbled back and cried out in pain. The bullets ripped through parts of her body, but the hardened patches of skin prevented any penetration. The people standing in the hallway darted towards the staircase as Karen chased after them. Karen's screams echoed down the hallway as her long neck weaved back and forth while she ran, bobbing her head around. Her broken jaw snapped up and down. More infected were coming downstairs from the opposite staircase, leaving the soldiers to decide—chase after Karen and help the people running away or run down the stairs across the hall and escape.

"Let's go! Now's our chance!" One of them shouted, pointing to the staircase leading down.

"No! We have to save those people!" Another argued.

"Forget them! We don't know what that thing is!" Another solider argued back. "Go after that infected lady if you want, I'm getting out of here!" And with that, he and a few soldiers headed down the stairs.

Only two soldiers stayed behind and agreed to chase after Karen. The third truck was nearly full of people and the fourth one was getting ready to starting loading. Jeremiah and the rest of the survivors followed the military down another flight of stairs to the second floor. As soon as they arrived, the elevator door across from them opened. Emerging from the elevator, two men rushed out. The military immediately opened fire on them.

"Hold your fire! Hold your fire!" One of the soldiers ordered.

They approached the two bodies and realized they didn't show any signs of infection. The survivors standing behind the soldiers were dead silent, Jeremiah included.

"Come on, we have to get outside!" Another solider ordered.

Everyone stepped over the bodies and no one said a word. The fourth truck was now being loaded. Heading down another hallway and down another flight of stairs, they made it to the ground floor. They still needed to head down one last hallway, through the lobby, and out to the parking lot to reach the military trucks. The hallway leading to the lobby was packed; people shoved one another as they squirmed their way through the hall, each person pressed up against someone else. It was hard to hear the person next to you, especially over the shouting soldiers who were trying to take a quick visual inspection over every person before they were loaded onto a truck.

They mainly looked in and around their eyes; it was the best they could do in this situation and the fourth truck was loading up fast. Amelia held Pup tightly against her as she quietly whimpered in her father's arms. All the way in the back of the hallway, Jeremiah knew for sure that he wasn't going to be able to make it through the lobby out to the parking lot in time. But looking at his sobbing daughter, he knew he couldn't resolve to stay here. Just then, a pounding was heard overhead—like heavy footsteps, then a loud crash and people shouting from the floor above them.

Everyone in the hallway was silent for a moment, listening to what it might be. Then the screech, one Jeremiah had heard before.

"It's her," Jeremiah told one of the soldiers that had been with them when Karen emerged from her room.

The soldier nodded and began shouting over his radio for all available troops to head towards the staircase. Sure enough, Karen quickly stumbled down the stairs, dripping blood from her wounds and back as she came towards them. The sound of gunfire sent everyone in the hallway in a panic. People started shoving one another as Karen ran towards the crowd. She effortlessly killed each soldier, throwing them against the wall and biting one solider in the neck, decapitating him in the process.

One man took another person by the shoulders and threw them on the ground near Karen. The crowd started to push harder, some people shoving each other to the floor and stepping over them. Karen took the bait, but the person on the ground didn't buy much time; the fourth truck drove off, full of people. The fifth and final truck was now being loaded. By some miracle, Jeremiah was able to squeeze through the crowd as Karen tore into the person on the ground; people looked back at the attack, some unable to look away or move.

After what seemed like hours but was only a few minutes, Jeremiah made it to the lobby. Looking behind him as he pushed his way to the front, he saw Karen throwing people against the walls, making her way to the lobby as well. Once at the front door, a soldier stopped him by pushing him back and explaining there wasn't enough room. The final truck was nearly full, and he'd have to figure something else out.

"Please, just take my daughter! I *know* you can make room!" Jeremiah held out Amelia, causing her to start crying.

"Get back! We can't take any more people!" The solider barked.

"I'm begging you! She's only one year old! She deserves a chance," Jeremiah pleaded. He couldn't see the soldier's face due to the gas mask covering it, but the soldier seemed to pause and think for a moment. Jeremiah looked back; Karen was tearing through the crowd and had made it to the lobby. He knew time was running out. Panic rising, he managed to keep a calm voice so he wouldn't frighten Amelia any further. "Do you have kids?"

The soldier quickly nodded.

"I can't protect my daughter right now. I'm asking you one father to another, give her a chance to make it out of here. Do what I can't for her."

The soldier took her in his arms and told another soldier to get her to the truck. The other soldier hesitated.

"Sir, there's no room," the other solider said.

"*Make* room, private! That's an order!" The gasmask soldier commanded.

"Yes, sir. "He saluted and took a crying Amelia in his arms. "We need to get out of here, this whole block is being overrun."

"I know, I'm right behind you," the gasmask soldier responded.

"I love you," Jeremiah silently said to Amelia as she reached out for him.

"We're taking everyone to the school. Your daughter will be waiting for you there. I hope you see her again," the gasmask soldier said as he pushed Jeremiah out of the way to shoot down Karen.

A few soldiers followed behind the one wearing the gas mask and they tossed grenades at Karen. Jeremiah closed his eyes and turned away. The last thing he saw before closing them was a crowd of people trying to get away from Karen, the grenades landing by several people's feet, and Karen picking one of the grenades up. Jeremiah hit the ground for cover and his eardrums felt like they were going to explode as each grenade simultaneously went off. Karen was blown apart as two of the grenades denotated near her, pieces of shrapnel slicing through the people nearby. The other grenades made sure Karen wouldn't get up again, but at the cost of most of the people in the lobby. If the initial grenade blast didn't kill them instantly, the shrapnel did. The rest of the soldiers ran out of the building, along with a few remaining survivors, Jeremiah included. The solider told the survivors that they were on their own. Even the soldiers themselves were left without an escape vehicle and headed onto the streets.

No vehicle, but at least they had guns. That was more than what Jeremiah had to work with. Now on the streets, Jeremiah knew he had to make it to that school, no matter what it took. He took a deep breath and brushed himself off. He looked around at the other survivors in the parking lot, and they exchanged glances but no words. The streets were in complete chaos; a few people were smashing a car window to break in. Four people were fighting over what appeared to be a gun. The gun went off and shot one of the people in the stomach. Two others kicked the third person to the ground and took the gun, shooting him, then ran off together. People in the parking lot were screaming and trying to call loved ones to come pick them up.

Jeremiah pulled out his phone and tried to call the elderly store owners, but they never picked up. He at least knew where the school was; it wasn't far by car, but on foot it was going to be awhile. It was dark by now and Jeremiah knew it would be a long night. He began hurriedly walking down the street, careful to stay in the streetlights and out of view from anyone else on foot. A group of people across the street were ransacking a gas station, inside Jeremiah could see someone holding up the cashier at gunpoint.

Chapter 10

The car sped down the street, ignoring streetlights and stop signs. Not that anyone else on the road paid attention to them either; it was a race to the safe zones. The car narrowly zoomed by people running in the streets; inside the car, Miguel and Sam turned on the radio.

"…bloodshot eyes would be the most reliable sign at this moment. The CDC is issuing a warning to everyone to stay away from these infected individuals. What some are now calling, the 'Ghost Flu' or the 'Phantom Flu' is appearing to be worse than any of us originally thought. If your flu disappears rapidly, the CDC is urging you to isolate yourself immediately as you are infected. Your flu *will* return, and you will infect everyone around you. We repeat, for the safety of your loved ones and others around you, isolate yourself if infected. The CDC says that there's no way to tell how this flu will infect you once it returns but may have something to do with your genetic makeup. Therefore, the Ghost Flu will infect everyone slightly different but as far as we know, once you start showing signs of the infection, there is no cure.

"Also, they are evacuating several buildings in our local area with the help of the military. Their plan is to transport everyone to Black Bear School in the Dark Wood County district. We are urging everyone in this district to head there if you're not already. The CDC will issue further instructions there. If you are living in another district, we will now list other safe zones in your area starting with—"

Miguel cut off the radio as Sam instructed him where to turn.

"They're taking everyone to the boys' school. Please be there already," Sam whispered to herself.

"The boys are safe there, Sam. I know it. They're going to stay there and we're going to find them," Miguel said calmly. At least, as calmly as his nerves would allow.

The car continued through the city, passing people throwing rocks through car windshields and storefronts. Just ahead, Miguel and Sam noticed two people running from a small group of people chasing them. The small group chased them with exceptional speed and threw them to the ground.

"Are those people...*biting* them?" Sam asked aloud.

As the car got closer and quickly passed by, Miguel glanced over with just enough time to see the group tearing into the people with their teeth. He noticed a few members of the group without lips, fully exposing their teeth. Miguel said nothing and sped up, pressing his foot against the gas pedal with full force. Sam told him to slow down. Their car passed by people exiting the front door to a bar, stumbling out and screaming as more people came sprinting out, tackling them to the ground. Miguel averted his eyes from the scene and focused on the road. Sam told him to slow down again.

"We have to get to the school. We need to make it. We have to get the boys out of here," Miguel mumbled to himself, trying to keep himself focused on the road and not the chaos around him. Continuing to speed down the street, the car soon arrived in bumper-to-bumper traffic, causing Miguel to slow to a complete stop. "There has to be a way around this traffic. There must be! We need to reach the boys!"

"Miguel, calm down, we'll reach them in time. Obviously, everyone in this area is trying to reach the school too. There's going to be traffic; it's expected and normal. Everything's ok—" before Sam finished, Miguel switched lanes abruptly and squeezed between two cars. "Miguel, stop!"

There was a man walking between the cars, coming from the passenger side of the car so only Sam could see him. In Miguel's blind spot, the man walked in front of a few cars that weren't moving due to the traffic. Miguel continued to speed up, weaving between two more cars and suddenly slamming the car into the man. Sam shrieked and every muscle in Miguel's body froze. He slammed on the breaks as soon as the man flew back from the impact.

The man groaned and slowly made it to his feet. The pedestrian stumbled over to the car that hit him and approached the driver's side. Miguel rolled down the window and apologized profusely. Sam unbuckled herself and got out of the car, rushing over to the man. She instantly took note of his CDC uniform and asked what he was doing walking around traffic.

"I'm just trying to find someone to give me a ride. The CDC is meeting up at the Black Bear school," the man responded.

"Why aren't you already with them? We haven't seen any other CDC people around the streets," Miguel questioned. It seemed odd to him that a CDC worker would be walking around by himself in this mess.

The man thought quickly. "I got separated. A group of infected attacked us. Please, I'm not infected, I just need to meet up with everyone at the school. Will you be so kind as to give me a ride?"

Sam answered for Miguel. "Of course we will. Hop in, it's the least we could do for nearly killing you." She gave Miguel a dirty look.

Miguel reluctantly unlocked the car doors and let them both in. *This guy better not be infected, Sam. Our boys still need us,* he thought to himself. "So, you got a name, friend?" Miguel asked the man as he climbed in the passenger seat and Sam got in the back.

"Hugo," the man replied.

"You said you were separated from your team. Do you know if they're okay?" Sam asked, concerned.

"It's just me," Hugo answered.

"I'm so sorry. Did they get sick?" Sam asked.

"Sam maybe let's not pry in this guy's business," Miguel suggested, keeping his eyes on the road. He decided to take backroads to the school to avoid the heavy traffic.

***

The images of their broken corpses flashed in Hugo's mind. And the policemen… if they even were men any longer. *What kind of infection could do that…twist the human body into those things?* He wondered silently to himself.

A feeling of uncomfortable silence filled the car.

"Hugo? Everything okay?" Sam asked.

Hugo snapped out of it. "Oh, yes. I'm fine. Just a rough couple of days, that's all. Thanks again for the lift."

"No problem. I'm glad you're alright. You don't feel like anything's broken?" Miguel asked.

"No, I'm fine. I'm sorry for running in front of your car," Hugo apologized.

"It's my fault," Miguel corrected.

"Neither of you have come into contact with the sick?" Hugo asked.

"No, we haven't…have you?" Sam jumped in.

"No, me either," Hugo lied.

***

"That's good, I'm glad you're—" Sam paused. She turned for a moment to look at Hugo and saw Hugo's eyes clearly for the first time; watery and bloodshot.

"What's that?" Hugo asked, waiting for Sam's sentence to be finished.

"…just glad you're okay."

Sam gave Miguel a look through the rearview mirror and made a motion with her hand; she acted like she was scratching the side of her face, but pointed with her thumb towards Hugo, then rubbed her eyes. Miguel quickly glanced at Hugo and looked back in the rearview mirror at Sam, nodding.

"Are we getting close to the school?" Hugo asked, only to break the silence. He knew the way. They were roughly ten minutes from the school.

The car slowed to a halt and Miguel put the car in park.

"We need you to get out, please," Sam requested in a soft voice.

Hugo looked confused. "Is something wrong?"

"You're sick, Hugo. Please get out."

"No, no I'm not sick!"

"Hugo…please get out of the car."

"Look, I know how to cure this! I have the cure for this flu! Please, take me to the school with you."

"Do you really have a cure for this?" Sam asked.

"No, he doesn't, Sam. He's just trying to stay in the car. You need to leave, Hugo," Miguel said in a stern voice.

Hugo panicked and threw the car into drive, Miguel took his foot off the breaks and hit the gas. The car shifted into reverse during their struggle, sending it jerking back and heading towards a few other cars. Miguel shoved Hugo's head against the door, leaving Hugo stunned for a moment. Miguel took the car out of reverse and parked it again, taking his foot all the way off both pedals. He removed the belt from his pants and threw it in the backseat.

Sam grabbed it and threw the belt over Hugo's throat. Hugo gagged and thrashed his arms, trying to hit Miguel. Trying to kick Hugo out of the car, Miguel unlocked the passenger door and reached across Hugo to open it. Hugo punched Miguel and shoved him back in his seat, locking his door with the buttons. Miguel tried unlocking the door again. Hugo gagged louder, putting both hands on the belt around his throat to pull away. He tried to reach around the seat to hit Sam, but Miguel elbowed Hugo in the jaw to prevent this from happening.

Sam shouted at Miguel to open the door quickly before she lost her grip; she couldn't hold him much longer. Hugo fought harder, trying to get his feet up on the dashboard and locking his door every time he heard the click of Miguel unlocking it. Miguel managed to grab both of Hugo's hands for a moment while Sam let go of the belt, unlocked Hugo's door, and opened it. Once the belt fell from Hugo's neck, he started screaming and cursing, trying to break his hands free from Miguel.

"Hold him!" Miguel shouted.

Sam put her arms around Hugo's neck and held him against the seat with all her strength. Miguel immediately leaned all the way against his door so his feet faced Hugo.

"No! No, stop!" Hugo gagged.

"*Now!*" Miguel shouted.

Sam released Hugo and Miguel used both feet to kick Hugo out of the car, sending him flying out of his seat onto the pavement. Suddenly, they heard the repeated honking of car horns until one car slammed against the back of them, jolting the car forwards as another car simultaneously sideswiped them, flipping their car several times until it landed upside-down. Dazed and hurt, Sam and Miguel dropped down from their seats and started to crawl over broken glass and debris to make their way out of the car. Miguel made it out first, but Sam's leg was wrapped in a seatbelt, so she used a glass shard to quickly cut herself free.

Hugo stumbled towards them, eyes dripping blood and releasing a low growl as he got closer. Once he saw Sam climbing out of the car, he rushed towards her, violently dragging her out of the wreckage as she thrashed and screamed for Miguel. Two people from the car that hit them got out, also climbing out through the window and raced towards Sam. Miguel picked up a glass shard, cutting his hand in the process but too full of adrenaline to notice. The other car passengers made it to Sam first and one of them tackled Hugo to the ground. Hugo roared and vomited dark red blood all over the other person. Sam screamed and rolled away, avoiding the blood. The other person held Hugo's arms down and Miguel darted towards him, stabbing him in the neck.

Hugo made a gargling noise as his throat spurted blood and he fell to his knees. The other person kicked Hugo to the ground and all three of them watched in stunned silence as Hugo bled out in front of them, wriggling on the ground until he died. The passenger helped his blood-covered friend to his feet and brushed him off.

"Did you get any in your mouth, nose, or eyes?" The passenger asked.

"No, thankfully not. Mainly got it all on my shirt," the bloody passenger replied, checking himself.

"Thanks for the help," Miguel said to the two passengers as he helped Sam to her feet.

"Don't mention it. Are you both okay?" They asked.

"Physically, yes," Sam whispered.

"We were hit by two cars. Where's the other car? We should check on them too," Miguel asked the two men.

One of them turned around and pointed. A person was hanging out of the front windshield, glass shards sticking out of them and laying on the hood of the car motionless.

Chapter 11

Ellis wiped his tears with his shirt as he hid underneath his desk along with his other classmates. With sirens blaring and the teacher underneath her own desk, it felt like the world was coming to an end. In the mind of a child, if the grownups are scared, there's a reason to be terrified. Grownups don't scare easily. They're supposed to protect kids and tell them everything will be alright. The teacher was silent, carefully messing with her phone, trying to get a phone call out. Her hands were shaky, accidently pressing the wrong buttons on her phone, and she couldn't bear to look any of the children in the eyes; they would see how afraid she was.

The door burst open, all the kids jumped; Ellis even bumped his head on his desk. A CDC worker in a hazmat suit said the coast was clear and ordered everyone to leave the room. Single file and silent, the kids exited the room and went into the hallway. Ellis wrapped his arms around himself and followed the kid in front of him. Everyone in the hallway was shouting, and the grownups asked each other what the situation was. Ellis didn't know what "evacuation" meant or "contagious," but all the grownups were saying them. He also didn't know why so many people were being called, "contagious". Was that their name? If so, there were a lot of people named, "contagious." Maybe they were all related? Grownups his parents' age, old people like his grandma and grandpa, and kids just like him; the contagious family was huge. Ellis still didn't know why there were so many people at his school today. Many of them didn't go to school here.

A man in a scary mask carrying a big gun told this kid he was named "contagious", and the child took off running and screaming. The kid knocked Ellis to the ground and ran past him. More men wearing scary masks eventually grabbed him and carried him away to be with his huge family. That's when he felt two strong arms pulling him up, followed by a familiar voice.

"You okay, kiddo?" Louis asked.

Ellis started weeping and held his big brother as tight as he could. "My name's not 'contagious'. It's not! It's not!" he cried.

Louis made a faint smile and held his brother. "No, it's not. Your name is Ellis." Louis helped Ellis stand to his feet and told him, "we have to follow these guys wearing the masks. They're going to scan us just like the doctor does when we get our checkups, okay? They're just taking our temperature to see if we have a fever."

Ellis nodded. Louis was right. Just up ahead, the men wearing scary masks were holding a small device just like the ones at the doctor's office. They held it about an inch away from each person's temple and it made a small beeping sound. Sometimes the people would keep walking forward in line, and other times the people named "contagious" were dragged out of line and put into a different line only for the contagious family. Ellis couldn't understand why they didn't recognize their own family members. He figured the family was so big they couldn't remember everyone. Still, they didn't look happy to see each other.

"Ellis! Louis!" Miguel and Sam shouted. They rushed over to their boys, ignoring the line and embraced them. "Are you both okay?"

Louis and Ellis nodded. The other people in line made room for Miguel and Sam, sympathetic at the sight of parents finding their lost children. One of the soldiers scanned Miguel.

"Clear!" The soldier shouted as he allowed Miguel to go forward into the next line.

Sam stepped forward and stood motionless as the soldier scanned her.

"Clear!"

Louis stepped forward and allowed himself to be scanned.

"Clear!"

Ellis stepped forward.

"Contagious! Go! Go! Go!"

Ellis was furiously shoved into a different line, kicking and screaming that his name wasn't "contagious".

"No! Stop! Let him go!" Sam shouted as he pushed several CDC workers aside.

"Ma'am he's sick!" One of the people from the CDC shouted, shoving her back.

"No, he's not! Scan him again!" Sam continued to shout as Miguel held her back.

Miguel wanted to run after his son just as much as she did, but he knew how that would end.

"At least tell us where you're taking him!" Miguel yelled at a CDC person.

"You'll see him again. Now get back!" The CDC personnel answered. Behind him, a few soldiers aimed their weapons at Miguel and Sam. "Just get back in line," the CDC personnel said calmly. "You'll see your son again. We must separate the sick for the safety of everyone else."

Reluctantly, Miguel and Sam stepped back in line without a word.

"What's going to happen to him?" Louis asked, looking more worried than before.

"He's going to be okay. I promise," Sam said, trying to calm herself. She turned to Miguel and whispered in his ear, "I'm going to sneak in the sick line. Take care of Louis and I'll find a way back to you both."

Miguel's eyes widened. "Are you crazy?" He tried to keep his voice down as to not alert Louis. "You'll get sick yourself! What if they end up quarantining you both? How are we supposed to reach you?"

"It'll be okay, Miguel."

"No! No, you're not leaving us!"

The line quickly moved outdoors to a parking lot where several busses were located. Some busses had a red "X" mark painted on the sides, and some had a green check-mark. It didn't take long to see that the sick line was headed to the red X busses, and the healthy were going to the busses with the green checks.

"I love you, Miguel. I can't leave our son alone. Our boys need us both," Sam whispered as she quickly kissed him and rushed over to the sick line when the soldiers weren't looking.

The sick people wondered what Sam was doing, but she shoved her way to meet Ellis. She found him crying and following the line, telling the people around him that his name wasn't "contagious" and wasn't related to any of them.

"Mom!" Ellis shouted when he saw her. Sam scooped him up in her arms and told him it was going to be alright. "Where's dad and Louis?"

"They're going to stay together. And we're going to stay together. But later, we'll all be together again, okay?" Sam said as calmly as she could.

"Why am I in this line?" Ellis asked.

"They think we're sick. But we're not, okay? We're *not* sick."

"Why can't we just tell them that we're fine?"

"Because they're scared, Ellis. They don't believe anyone right now. But later, we'll find your dad and Louis."

"Then what? Do we go home?"

Sam genuinely didn't know. "We'll go someplace safe. All of us. Sound good?"

Ellis nodded.

"When's Mom coming back?" Louis asked.

"Soon. She's going to get your brother and meet up with us later," Miguel answered.

"But how can she do that if she's going to the other busses? You know they won't take us all to the same place if they're separating us now."

"I don't know, Louis!" Miguel fired back. It came out angrier than intended. "Your mother will find us again, Louis. I need you to trust that, alright?"

Louis nodded, unsatisfied. He looked over at the sick line to where Sam and Ellis were. He gave Ellis a small wave. Ellis wiped his tears with one hand and waved with the other. Miguel stepped forward in line and tripped a little, bumping into the man in front of him.

"I'm sorry, sir. Just tripped," Miguel apologized.

The man turned around, gave a weak smile, and nodded. "That's okay," he said in a soft voice.

The man looked like he'd been rolled down a hill, hitting every tree and rock on the way down. Clearly, this guy had seen some events before arriving here.

Miguel had to ask. "How did you get here?"

The man looked at the ground as he spoke. "Barely in one piece. Had to walk. Made it here early this morning when they started to evacuate the school."

"You mean this has been going on all day? Why are you just now leaving?"

"I thought I would find my daughter here. They told me about an hour ago that everyone is being taken to some military base farther away. Apparently, this area won't be safe for long. I overheard some of the soldiers talking about something coming this way. I couldn't tell what exactly they were talking about, but it must be pretty bad if we can't stay here." That's when the man noticed Louis standing behind Miguel, listening to their conversation. The man looked back up at Miguel. "I'm sorry, I didn't mean to scare him."

Miguel looked down at Louis. "He'll be alright. He's tough. How old is your d—"

Just then, a loud booming sound was heard overhead. Everyone in the parking lot, stood motionless. The sick, the healthy, the CDC, the soldiers, they all stood still, looking up at the sky. Two large planes were falling right out of the sky, leaving a trail of fire and smoke behind them. One of the plane's wings came too close to the other plane, causing a deafening explosion, and both planes tore apart, raining down pieces of debris and rubble.

"Everyone on the busses *now!*" The soldiers started barking.

The lines broke and everyone made a mad dash to the busses. If any of the sick tried to run across the parking lot to the Green Check busses, they were immediately shot down. Smithereens from the planes came crashing down, landing all around them. A turbine from one of the planes fell several feet away from the sick busses, proceeding to explode as soon as it hit the ground. Miguel picked up Louis and ran, along with the man, to one of the busses.

The man let Miguel and his son inside first, then sat down with them. A few more people scrambled in, and the bus driver took off. Fragments continued to rain down, landing on the busses, making it sound like heavy rain. The Red X busses followed each other down one street and the Green Check busses went off in a different direction. Nobody asked where they were being taken; anywhere was better than here. As they drove away from the school, gunfire was still heard in the distance along with people screaming.

If they didn't make it on a bus, they'd been left in that parking lot. If they were sick and didn't get on a Red X bus, they were shot. The remaining military and CDC piled into tanks and trucks, following closely behind the busses. Each bus had one soldier on it. The people on the Green Check busses were given face masks to wear.

"What just happened?" Louis asked his dad.

Miguel looked at the man and they both shook their heads.

"Something happened on those planes," the man whispered.

"We're okay now," Miguel whispered to Louis.

"What about Mom and Ellis?"

"They made it on the bus. I saw them," Miguel answered. He made sure to keep his eyes trained on them as he ran towards his own bus with Louis.

"Promise?"

"Pinky promise." Miguel stuck his pinky out and wrapped it around Louis' pinky. He looked at the man, "I'm sure your daughter is wherever they're taking us next."

The man slowly nodded. "I hope they were right about that military base being safer."

"You sure that's where they're taking us?" Miguel asked.

"I hope so. Although I can't say the same for the sick busses. There's no way they'd bring us all to the same location."

"I have to find my wife and other son again," Miguel said, growing frustrated.

"I understand." The man nodded. "I don't know if they sent my daughter with the sick or the healthy. I'll have to check *both* places. I'll help you find your wife and son if she's not where they're taking us."

"I appreciate the help, but you don't need to do that."

"Maybe I don't, but from one father to another: I know how you feel right now. The offer stands if you change your mind."

Miguel nodded and stuck out his hand. The man shook it and nodded back. "I'm Miguel, and this is my son, Louis. What's your name?"

"Jeremiah."

Chapter 12

There were whispers on the Red X bus about where they were being taken. Thinking quickly, Sam started talking to Ellis so he wouldn't hear the conversations around him.

"It's been a long time since I've been on a school bus," Sam said, faking her best smile.

Ellis looked behind them. "Why is there a tank following our bus?"

"Oh, they're just making sure we travel safely."

"What about the people back at my school? Why did we leave them? Couldn't we fit them on the bus? I'll sit on the floor!"

"They're going to wait for someone to pick them up."

"And why did those planes crash?"

"Remember those remote-control planes you and Louis had?"

"Yeah!"

"Well, those were really big remote-control planes. And someone crashed them on accident."

"But they could've hurt someone! The pieces were falling on us!"

"That's right. It could've hurt us. But it didn't. The person should've been paying better attention, right?"

"Right!"

On the Green Check bus, a soldier walked up and down the aisle, wearing a gasmask and carrying a machine gun. This scared Louis, and Miguel could tell. Jeremiah noticed the uneasy look on Louis' face, too. Jeremiah reached in his pocket and pulled out a pen. Jeremiah drew a tic-tac-toe board on the back of the seat in front of them. Whenever the soldier would walk past their seat and back towards the front of the bus, Jeremiah placed a circle in one of the squares, then handed the pen to Louis to make an X.

Miguel smiled and silently mouthed the words, "thank you" to Jeremiah.

"So, two boys, huh?" Jeremiah asked Miguel.

Miguel laughed a little, "yeah, they're a handful."

Louis looked up and gave his dad a mean look.

"I haven't felt this lost since my daughter was born," Jeremiah mentioned.

"I know what you mean," Miguel nodded.

"You feel like you will make a good father, then you hold them for the first time, and you wonder what you're supposed to do next. You wonder if you're the kind of man they should look up to."

"If it makes you feel any better, I felt that way even after both boys were born."

"To be honest, I wasn't even sure if I was ready to be a father. A part of me didn't want to be. Not because I don't love my daughter, but because I was just so scared."

"I know you weren't ready," Miguel said, looking at Jeremiah and smiling. "Nobody is ready to be a parent for the first time. You can read all the parenting books and take all the classes you want. But you take it one day at a time. Some days you're going to feel like you make a good parent. And other days… you do the best you can."

Jeremiah looked away for a moment, feeling something in his eye. "I shouldn't have given her away like that. I should've kept her with me. I just wanted her to make it out."

Miguel reached over and put a hand on Jeremiah's shoulder. "You did what was best for her. You'll find her again. I *know* you will."

Jeremiah shook his head. "How can you know that?"

"When you first held her and she looked up at you, what was your first thought?"

Jeremiah looked back at him. "What did I do in life to deserve something so wonderful?"

"*That's* why you'll find her. You love her too much to quit looking."

The soldier walked past them, and Jeremiah took back the pen and made another circle. Louis took the pen and made another move, drawing a line through his x-marks; he won but only because Jeremiah let him.

On the Red X bus, Sam looked down at Ellis. His eyes were watery and puffy; the whites in his eyes were now red.

"What's wrong, mom?" Ellis asked, looking up at her.

Sam fought back the tears. "Nothing honey, everything's okay. Hey, remember that day we went camping, all four of us?"

Ellis smiled, "yeah, and we were roasting marshmallows when Louis dropped one in his lap!"

"I've never heard him shriek like that," Sam laughed.

"It burns! It burns!" Ellis said, imitating Louis' voice.

"Remember how the stars looked when we all laid on the ground?"

Ellis closed his eyes and leaned against his mother. "Yeah, they didn't seem so far away either, like I could reach up and grab one!"

A small stream of blood dripped down from Ellis's eyes and Sam immediately wiped it away.

"I remember how quiet it was out there. No cars or police sirens going by. Just the rustling of the leaves in the wind."

"Am I crying?" Ellis asked, opening his eyes.

"No, sweetie. You just had something in your eye," Sam said, gently putting a hand over his eyes to let him close them again.

"Can we go camping there again someday?"

Sam looked up, trying not to cry and holding her breath, afraid her exhale would result in the stream of tears she was holding back. "Yeah, we'll go back when this is over, okay?"

"And fishing! We were going to go fishing last time, but Dad forgot to pack our poles! We have to fish next time!"

"We'll go fishing too. You think you can catch a big catfish?"

"Sure, I can!"

"I don't know, catfish get pretty big. You'll need big muscles to reel it in!" Sam said as she squeezed Ellis' little arms.

Ellis giggled as he tried to get away. Sam pulled him in and started tickling his sides, resulting in Ellis laughing even louder. Everyone on the bus turned around at the sound of Ellis' laughter. They looked at each other and decided not to interrupt.

The soldier on the bus pulled out a walkie-talkie and whispered that, "one of them might be turning soon. A few others have the eyes too. Maybe thirty minutes. Maybe less."

A voice responded through the walkie. "We're almost there. Don't fire unless they're actively mutating. Keep your gasmask on."

"Understood," the soldier whispered back.

Chapter 13

In total, there were ten Red X busses and twelve Green Check busses, each packed with people. The Red X busses drove in a single file line, a tank or a truck full of soldiers driving between each one. Same for the Green Check busses. The path the Red X busses took was not far from the Green Check busses; they could just barely see each other in the distance. Every attempt the groups made at asking where they were being taken was met with silence from the solider on their bus and a gun in their face. After a short time, everyone stopped asking.

"If they're taking us someplace safe, why keep it hidden from us?" Someone on a Green Check bus whispered to the person next to them.

"Did you want to stay in that parking lot? At least we're getting away from the city! Now, keep your voice down and try to get some rest," the person next to them whispered back.

Louis woke up to the sound of whispers all around him.

"It's the military, I know it! They had something to do with this infection!"

"I know! This 'Phantom Flu' isn't a flu at all, we all figured that out by now."

"Well I say it's aliens, it only makes sense! I mean, why come down to Earth and invade when they can attack us with a disease, then move in when we're all dead!"

"You're crazy, you know that?"

"You're both wrong! This infection came from someplace else."

"You think this is a terrorist attack?"

"No, you idiot! Didn't you hear the news? This so-called 'Ghost Flu' is everywhere! Maybe we discovered something in nature we weren't supposed to find."

"I still say it's aliens, man."

The whispers continued as he looked out the window; it was dark outside with little visibility of the other busses or the truck following closely behind them. He looked at his digital watch. Louis pressed the backlight button and the watch lit up, displaying 10:36 p.m. on the small screen. "Dad, how long have we been driving?" Louis asked.

"A few hours, I'd figure," Miguel whispered back.

"About four hours," Jeremiah added.

With nothing else to do but sleep, Louis closed his eyes again.

"Alright, so continue," Miguel whispered to Jeremiah, smiling.

"Right, so Amelia likes those little pancakes. You know the ones? They come frozen," Jeremiah continued.

"Yeah, I remember."

"So, I just poured a little syrup on her plate." Jeremiah tried to hold back his laughter as he whispered, "and I turn away for a *second*."

Miguel smiled, covering his mouth. "I can see where this is going," he laughed.

"This girl smacks her hands into the puddle of syrup and her hair gets in her face so she takes both hands," Jeremiah made a motion with his hands to brush back his hair to illustrate, "and brushes back her hair with both hands, getting syrup all in her hair!"

"Oh man, that sounds like a one-year-old alright," Miguel laughed.

"I had *just* given her a bath that morning too," Jeremiah laughed. "It took like ten minutes of just rubbing shampoo through her hair to get it to stop being so sticky."

Miguel settled down and exhaled as he sat back in the bus seat. "I kind of miss our boys doing stuff like that, as frustrating as it was. It always made me laugh afterwards."

Jeremiah sat back in his seat too and smiled. "I can't wait to see my little troublemaker again."

Just then, they heard what sounded like a popping noise in the distance. The soldier on their bus, who was sleeping a moment ago, popped up from his seat as chatter came over the radio.

"Stop the bus! Now!" The soldier ordered.

Every Green Check bus in the line promptly came to a stop. Dead silence waited in the air as everyone looked over in the distance at the Red X busses; they were stopped, too. The popping noise started to become louder and bright flashes of light appeared to be coming from inside the busses.

"Open fire! Open fire! We have Ghost Deltas on busses One Twenty-Five, One Twenty-Eight, and One Forty! Repeat! Ghost Deltas on busses One Twenty-Five, One Twenty-Eight, and One—Retreat! Get off the bus! Green Tango, we need back-up!" a voice screamed through the soldier's walkie talkie.

The solider on the bus froze for a minute, then came another voice over the talkie. "Red Tangos have been compromised! Repeat, Red Tangos compromised!"

The solider seemed to snap out of his frozen state and picked up his rifle, getting off the bus and calling over his walkie that all tanks aim at the "Red Tangos".

Miguel and several others on the bus stood.

"They're going to shoot the sick busses!" One person on the bus shouted.

In a crazed panic, everyone on the Green Check busses poured out of the bus and headed across the field just behind the tanks rolling in that direction.

"Why aren't the tanks following the sick busses firing?" Miguel asked aloud while running.

"I don't know, but it can't be good if they need our tanks. What are 'Ghost Deltas'?" Jeremiah asked, running next to Louis and Miguel.

One tank fired, deafening everyone around it. The blast lit up the darkness around them, and for a moment, they saw them; several people up ahead, attacking the sick busses. As they got closer, Jeremiah and Miguel could see that the people attacking the busses weren't people. They didn't *stand* like people. Another tank fired, hitting a Red X bus directly, causing a massive explosion. Everyone running across the field hit the ground.

"*No!* Stop shooting!" Miguel shouted. He ran and tackled one solider to the ground, wrestling with him for the rifle. "My wife and son are on those busses!"

"Get off me!" The soldier socked Miguel in the stomach with the butt of his rifle, causing Miguel to roll back in pain. "Ghost Deltas attacking Red Tangos! All tanks fire! Repeat, all tanks fire!"

"No, stop!" Miguel shouted again, still unable to stand from the pain.

Miguel looked over in the distance at the sick busses as the tanks in front of Miguel fired their main cannons. Each of the Red X busses jumped in the air and exploded as they were hit. The few people that ran from the wreckage were on fire and quickly fell to the ground if they weren't shot first. From behind the people and soldiers, came a sound that didn't seem human or animal. Looking behind them, they saw the Green Check busses rocking back and forth, with figures inside them, but it was unclear who they were.

"Green Tango busses compromised!" A solider shouted over his talkie. "Ghost Deltas inside busses! Open fire!"

"Sir, that's our only way to the base!" Another soldier called over the walkie talkie.

"These people can *walk* for all I care! I gave you an *order*!"

"You heard him! All tanks fire at Green Tango busses! All of them!"

The tanks unloaded on the remaining busses as the screams of infected rang out in the air. After a few minutes of deafening explosions, there remained only a handful of tanks, a few trucks carrying soldiers, and the large group of people that were healthy. The soldiers from the trucks got out and loaded what few people they could carry.

"Where did those Ghost Deltas come from?" One soldier asked.

"I don't know, but we should've spotted them sooner! We just lost half our men and resources!" A higher-ranking soldier responded.

"What about all these people? Now how are we going to get them to the base?"

The higher-ranking solider pulled out his walkie-talkie and gave an order to load the people they could in the remaining trucks, the rest will have to walk. Miguel remained on the ground, weeping next to Louis. Jeremiah knelt next to him.

"Miguel…I'm so sorry. Truly, I am. But we need to go," Jeremiah said through a cracked voice.

Off in the distance behind them, the echoed screams of infected were heard.

"Everyone, we need to move out! Ghost Deltas are coming!" A few soldiers called out to the people.

The crowd began piling into army trucks and the rest formed little groups, depending on what bus they were on, and slowly jogged along with the soldiers. Tanks in front, trucks slightly behind, then the jogging groups in back.

"Miguel. Louis. I can't understand what you've just lost. But there's more of those things coming. We can't stay here," Jeremiah said quickly.

Jeremiah extended his hands and helped Miguel and Louis to their feet, then joined the jogging groups. Miguel said nothing to Louis, but they stayed close together as they jogged, weeping bitterly as they went. Only Jeremiah looked back at the burning wreckage they were leaving behind. The screams of the infected grew louder behind them, but they were unable to see them coming in the dark. The soldiers continuously looked back as they jogged, rifles ready.

Chapter 14

The group ended up stopping in the middle of the night to rest; the military keeping watch and shooting down any infected that caught up to them. In the early hours of the morning, orders were given for everyone to keep moving. Restless and groggy, Jeremiah stood, helping Louis and Miguel to their feet as well.

"What time is it?" Miguel asked.

"A little past six," Louis yawned.

"They couldn't give us a few more hours to rest. We were running all night. Not to mention the gunfire that kept us up. Did you see any of them?" Miguel asked Jeremiah.

Jeremiah shook his head. "They were shooting off in the trees there. I heard them but couldn't see them. Good thing, I suppose."

Miguel nodded in agreement. Louis wiped his eyes and sniffled.

"Are you sure mom and Ellis didn't make it out?" Louis asked.

Miguel looked at Jeremiah, neither of them sure of what to say. Ultimately, Miguel went with the truth.

"I'm sorry, son. Nobody could've made it out of those busses. I wish it weren't true," Miguel said, trying to hide his own internal pain from Louis. He knew his boy just lost his little brother and mother the night before, and he was now without his wife and youngest son; how either of them slept at all was a miracle. *It just feels like a bad dream. I'd give my very soul to let Louis wake up from this nightmare*, he thought to himself.

"Keep moving!" A few soldiers shouted.

"I know this isn't easy for either of you, but we need to keep moving. We can't get left behind," Jeremiah said impassively.

Miguel looked down at a distressed Louis and nodded. "He's right. Let's go."

Citizens and soldiers jogged beside each other, neither one of them caring to make conversation. Many were still yawning and if anything was said, it was mostly to complain about how early it was. Still, the cries and screams of the infected could be faintly heard far off in the distance behind them. The night before, only a few infected managed to catch up to them, but more were heard trailing behind. The military seemed just as confused as everyone else as to where they came from.

Many speculated they were from the city; it made sense, but nobody recognized the infected. Not that there was much to recognize, anyway— their faces distorted and bodies horrifically changed from the virus; it was hard to tell if they were once human. Many of the infected had similarities in their faces; bloodshot eyes, nose and lips completely missing, skin around the cheeks peeling off. But some appeared worse, the few CDC workers that were with them theorized that those that appeared worse had been infected much longer, perhaps even weeks longer.

The eyes of the most infected were gone. The eyeballs, that is. Sprouting from the sockets were bloody antenna that moved around when the infected person was agitated. The arms were the most deformed part of the infected person's body. *The looser the arms appeared to be, the longer they've been infected,* the CDC workers deducted. Eventually, both arms would fall off, quickly leading to "new arms", the CDC called them, growing in their place.

The "new arms" weren't always the same with every infected person, but they were never like the human arms that fell off. These new ones were much longer, roughly twice the size of the person's full body length. The arms themselves were usually a dark green or dark purple color, depending on the person. The skin on the arms differed depending on the amount of time the person had been infected. Longer periods of time resulted in skin that resembled a crustacean shell.

The military would call these ones, "Tank Ghost Deltas". The crustacean-like shell that replaced human skin on these infected made bullets almost useless against them. The hands were a pair of pincher-like hands covered in a thick layer of skin, feeling almost like a rock or the crustacean shell. If not pincher hands, then the infected person would have a long, serrated blade formed by the crustacean shell, replacing the hands altogether. The CDC referred to these as, "Sawblades". The most lethal form of the infection, coming from the infected person carrying the Phantom Flu for at least a month.

A mystery even to the CDC, the infected person's legs normally remained unchanged. The skin would peel off and to reveal a thicker layer of skin underneath but not nearly as tough as the crustacean-like shell that covered the upper body. Jeremiah attempted to explain to a CDC worker jogging next to him that a friend of his didn't look like any of those descriptions. Describing Karen, Jeremiah believed that not every infected person took on this "Tank Ghost Delta" or "Sawblade" appearance.

To which, the CDC worker replied, "this is just what we've seen so far. We don't know why there's still different forms of this infection or what makes one person change appearance, and another change into something else altogether. It has to do with our genetic makeup, as well as the time elapsed while carrying the virus."

"Have you guys met anyone immune to the Phantom Flu?" Miguel asked the CDC worker.

"Not yet, I'm afraid. But I pray that one day we find those people. Perhaps they could be the key to finding a cure. Maybe even reverse the effects of the virus," she replied.

Before Miguel or Jeremiah could ask her anything else, a person nearby started coughing. Two soldiers jogging ahead spun around, aimed their rifles, and fired at the offender. The bullets zipped through the air, straight through the person, killing them before they hit the ground. Everyone stopped dead in their tracks, the people who had just witnessed what happened screamed and backed away from the scene.

"Attention citizens!" One man in a general's uniform announced through a megaphone. He stood on top of one of the tanks as he made his announcement. "Anyone who appears sick, even in the slightest, *will* be shot on sight! I will not have our group be compromised by infected individuals. We will arrive at the base in a few hours, and we're *only* bringing healthy individuals inside! All citizens will now march in front, soldiers will be marching behind you! This is non-negotiable and there will be no questions!"

All the citizens who were previously riding in the trucks were forced to get out. Everyone who wasn't military, or CDC were now travelling in the front, soldiers and trucks behind them, and tanks in the back. Those who had to cough or sneeze now did so as quietly as possible. A few people nearby would start talking loudly, to mask the sound of the faint cough or sneeze. Jeremiah, Miguel, and Louis traveled in silence. After a while, the group soon arrived at a farm.

"Did you know this was here?" a soldier asked a few CDC workers, pointing to an abandoned CDC truck.

They shook their heads.

"Speculate then! Why would the CDC be at this farm?" The soldier asked again, a few other soldiers gathering around.

"We really don't know! A few months ago, we did send a few of our guys out to a farm in this area to test for rabies. But I didn't hear anything about it since then. I didn't know any of them personally, honest!" A CDC worker explained.

The general pushed a few soldiers out of the way and inserted himself in the conversation. "*Rabies?* Are you saying this flu is some form of rabies?"

The CDC worker shook her head and put her hands up defensively. "No, I doubt that this test had anything to do with the flu we're currently experiencing. When we first started investigating the Ghost Flu, we were trying to rule out possibilities, so that's why some of our guys came here. I do remember getting a call from a farmer about his animals acting strange, so we sent some of our people out to investigate; see if his animals had some connection to the Ghost Flu. But that still doesn't explain why their truck is still here. Like I said before, we got that call months ago!"

The general's eyes narrowed. "And it didn't seem suspicious that they didn't come back?"

"The people that were called out don't report back to me. We have a big team and I didn't know the individuals who came here."

"Then *who* did they report back to?"

"I don't *know!*"

"You're hiding something." The soldiers around the general slowly raised their weapons to the CDC workers. There was a silence that came over everyone. The general continued, "now that I have your attention, you're going to tell me *exactly* where those CDC employees are. And you're going to tell me right now. I'm sick of you people not telling us everything. I won't have my men running around in the dark, uninformed about what they're up against. You people know more than you're letting on!"

The CDC workers looked at each other, everyone afraid to speak up. Only one did. "We can't tell you," they said, nervously.

"And why is that?" The general asked calmly.

More soldiers gathered, weapons pointed at the CDC workers. The citizens all backed away from the scene, still within earshot. Miguel had

Louis stand behind him and Jeremiah, just in case the situation went sideways.

"We can only tell you that this isn't a flu," the CDC worker continued.

"Well, you don't say," the general said in a fake surprised tone. "Give us something we don't know already."

"The caterpillars. We don't know where they came from. Only that they caused all this," the CDC worker said in a shaky voice.

The general pulled out a pistol and touched the barrel to the CDC worker's head. "That's very funny. It's so creative that I'm almost jealous I didn't think of that myself. *Of course!* It was the caterpillars! How did I not see this coming?" The general said sarcastically.

The soldiers around him chuckled with amusement.

"I—I'm telling you the truth. They're black and purple. Their hollow spines produce toxic particles in the air. J—just barely visible to the naked eye. But you breathe those particles in…and—and you're done. T—t—that's how you get it."

"Listen to this, men!" The general declared. The soldiers around him laughed again. "Somebody's been watching too many science fiction movies on late night tv! It appears all those movies ruined your brain, young man. You've spread your psychosis throughout the CDC, and now you're trying to spread it throughout my ranks, aren't you?!"

"No! No, I'm not!" The CDC worker protested.

"Kitten," Miguel whispered under his breath.

"What?" Jeremiah turned to Miguel.

"Kitten the caterpillar. It's what my youngest son, Ellis called this black and purple caterpillar we found in our backyard. My friend found one just like it too. Particles floated throughout his home. I think this guy might be telling the—" before Miguel could finish, a shot rang out and everyone around them screamed.

The citizens hit the ground as every CDC worker was shot down. The next thing to follow was the sound of a distinct croaking noise coming from inside the barn house. The front door burst open and out poured the vilest of creatures, wearing police uniforms. Bloated and sickly, their throats swelled up and exhaled a croaking noise every few moments. Everyone stood motionless, even the general, stunned at the scene before them.

"O—open fire!" The general stuttered.

In an instant, a long sticky tongue lashed out and wrapped around the general's neck, then jerked him forwards, snapping his neck in the process. Each soldier unloaded on the mutated cops but stopped when they heard the screams of people behind them, followed by what felt like an earthquake. Miguel, Jeremiah, and Louis followed the crowd of people as they ran for cover. The only thing worse than the sight was the low-pitched, numerous mooing the creature made.

Four heavy arms pounded the ground with striking force, the massive body held up by each arm; its slim legs did little to maintain balance. Muscular and covered with white hair, featuring black splotches all over. The head was an ugly fusion of several cow heads. Random cow horns sprouting from the top of each head, some eyes fused together, and some eyes scattered across the heads, ignoring normal anatomy. Several snouts and mouths of the cows were located on the bottom parts of the fusion heads. Puss and blood dripped from the hideous eyes, and disgusting green mucus poured from the snouts. Siliva was flung from the mouths each time the mouths let out an unnerving, "moo".

"What on earth…fire! Fire!" The soldiers shouted, caught between the monstrosity behind them and the mutant cops in front of them. "All tanks, focus fire on the Cow Ghost Delta!"

As the order was being given, the walking fusion of cows lifted one of the tanks above its many heads with two massive arms, the other two arms remaining on the ground to maintain balance; the tiny legs crouched down to help lift the tank. The Fusion Cows threw the tank forwards at the other tanks, destroying two of them in moments. One tank fired off a shell from its main cannon. Seeing the shell with its many eyes, it instinctively caught the shell with a large hand formed by many hooves. The hands on the end of each of its four arms resembled a gorilla hand, and it walked on the knuckles formed by the hooves. The six short, stubby fingers were formed by rough tissue, much like the snouts of the cows, bumpy and darkened. Four fingers were on each hand, featuring two apposable thumbs on each side of the hand.

When the Fusion Cows had caught the tank shell on one hand, it spun its body around, then tossed the shell back at the tank with a loud grunt, obliterating the tank along with the two tanks next to it. The Fusion Cows moved towards another tank, using its strength to pick up the tank by the main cannon, and slam it down repeatedly on another tank like a hammer, demolishing both.

"Sawblades!" One soldier shouted as a group of infected rushed towards them.

The Sawblade infected used their serrated arms to slice through the soldiers' flesh, moving their arms back and forth rapidly to cut through bone.

"Retreat! Retreat!" The soldiers began shouting.

The group of citizens, seeing what was going on, decided to come to their aid after realizing without the soldiers' protection they wouldn't make it much farther on their own.

"I have to go. Without those guns, we don't stand a chance making it to that military base," Jeremiah said. The sound of low, repulsive mooing was heard traveling closer to their location. Jeremiah knew they didn't have much time. The Fusion Cows were nearly done eliminating all the tanks, using them almost like toys as it tore each tank apart. "Get inside the barn house with the women and children. Send anyone willing to help my way," Jeremiah instructed before running towards the soldiers.

The Fusion Cows picked up any soldier who dared to get too close; crushing their bones in its hands. The mutated police and Sawblades made quick work of the soldiers; a massacre Jeremiah wasn't sure he'd live through. But if he was ever to see Amelia again, he knew he had to get ahold of one of the soldiers' guns. Seeing his opportunity, Jeremiah dashed towards a fallen soldier, but another citizen reached it first.

"Behind you!" Jeremiah pointed behind the citizen.

The person turned around, only to have their lower jaw sliced off by a serrated blade. The Sawblade shrieked as the person, bleeding and tongue drooping down, crawled forward towards Jeremiah. Jeremiah darted towards the person, grabbing their hands but the Sawblade was faster; the serrated blade on its arm cutting through the person's back and spine, quickly separating the person into two parts. Jeremiah shoved the Sawblade off the dead person and fell forward. Seeing the rifle on the ground a few inches away, he quickly crawled towards it. With the shrieking of the Sawblade clearly behind him, he knew he only had moments to reach the gun.

Jeremiah grabbed the rifle, heard the serrated arm cutting through the air, and rolled over on his back to face the Sawblade. He fired off two rounds, sending the bullets into the bottom of the Sawblade's mouth and out the top of its skull. The Sawblade fell to its knees, then face down on the ground. Jeremiah quickly got to his feet and looked around as citizens used the military's rifles to defeat the infected around them. Startled by the gunfire and bullets whizzing by, the Fusion Cows let out several moos as it dashed away, disappearing.

Many of the military had dropped their weapons once they saw their comrades being torn apart and fled from the scene. The few military personnel that stayed to fight off the infected were held up at gunpoint by the citizens. The infected were dead or bleeding out, all the tanks were destroyed, only a few trucks remained, and a handful of people and soldiers were alive. The few women and children that didn't initially run off, exited the farmhouse with Miguel. The citizens ordered that the military drop their weapons, which they promptly did. They forced the military to march ahead as the citizens followed closely behind, weapons pointed at the soldiers.

Women and children were loaded into the few trucks that were left. Louis rode in one of the trucks as Miguel and Jeremiah walked just ahead with their weapons pointed at the soldiers in front of them.

"We're in charge now!" One citizen shouted, causing everyone around him to cheer in agreement. "No more getting shot!" He shouted, followed by more cheers.

The soldiers were silent as they marched at the front.

"Jeremiah…what in the world *was* that thing?" Miguel whispered.

"The cows, you mean?" Jeremiah whispered back.

Miguel nodded.

Jeremiah shook his head. "I don't know. But this flu isn't just infecting people. It looks like the livestock are experiencing the worst this infection has to offer. I don't know where that mutated cow thing ran off to, but let's hope it's the last time we see it."

Miguel focused his eyes forward and nodded. "Agreed."

CHAPTER 15

Riding in the truck, Louis turned his head and held his breath. Unable to contain it, he let out several loud coughs. A few soldiers turned their heads to see a child coughing in one of the trucks.

"Keep your eyes forward!" Miguel commanded, pointing the gun barrel at one of the soldiers.

"If you guys were smart, you'd put down that sick dog now, before he infects the rest of you," the soldier muttered.

"He's *not* sick! Keep your mouth shut or I won't hesitate to shoot!" Miguel shot back.

"You're not a killer, none of you are. And judging by your defensiveness, I'd say that boy is your son, right? You won't shoot him for the same reason you won't shoot any of us: you don't have it in you."

"Say one more word and you might find out," Miguel said coldly.

Jeremiah put a hand on the barrel of Miguel's rifle, lowering it. "Easy. Let's be calm," Jeremiah said in a gentle voice, not wanting the escalate things.

"There could still be a cure out there somewhere," a person next to Miguel whispered. "Don't give up on hope yet, even if your son *is* infected."

"He's *not*," Miguel replied.

"I didn't say he was. I'm just saying… *if.*"

"There is no 'if'. He's not infected. He just has a cough."

"That's how it starts. Then your boy won't be your boy anymore," another solider chimed in.

"Shut it!" Miguel shouted.

"Hey, calm down," Jeremiah said calmly. "Louis is fine. Everything is okay. Just take it easy, okay?"

Miguel was silent. After another hour of walking, they came to a small town, empty with no visible sign of life.

"We ought to gather some supplies, you know?" One person suggested.

Everyone agreed and helped the women and kids off the trucks. The military was instructed to stay at the entrance of the town as a few people guarded them. Jeremiah, Miguel, and Louis walked to a nearby drugstore, just in case Louis wasn't okay. It wasn't vocalized, but Jeremiah and Louis knew why Miguel was taking them there.

"You're all going to be infected soon," a few soldiers taunted the people guarding them.

"Shut up!" One of the guards ordered.

"Yeah," another soldier added, "you'll tear each other apart. You got a family? You won't see them as your family when you turn into one of *them*. They'll just be food in your eyes."

"I said to shut up!" The guard shot back again.

After a few minutes, the group of citizens met back in the center of the small town, supplies in hand.

"Sick! The sick ones are here!" One person shouted, pointing to a small group of infected stumbling towards them.

Missing noses, lips, and some even missing eyeballs, the infected growled and snarled as they stumbled forwards. Their skin was hardened, tiny spikes formed by bone covering their shoulders. The citizens with guns ordered everyone else to get behind them as they fired off several rounds into the group. The infected shrieked and cried out in pain as the bullets zipped through them, splattering blood and bone fragments into the air.

Once they were all put down, the civilians checked ammo and carried their newly found supplies back to the trucks. Jeremiah stopped dead in his tracks when they reached the trucks. Miguel instinctively covered Louis' eyes. All the soldiers were bullet ridden and lying dead on the ground. The guards were covered in blood and stood like statues over the bodies.

"W—what did you do?" Someone asked the guards.

"They kept spreading lies. Telling us that *we* were infected. We think *they* were infected! Trying to cover for themselves! We had to! We didn't have a choice!" One of the guards said, laughing wildly with his eyes wide and looking at the bodies. "We had to! We *had* to!

The guards kept their backs to the citizens, their eyes fixed on the bodies. The citizens looked at each other. A few armed citizens stepped forward and aimed their guns at the guards. Children's eyes and ears were covered by their parents as bright flashes of light and deafening pops occurred until there was silence. Everyone was loaded onto the trucks and they drove through the small town. Louis told Miguel that he was already starting to feel better. Miguel looked into his son's eyes.

Chapter 16

After a few more hours, the sun began to set and the people were growing weary. While gathering supplies at the previous town, they'd managed to find more food, so they took the time to pass out small portions. Children ate first, then women, then the men. There were so few people left by this point, that everyone fit in the four remaining trucks, so there was no need to stop. As a courteous gesture by the citizens, they agreed to give the truck drivers the biggest portions of food since they didn't get to relax like everyone else.

Miguel picked out some large carrots and a loaf of bread and passed the bread to his son. Jeremiah grabbed a vanilla pudding cup.

"You know, I used to eat these every day when I was a kid," Jeremiah said to Louis.

Louis laughed with a mouthful of bread.

"Did your parents know about that?" Miguel teased.

Jeremiah smiled and shook his head. "In school, I would trade my lunch with this other kid. He always had pudding, I always had rice cakes."

"Gross. Your mom packed you rice cakes?" Louis said with a scrunched-up face.

Jeremiah's smile faded. "My parents weren't around much. I tried to stay out of their way when they were home. Rice cakes were all I could find in our pantry that wasn't expired."

Louis' smile faded as well. "Oh, I'm sorry."

Jeremiah sat up, taking in another spoonful of pudding. "Don't be," Jeremiah glanced at Miguel, "you know, you have a pretty cool Dad."

Louis looked at Miguel and smiled. "I know." When Miguel met Louis' eyes, he noticed how red Louis' eyes were getting. He didn't say anything. Louis wasn't sick. That was impossible. He wasn't going to lose another son. "You going to eat that?" Louis asked, pointing to another carrot.

"What?" Miguel said, a little distracted.

"I asked if you're going to eat that other carrot," Louis repeated.

Miguel shook his head.

"You okay, buddy?" Jeremiah asked Miguel.

"Y—yes. I'm okay," Miguel replied. He glanced at Louis' eyes again. "I'm okay."

There were two armed citizens in their truck, both sitting near Louis, and both carefully observing. It was clear that they noticed his eyes, too. Miguel moved closer to his boy. Louis bit into the carrot, snapping the end off with his teeth, and halfway into chewing. Louis spit out the carrot and coughed. Every head turned towards Louis.

"Is everything okay?" Miguel asked.

Jeremiah put down his pudding cup as soon as it happened. The armed citizens placed their hands on their weapons.

"Yeah, it's nothing, I promise," Louis calmly replied.

The armed citizens kept their eyes on Louis for several minutes. Everyone else on the truck began to whisper about whether they should allow the boy to be killed or not. Overhearing this, Jeremiah sat in front of Louis, not saying a word but giving everyone around him a look.

CHAPTER 17

The moon was up, and the people in the trucks used their newly acquired flashlights to see around them; they had found a handful of flashlights during their supply hunt in the previous town. Many people were asleep, but a few people were selected to stay awake and shine the flashlights around; nobody wanted to be attacked at night. During the day was difficult enough when they could *see* the infected. Miguel had cried until he fell asleep and Jeremiah volunteered to stay awake with a flashlight. It's not like Jeremiah wanted to sleep even if he could. He kept seeing Louis' face light up, and his ears were still ringing from the gun blast.

"We should've been there by now! Where's this military base?" Somebody asked Jeremiah with a whisper as to not wake up anyone.

"I wish I knew, but we can't be far," Jeremiah whispered back, shining the flashlight at some moving trees; *just the wind.*

"At least when those army guys were with us, they knew the way. But since we've been using their maps, I've lost count of the times we've gotten turned around."

"It's not like any of us have been there before. Just hang tight, we'll get there soon enough."

"And if we don't?"

Jeremiah put the flashlight down and looked into the person's eyes. "We will. We have to." Jeremiah picked up the flashlight and shined the light on some more moving trees; only they weren't trees. "What is that?" He whispered to the person.

The moving figures shot into the sky with a screech. It looked like five or six figures the size of fully-grown men. Only, they had large wings with a wingspan of at least ten feet across. The bodies looked human enough, but the heads were something entirely different. Jeremiah shined the light up at them and dropped it when he saw their faces, human skulls but insect features. They swooped down, knocking over one of the trucks ahead, flipping it over and sending everyone flying.

"Infected!" Jeremiah shouted, waking everyone on their truck. The armed citizens began firing in all directions, unable to see the flying infected. The bullets whizzed through the air, hitting a few people on other trucks, and hitting only one of the flying infected. The flying creature that was hit came falling out of the sky, landing in one of the trucks onto a few people. They screamed to get it off and a few people helped lift the creature's body when the corpse suddenly erupted, exploding green goo all over the people on that truck.

Jeremiah couldn't see why the people were screaming until he shined the light at that truck. The people covered in goo were shrieking in a way that Jeremiah had never heard before. Their flesh was falling off their bones, their vocal cords dissolving and creating a horrible noise as their screams distorted. Their bones quickly liquified in a matter of moments, the green goo breaking down the truck soon after. The truck and everyone on it were reduced to a nasty puddle of gore and liquified machine parts within the span of a minute.

With little time to react, Jeremiah's truck was lifted into the air by two flying creatures. Jeremiah began shouting not to shoot but the armed citizens fired anyway in a crazed panic. The creatures dropped the truck after lifting only a few feet in the air and exploded in the sky into a gooey mess raining down above them. Jeremiah leaped out of the way, tackling Louis in the process as the goo began to fall onto everything below it when he saw Miguel racing towards him. Droplets of goo landed on Miguel's head and he began screaming, smacking himself wildly to get it off but only getting it on his hands.

The flesh on Miguel's hands melted away, reducing them to bone and then a liquid state. The same happened to his head and shoulders; his eyes liquefied before melting into his skull as his entire face dissolved. Unable to touch him, Jeremiah stood helplessly as he watched Miguel and most of the people on the truck liquefy before him. Jeremiah fell to his knees as the other armed citizens from the last two trucks finished off the remainder of the flying creatures. Louis began screaming hysterically and Jeremiah felt a hand on his shoulder.

"Time to go, friend. There's probably more of those flying things nearby. You're welcome to stay, but we're leaving with the last truck. Unholy things destroyed our truck too, so we only have the one left," a person explained.

Not wanting to leave but remembering Amelia, he followed the last survivors on the truck as they pulled away from the scene. Jeremiah held Louis in his arms, letting him cry.

They drove in silence for a few minutes before the person leaned towards Jeremiah.

"I want to mourn too, but there just isn't time for that," the person told Jeremiah while they sat on the truck.

"Can't these things just give us a break!" One person stood up and shouted.

Another pulled them back to their seat. "Keep your voice down, idiot!" They scolded, "there could still be more overhead. Keep those flashlights in the sky! We lose this truck, we're toast. We won't make it on foot."

"Doesn't matter now," someone else mumbled.

The truck stopped. Everyone looked around to see why they stopped so soon. Jeremiah looked ahead and saw it; the military base was a few yards away. Louis felt something dripping from his nose and quickly wiped it away before anyone could notice; blood stained his hand as he wiped his nose.

CHAPTER 18

Jeremiah looked around, several people embracing loved ones while CDC and military personnel kept watch. After several minutes of walking around the huge building, Jeremiah saw her. He raced over to a CDC worker carrying his daughter and the worker handed Amelia over to her father. When Amelia saw Jeremiah running towards her, she began crying.

"Daddy! Daddy!" She shouted.

Unsurprisingly, Amelia was still holding onto Pup, which made Jeremiah smile and cry at the same time.

"You never let go of Pup, did you? I'm sorry I let you go, baby. I had to make sure you made it out of there," Jeremiah explained through his sobbing as he held her. "I won't let you go again; I promise."

The CDC worker who was holding Amelia put a hand on Jeremiah's shoulder. "I don't mean to interrupt your happy reunion, but I assume you are the girl's biological father?" The CDC worker asked. She was a stern looking woman, but Jeremiah didn't feel intimidated by her. Her soothing voice helped to put him at ease. Jeremiah nodded. "Can I ask you to come with me, Mr. Carter? I'm afraid it's urgent."

"How did you know my last name?" Jeremiah asked.

"All will be explained, rest assured. Please, follow me," she said.

Jeremiah looked over to see Louis waiting in the main lobby to grab some of the food the workers handed out. The CDC lady led Jeremiah into a small room. The room had a table in the center with two chairs. Armed guards surrounded the room. She sat in one of the chairs and offered the other chair to Jeremiah.

Jeremiah sat Amelia and Pup on his lap and nervously looked around the room at the armed guards. "What is this about?" He asked, making eye contact with her.

The CDC lady cleared her throat and began. "Your daughter was brought here along with a few others. I overheard you tell Amelia that you let her go. I assume you're talking about when you released her to our care when we evacuated those apartments?"

Jeremiah didn't know how long it had been. Weeks perhaps? He nodded. "It was the last truck out of there. They wouldn't let us both on so I gave her to them so she could escape."

"And now, here you both are! How wonderful," she smiled as she raised her hands to Jeremiah and Amelia. "Reunited at last."

"Is she okay?" Jeremiah asked abruptly.

The CDC lady's smile faded, and her voice changed. "Well, that's why I asked you in here. I have good news and bad news for you both."

Jeremiah's eyes narrowed. "Well don't keep me in suspense."

"A man who likes to get straight to the point; I like that. Well, we took blood samples of every person who first arrived, your daughter among them. We discovered that your daughter is carrying the Phantom Flu virus."

Jeremiah sat up. "What? No, that's impossible! She doesn't even look sick!" He said, trying to keep his voice down so he wouldn't startle Amelia.

"I'm afraid it's true. I'd like to test your blood as well. But you're right; she doesn't look sick. And that's where the good news comes in," the CDC lady said, clasping her hands together. "Your daughter is immune to the virus. She won't turn into one of those…well, you know."

"How did she get infected? She never came into direct contact with any infected person. At least…not that I know of."

"We believe she caught the airborne strand of the virus. We didn't see any visual damage to her body and like I said, she's been fine this whole time. If she was going to…*turn*…she would've done so by now. And since you're her biological father, we want to test your blood to see if you carry the same immunity."

"Of course. I guess I should know."

"Good, very good. Well, it seems there's a bit more good news I must tell you!"

"It's my lucky day," Jeremiah mumbled under his breath.

Amelia looked up at him and smiled. Jeremiah smiled back. "Good news," Amelia repeated. She looked at her plush dog and repeated, "good news, Pup."

The CDC lady smiled. "That's right, young lady! There are more people like your daughter."

Jeremiah leaned forward. "Really?"

"Oh yes," the CDC lady continued, "more immune people just like her. A whole community, in fact. They're not far from here, just a few miles north in Wyoming. We want to send her there, and you, if it turns out you're immune as well."

"Wait, the community is *only* immune people?"

"Yes, that's correct. Why do you ask?"

"Why are you separating them? Why can't we be with everyone else who isn't infected?"

"Come on, Mr. Carter. Surely you realize that you'll infect them as well, if you haven't already. Turns out, most people here on base are immune. We're sending them all to the community."

"Wait…you mean…"

"Yes, Mr. Carter. You've most likely infected anyone you've been around without even realizing it. Turns out, every time an infected person exhales, they release tiny particles into the air; the same particles that probably once infected you and your daughter. Once you carry the virus, you spread it every time you breathe. At first, we couldn't figure out why the infection was being spread so fast. But once we captured a live infected…we found out the truth."

Jeremiah hung his head down and closed his eyes. "Louis…it was me," he whispered.

"If you believe you're the cause for infecting someone on your way here, I wouldn't be so hard on yourself. The people you were traveling with might also be carriers too. It could've been any one of them. We'll find out who's sick and who's not soon enough."

"And the healthy who never got infected?" Jeremiah looked up at her.

The CDC lady stood up from her chair. "We're all infected by now, Mr. Carter. The Phantom Flu will come for us all eventually. Just like death and taxes. The healthy won't stay that way forever. If you haven't changed within a few days of being infected, you're immune. The human body is an extraordinary thing, Mr. Carter. Consider yours lucky. And be thankful your daughter is still alive. Be thankful you didn't witness your child change into a monster. Someone will be in to take your blood sample momentarily," the CDC worker finished and walked out of the room.

Jeremiah left to grab Louis from the food table, and a few moments later, another CDC employee came in to take Jeremiah's and Louis' blood and they were told to wait around for the results. After a few hours, they both tested positive; carrying the virus yet immune to the deadly effects. Jeremiah held Amelia and Louis and cried. Jeremiah knew he had the responsibility of looking after Louis. For Miguel's sake, he was going to get Louis out of here alive. The CDC lady's words reverberated in his head.

"We're all infected by now, Mr. Carter. The Phantom Flu will come for us all eventually."

CHAPTER 19

"We'll take all the immune we have to the community now. Better to do it in small groups anyway. Otherwise, we'll risk losing most of them if things go south," the CDC lady ordered.

The man in the gasmask nodded. "And the healthy?"

"Expose them to a carrier. If they start to turn, get rid of them. If not, they can join us in our community."

"Any eyes on the Demon Ghost Delta?"

"It was last spotted near our community. They managed to drive it off but they're afraid it might be heading back this way. Bring a few RPGs with you, just in case you encounter it."

"Yes ma'am. That hellish thing just won't die."

"Be careful and I'll see you soon."

"Yes ma'am." The man in the gasmask saluted her and walked out of the room.

Hopefully, it's the only one, the CDC lady thought to herself, *if I never see another cow again, it'll be too soon.*

Jeremiah and Amelia were loaded onto another military truck, along with a few other immune people. Jeremiah wasn't thrilled to see another military truck, especially after seeing how easily they melt. However, a colony of people where they would be safe was better than being killed by whatever monstrosity was lurking around.

"Have you heard anything about this community?" Jeremiah asked aloud.

One person nodded. "Oh yeah, it's going to be great. Walls thirty feet high, snipers in towers, and plenty of food and shelter for everyone. Plus, when was the last time you've had a hot shower?"

Jeremiah shrugged. "Too long."

"It's real nice."

"You've been there already?"

"I have. I only came back because my cousin reached the base and I wanted to be there to greet him." The person smiled at the man sitting next to him.

Amelia waved.

"Is this journey there safe? I don't know if you realize how bad it is out there."

"Oh gosh, yeah. I've heard stories about the infected. But no, it's a relatively short journey and I've never seen any infected on the path we take."

"Well I've seen enough of them to know that if we do come across any…" Jeremiah stopped himself. Amelia was with him.

The strangers looked at Amelia and then back at Jeremiah, smiling faintly. "It'll be okay, I promise. Hey, look! It's snowing!"

An overcast day, the snow gently drifted from the sky. It was kind of nice and Jeremiah smiled at how pretty it looked as it covered the ground. He bundled Amelia up in warm clothes and held her tight as she held Pup. It was almost easy to forget how awful things were. Almost easy to forget all the death he had seen. But not easy enough to get Miguel's face out of his mind. He looked down at Louis and snapped out of it.

"Where are we?" Jeremiah asked.

"Right now, we're going through a ghost town, so don't worry. Just a shortcut to reach the community," someone explained.

Jeremiah nodded and sat back in his chair. He held out his hand and let the snow fall onto his palm. He smeared it against his hands out of boredom. He rubbed a little of the snow on Amelia's face as she giggled; she had never seen snow before. Jeremiah only wished her first snowfall was a happier occasion, not in the middle of a massive deadly flu epidemic. Jeremiah held out his hands and smeared some white particles on them again. Only this time, when it smeared, it created a dark brown looking substance.

"Some of this isn't snow," Louis realized.

One person held out their tongue to catch a little snow, and Jeremiah shouted for them to stop causing Amelia to jump, startled at the sharp change in her dad's voice.

"Hey, what's your problem, dude? I was only—" the person began, but Jeremiah cut them off.

"There's something in the air! Don't touch the snow!" Jeremiah shouted.

"This guy's gone nuts," one person said.

"No, look!" Jeremiah displayed the dark brown substance smeared on his hands. "There's something mixed in the snow!"

"Like dirt?" One person teased.

"No! Listen!" Jeremiah held up a hand for everyone to hush.

Just overhead came a noise. The wind? A bird? The flapping of wings. A large creature with wings flying overhead. Each time it flapped its wings; tiny particles were released into the air. Jeremiah silently motioned for everyone to remain still.

"It hasn't noticed us," one person whispered softly.

A soldier on the truck slowly raised a weapon. Jeremiah began silently but franticly trying to get the soldier's attention.

"Stop! Stop! Don't shoot it!" Jeremiah whispered, trying to remain as quiet as possible.

Everyone froze. The soldier wore a confused look.

"Why?" The soldier silently mouthed.

"The blood," Jeremiah whispered, "I've come across these flying ones before. They bleed a strong acid. Don't shoot. *Please.*"

The soldier thought for a moment, deciding whether to take his word or not. The soldier lowered his weapon and nodded. The creature began to fly faster, releasing more particles into the air, mixing with the snow, then flying ahead of the truck and disappearing into the clouds. Everyone exhaled. Amelia looked up at Jeremiah.

"It's okay, baby. Everything is okay," he comforted her.

"Oh no…" the soldier whispered.

"What?" Jeremiah asked, still whispering.

"Demon Ghost Delta up ahead. Stop the truck."

"What are you…" Jeremiah's voice trailed off when he heard the moos.

***

Smack! Splash!

The monkey tossed an object high into the air.

Smash! The object crashed into the ceiling.

Splash! The object landed back into the puddle.

The monkey looked around, alone in the room. Blood dripped from the walls.

Smack! Smack!

The monkey clapped its hands together, amusing itself with the blood splattering in all directions as it clapped with its wet hands.

***

An hour earlier, the General walked down the hallway with his two guards.

"Sir, we've done it!" One man in a lab coat reported. "Just watch."

The man in the lab coat took a syringe, went over to a small bag filled with liquid, and filled the syringe with the strange liquid. He then walked towards the Sawblade. It was chained to the floor with shackles around its feet, and it thrashed around in a straitjacket. It began to growl and gnash its teeth when the man in the lab coat approached. He injected the Sawblade with the syringe and the Sawblade fell to its knees, then to the ground as it convulsed violently.

"Wait for it," the man in the lab coat said.

The General and his guards stared intensely at the Sawblade. After a few moments the Sawblade grew tranquil.

"What are you showing me? You found a way for the infected to take a nap?!" The General asked angrily.

"Sir…this is the cure. Look at this." The man in the lab coat walked the General over to some rat cages.

"They look like normal rats. Again, what are you showing me?"

"Exactly! They *are* normal rats, sir," the man in the lab coat exclaimed as he pressed play on a video of some demonic looking creatures.

The tiny creatures possessed long fangs and muscular bodies, totally void of hair. Their eyes were bright red and bloody, oozing puss.

"What are these?" The General asked.

"The rats. A few days ago," the man in the lab coat replied.

"*Days?*"

"That's right. I tested the cure on them, and it worked! See this." The man walked the General over to a naked man who was also chained to the floor. "I tested the cure on him shortly after the rats returned to normal. This man was a Sawblade *last week.*"

The man looked severely malnourished and barely alive. But he looked human. The General looked at one of the guards and signaled for them to cover over. A guard pulled out a pistol and fired off three shots into the healed man.

"What are you—" the man in the lab coat stopped as soon as he saw the gun pointed at his head.

The General calmly walked over to the lab tech until he was inches away. "This cure…where is it?"

The lab tech, with both hands raised, pointed towards the back of the lab where a safe was located. The safe didn't have a keypad on the front or any obvious signs of opening it. Only a small red light was shining on the front door of the safe.

"Open it." The General demanded.

"The safe is only opened by entering the password on that terminal." The lab tech explained slowly. He felt the barrel of a gun touch the back of his head.

"Well, then I guess you better enter it." The guard threated.

The guard in front of the tech, originally holding him at gun point, lowered his weapon, allowing the second guard to walk the tech over to the terminal, and warned the tech not to try anything stupid.

"I don't understand, General." The tech pleaded as he logged into the computer.

The General exhaled and nodded. "There are certain things in life we never get answers for. This is just one of those times for you; it's not for you to understand."

The lab tech stopped typing on his keyboard.

"I didn't tell you to stop!" A guard shouted.

The tech calmly nodded. "I was just thinking."

The barrel of the gun pushed hard into the back of the tech's head.

"If you can't remember the password, I'll kill you right here and shoot the safe open myself." The guard threatened.

The lab tech faintly smiled. The red light on the safe turned blue and shutters slammed down over the exit doors. An alarm began blaring.

"What is this? What did you do?" The General shouted.

"I opened a cage. You may shoot me now because none of us are leaving this lab now, especially the cure."

The alarm continued to blare and pounding began to grow closer. The lights began to flicker as a wild scream rang out. The guards began screaming as the General drew his pistol and began firing in all directions. The guards did the same, shooting into the darkness, exploding beakers and destroying various glass lab equipment. The lights flashed again, illuminating the source of the screeching, allowing the military and lab tech to see a glimpse at what their last sight would be.

A monkey with blood red eyes, dark purple hair, and patches of skin peeling off exposed its fangs as it shouted at the humans. The missing sections of flesh displayed pale, grisly muscle fibers that gave off a faint glow of dark blue, which continued to radiate when the lights gave out, plunging them back into darkness, and leaving only the dim luminosity of muscle from the monkey as it leapt into the air, sinking its fangs into the General first.

*****

Smack! Splash!

The monkey tossed a severed arm into the air, sending it crashing into the ceiling again, amused as gravity dragged into down into the puddle of blood before it. Only the soft blue glow of the monkey kept the room from total darkness, and the sound of severed body parts being flung into the ceiling kept the lab from complete silence.

Chapter 20

The Fusion Cows picked up the soldier, crushing all his ribs in its enormous hand, and threw him to the ground. It began furiously pounding him into pieces as it repeatedly smashed each of its fists into his body. The Fusion Cows bent down, picked up a car, and swung it into the air at the other soldiers who fired at it. With little time to react, the car flew and crashed into the soldiers, sending them crashing against a building in a bloody mess. The people scattered, going in random directions to get away. Jeremiah held a screaming Amelia as she gripped Pup will all her might. He ran as fast as his legs would allow, remembering which way the person on the truck told him the community was located.

A soldier's body flew past them as Jeremiah heard the loud mooing behind him. He covered Amelia's eyes as they ran. The earth shook every time the Fusion Cows moved on its four arms, the air around him seemed to vibrate each time one of the heads would moo. Jeremiah wasn't sure if he should be covering Amelia's eyes or her ears at this point.

"Duck!" He heard someone shout.

Jeremiah turned around and immediately ducked, pulling Louis down and holding Amelia tight. A car flew over them and crashed through a window. Amelia screamed and cried.

"I know, I know. We're going to get out of here. It's okay, baby. I'm not leaving you," Jeremiah told her.

People scattered; Jeremiah didn't rely on following anyone. Besides, those who didn't run fast enough were crushed and dismembered by the Fusion Cows. So, he ran; he picked the one direction he remembered and ran towards it like he saw the finish line. He ran despite his lungs and chest hurting from the cold air. He ran even though his legs were going numb. He ran because he had made it too far to die right here. He ran until that awful mooing couldn't be heard anymore. He ran until the screams were too far away to ring through his head. He ran until he came to the gates. Jeremiah panted and dropped to his knees, letting Amelia down.

"S—stay back," Jeremiah said to her, out of breath.

The gates opened and a few people stepped out. Jeremiah stood and picked up Amelia, spinning her so she wouldn't see what was inside the community walls. He covered her eyes and turned back around to face the few people. They were riding horses, healthy normal horses. Behind them was a bloodbath. Body parts and entrails covered the ground inside the community.

"What happened? Where's the community of immune?" Jeremiah asked, looking away from the grisly sight.

"That big thing. I know you've seen it. It was headed straight towards the base. That's where you came from, right?" One person answered.

Jeremiah nodded, speechless.

"It climbed the walls and got inside. We tried to warn the base that it was coming once we drove it out. I don't know why they sent another group. They should've evacuated everyone," another survivor added.

Jeremiah still didn't know what to say.

"You're welcome to ride with us. We can take you back to the base. It's not safe here knowing that thing can get over the walls," another chimed in.

"No…no, we can't go back. We were attacked by that thing. It's just me, my daughter…and my son," Jeremiah explained, still in a state of shock.

The small group on horseback looked at each other; only five of them were left from the community and the two people in front of them— a small group of seven with no weapons. They didn't say it, but they knew they were out of ideas. The military base was covered in smoke and fire. People ran out of the base, coughing and wheezing from the smoke. Soldiers shouted as they loaded what weapons they had left into a truck and headed away from the burning building. Farther north, the distant sound of mooing could be heard.

"I don't know how well these things handle the cold. If you want, we could just keep heading north. Maybe find more people. Besides the big cow thing, we haven't seen many infected since it started snowing. It'll be winter soon too, so that could help our odds," one person suggested.

Jeremiah nodded. "I just want my daughter to be okay."

"Pup! Pup come too?" Amelia asked, holding up her plush dog.

One young lady, about Jeremiah's age smiled. "The doggy comes too."

The young lady helped Jeremiah and Amelia on her horse. Louis got on a horse with one of the others, staying within eyesight of Jeremiah. She wrapped Amelia up in a warm blanket and covered her head with a beanie that was too big for her but better than nothing. Jeremiah smiled and thanked her for the kindness. The young lady smiled in return and asked if they were both ready. Jeremiah nodded. She asked Amelia if Pup was ready to go too. Amelia nodded.

Jack and Alexandra's Sea Trip into Hell: A Zombie Tale

Mark Mackey

PART I

There was one and only thing Alexandra Hexingmore could think about sitting in the eight to eleven Crestenmore University English Lit class she had enrolled in for the spring semester. This afternoon she was going to embark on a trip with her boyfriend Jack Skariff on his family's yacht. Their pre-planned destination would be a small island not far from their hometown of Glasswind, Massachusetts. She and Jack had been dating since their freshman year at Faircrest High and throughout the entire time of their relationship, there hadn't been a sour moment or anytime that either of them developed a straying, wandering eye for anyone else. She and Jack were completely devoted to each other.

***

Immediately stepping out of the building, Alexandra was met with a depressingly gray and overcast sky. This filled her with a dose of crushing disappointment. Was Jack's and her upcoming sea trip going to be ruined by the sudden arrival of a terrible rainstorm? It sure would suck if that were to occur invaded her mind. It wouldn't be the end of the world however; she and Jack would just discover an equally pleasant activity to spend their weekend doing. And if that happened to be shacking up in a hotel and engaging in you-know-what for the first time ever in their relationship, then so be it. In her mind, she and Jack getting intimate with each other was long overdue.

A first-generation university student, both her parents decided to skip out on getting a higher education and dive right into the workforce, she belonged to the Delta Theta Omega sorority. Several minutes after class ended found her heading for the house the sorority called home for the past few decades. She had grown incredibly close to one of the sorority sisters;–Gemma Clairemont, as a result, they were roommates. She and Gemma looked the complete opposite from each other. While she was tall and slender, a couple inches shy of six feet tall and had waist length jet black hair; Gemma was small and pixie-like, her shoulder length hair dyed a shade of bright blue. Another major difference between Gemma and her, she had a distinct Bostanian accent, while her roommate's tone of voice strongly revealed her southern lineage. Yeah, she sure sounded like a true blue, authentic southern belle all right.

The final difference between Gemma and her was the fact her roommate was one hundred percent obsessed with everything zombie. The truth of the matter was, she was deathly afraid of zombies. Thankfully, Gemma cared and respected her enough not to push her obsession onto her.

***

"I know you can't wait to spend the weekend on that island with your gorgeous frat boyfriend, who you've been involved with since high school," Gemma greeted her as she opened the door and stepped in, shutting and locking it back. Gemma's obsession had her decorating the walls of her side of the room with zombie movie posters-the two disturbing her the most out of all of them, *Dawn of the Dead* and *Return of the Living Dead*.

"Damn right I can't," Alexandra answered seconds before she turned away from her roommate to not only escape the sight of those frightening as all heck posters but to get packing. She closed the distance on her dresser in seconds and had the middle drawer open, pulling out her one and only bikini-black. "What's your plan for the weekend?"

"I just found out there's going to be a zombie film festival in town tomorrow afternoon," Gemma said. "That should answer your question."

"Well at least you won't be feeling miserable in my absence," Alexandra said as she began stripping off the clothes she wore to put on the bikini.

"You know Jack's really going to want to devour you when he sees you dressed in that," Gemma commented.

"Yep, that's my plan," she said and flashed her roommate a pleasant smile.

Over the course of the next several minutes, Alexandra covered up her bikini and finished packing her suitcase. As she did, Gemma took to reading a paperback edition of the *Dawn of the Dead*.

As soon as Alexandra zipped up her suitcase, a vigorous knock sounded against the door.

"Guess who's arrived, the great love of your life," Gemma said without taking her eyes off her reading.

Instead of answering her roommate, Alexandra hurried over to the door eager to answer it and let Jack in. The moment she laid her eyes on her boyfriend, she threw her arms around his neck and gave him one heck of a powerful, passionate kiss.

"I see someone's glad to see me," Jack said as soon as she removed her lips from his. Like her, he had a distinct Bostanian accent.

"Uh-huh, I sure am," Alexandra answered, continuing to keep her arms wrapped around his neck, the glint of desire in her eyes.

"I'm not surprised you're reading that, given your obsession with zombies, Gemma," Jack said, glancing over at the other woman in the room and seeing the novel gripped in her hands. "What are your plans going to be when Alexandra and I are spending our weekend on that island?"

"I don't know about the rest of today or Sunday, but tomorrow afternoon there's a zombie film festival in town," Gemma answered, taking her eyes off her novel and placing them on Alexandra and Jack.

"Well at least you won't be feeling miserable without your roommate around," Jack replied. "So, are you ready to take off Alexandra?"

"Uh-huh, just let me grab my suitcases and we can get the heck out of here," Alexandra said.

"You two be sure to have a blast," Gemma said as Alexandra distanced herself away from Jack, launching herself over to her bed so she could grab her suitcases.

"I guarantee you we will," Alexandra answered as she arrived at her bed and grabbed up her suitcases. "I hope you have an equal blast attending that zombie film festival tomorrow afternoon."

Two minutes later, Alexandra and Jack made their departure from the room.

***

Whatever disappointment Alexandra had with Jack's and her weekend plans being crushed by a rainstorm was extinguished as soon as they stepped from the Delta Theta Omega house. The depressing, overcast sky had been replaced by bright sunshine and crisp clouds.

"I almost thought our sea trip was going to be ruined with the sky dreary and downcast back when I was making my way from the classroom to here," she admitted to her boyfriend. His Ford Bronco was parked right in front of the Delta Omega house.

"Good thing this beautiful weather decided to make a sudden arrival," Jack answered as they began closing the distance on his vehicle. "I have a question for you, have any interest in grabbing a bite to eat somewhere before our island journey?"

Considering this, it only took Alexandra a few seconds to decide that yes, she was definitely going to say yes to this. It was just turning 11:47 a.m. which meant they had plenty of time to sit down, stuff their faces with the food of whatever restaurant they chose and make it to the harbor to board Jack's family yacht and arrive on the island while it was still daylight. And hopefully this weather would remain the way it was the entire time. "It's exactly what we should do, since it's going to be a while before we arrive at the island and find somewhere to eat."

"It's exactly what I was thinking," Jack informed her. "Come on, let's get your suitcases loaded in so we can get into town and do exactly that."

***

Thirty minutes after pulling away from the Delta Omega house, she and Jack were driving through the downtown section of Glasswind. The first thing to catch her sight, the prom dress shop, named Lucera's after the woman who owned it, Lucera Washerstone. She was well aware of the fact it had been in Lucera's family for decades. It was sandwiched in between Cavernors' Books specializing in horror and science fiction and J and H's compact discs, owned by twenty-seven-year-old identical twin sisters, Julia and Heather Virson.

"Do you have anything in mind for us to eat?" Jack asked as they continued driving forward.

Glancing around, Alexandra caught sight of a restaurant she'd never tried. Right smack square on the corner of Darson Street and Heckers Avenue, it was called Black Thimble and it didn't stick to serving one single particular type of food. No, it made a whole slew of various meals and it took her only a couple seconds to make the decision this was where she really wanted to eat.

"We should check out the Black Thimble," she informed Jack before they had a chance to drive too far away from it. "It advertises it serves multiple things, meaning there's something there for both of us."

"Sounds good to me," Jack replied.

***

Stepping into Black Thimble, Alexandra's nostrils were immediately filled by a delicious smelling aroma. This instantly told her she had chosen the perfect restaurant for her and Jack to dine in. Seconds into stepping in, they were approached by a woman wearing a Black Thimble uniform with the name tag Betsona over the left side of her chest.

"Welcome to the Black Thimble," Betsona greeted them with a pleasant demeanor, and like she and Jack, she spoke with a genuine Bostonian accent. "Is it just the two of you who will be dining here this early afternoon?

"You guessed right," Alexandra answered.

"All right, follow me and I'll get you seated and you can check out the menu and order," Betsona replied, and together Alexandra and Jack began trailing obediently after her.

It was Jack's intention to propose marriage to Alexandra during their yacht trip; but he made the sudden decision not to wait until then. He was going to pop the question to her right here and now in this restaurant. Not right away of course; he was going to do it while their waitress was off taking care of whatever they decided to order. Bringing a sudden end to his thinking about this, the Thimble employee, who he had to admit was a real looker, came to a sudden stop in front of a booth which was able to seat four. She wasn't as attractive as Alexandra but a close second.

"Here we are, and I hope it's to your liking," Betsona said, turning to face Alexandra and him.

"It's fine," he informed her seconds before he and Alexandra slid in on either side of the booth. "And I'm pretty sure the great love of my life will have no problem agreeing with me."

"You better believe I won't," Alexandra replied in an enthusiastic tone.

"Excellent," Betsona said. "I'll give you say ten minutes to check out the menus and decide what you two want."

"Ten minutes should be fine," Alexandra replied, and the next thing they knew, Betsona turned and was heading away from them. "I need to use the bathroom and then we can order," Alexandra continued.

"Sure go on," Jack informed her seconds before Alexandra and headed off to hunt down the bathroom.

As Jack sat there waiting for Alexandra to return, his thoughts were invaded by what he planned to do when he and Alexandra were on the yacht and well on the way to the island, to propose marriage to her. Seconds passed and he settled on the sudden decision not to wait until then. He was going to pop the question to her right here and now in this restaurant. Not right away immediately of course, he was going to do it when Alexandra made her bathroom return. The next thing he knew, Jack reached into his blue jean pocket and took out the engagement ring, it was the same one his deceased grandfather gave his deceased grandmother, and placed it down right in front of Alexandra's side of the booth.

"I'm back, did you check out the menu while I was gone?" Alexandra asked, sliding back into her side of the booth. And that's when she saw the ring placed down before her. It wasn't any old ring, it was an engagement ring, she had seen plenty of them in the past.

It took Alexandra only a second to realize why it was there and the reason for Jack placing it down there. It was his way of saying he wanted them to eventually get married.

"Wow, I sure wasn't expecting to see this when I returned," she said, focusing her eyes on Jack.

"Tell me what you think of it?" Jack asked.

"If you want to know if I'm going to accept your marriage proposal, my answer is an instanr yes." Alexandra wasted no time in answering him. "Jack, we've been involved since high school, and it was during that time I fell in love with you."

Today cannot get any better for me as far as I'm concerned, Jack thought as a result of Alexandra saying yes and accepting his marriage proposal.

"I promise you aren't making a mistake accepting my marriage proposal," he informed Alexandra as she picked up the ring and slipped it on her right ring finger. "Now come on, let's check out these menus and order."

"All right, but first I want to text Gemma and break the good news to her," Alexandra said and hurried to take out her cellphone. "You go right on ahead and order anything for us. I'm way to excited and want to break the good news to my roommate."

Alexandra: Hey, I have some great news to share with you.

Gemma: What, you and Jack are shacked up in a hotel and are about to take your relationship to the next level in a real physical way?

Alexandra: Not even close.

Gemma: Well don't keep me in suspense. What is it?

Alexandra: Jack proposed marriage to me. I'm going to be the future Mrs. Skariff.

Gemma: It's about damn time for that. Now you'd better be sure to name your first female child Gemma.

Alexandra: Yeah sure, you've got it. Provided Jack doesn't want to name our first female offspring after one of his relatives.

Gemma: See you when you get back.

"Are you two ready to order?" Betsona asked a few minutes later, making her return to them.

"Uh-huh we sure are," Jack immediately answered. "Alexandra here settled on the crispy shrimp and fry combo meal and I'll go with the seaman's meal."

"Both are excellent choices," Betsona said, flashing a smile. "I'll be back before you know it."

***

"Are you all ready to get to the port and take a yacht trip, future Mrs. Skariff?" Jack asked the moment they stepped from the Black Thimble. Luck was on their side as the bright sunshine and crisp clouds remained in the sky.

"You'd better believe I am," Alexandra replied with full blast enthusiasm.

Part II

"I've got a big surprise for you when I get back from throwing my suitcases in the room," Alexandra announced the moment she and Jack set foot on the yacht.

"I can barely wait to see what that is," Jack replied. "In the meantime, I'll get the yacht started up, destination island."

***

While Alexandra was heading for the room, she decided the moment she set foot into it: she was going to break the news to her parents as well.

***

It took Alexandra no time to reach and set foot in her room. As soon as she did, she moved over to the bed, anchoring herself down on it, getting out her cellphone and calling home. She flashed a pleased smile as her mother answered immediately.

"Yeah, hey Mom, I'm sure glad you were home and decided to answer. Uh-huh, college is going great and Jack is doing perfectly fine. I've got a big surprise for you, Jack finally got around to proposing marriage to me. Uh-huh, heck yeah I accepted it! Yeah, I'm glad you think so and are happy for me, and I'll tell Jack you can't wait for him to become part of our family. All right, I'll talk to you later."

Seconds later, Alexandra placed her cellphone down beside her on the bed to the right and stood. Wanting to get back on deck and spend what was left of the afternoon sun with Jack, she hurriedly stripped down to her bikini. A minute later, she took out her StarBay slip on flip flops and slid her feet into them, stepping from her room to do exactly that.

***

Returning to the deck, she met Jack, standing at the edge of the deck, his hands gripping the safety guard rail. The bright sunshine was still out and powerful-it hadn't let her down, and she moved quickly to join him. While she was in her room Jack removed his shirt so that the only thing he had on were blue jean cut off shorts and like her, his feet stuck into a pair of men's flip flops.

"Enjoying staring down at the Atlantic Ocean?" she asked, arriving at his side within moments.

"Yeah, you'd better believe it he answered, turning to face her. And when he did, seeing her in the bikini she had on caused his face to brighten with pleased excitement.

"What do you think?" she asked, wrapping her arms around his neck-the look on her face matching his.

"You sure didn't let me down with the surprise, that's for sure. Anyway, changing the subject, I have the yacht on autopilot so we can relax and enjoy the sights of the ocean for a little while."

"You're intelligent, that's for sure," Alexandra said as she removed her arms from around his neck and together, they positioned themselves to face the ocean. "Anyway I filled my mother in on our engagement and forthcoming marriage."

"Really, what was her opinion of it?" Jack asked.

"She's all for it and gives her blessing," Alexandra replied. "It's too bad my father wasn't home when I called there, however I'm pretty sure he won't have a problem with us getting married. He's always been a fan of our relationship ever since our high school days. So I'm going to take it easy on the ever-present lounge chair, are you interested in joining me?"

"I'll join you in a few minutes," Jack answered her.

"Suit yourself," Alexandra said. She turned around and headed for the pair of lounge chairs placed next to each other.

Continuing to stand there and stare down onto the ocean below allowed the hot afternoon sun to finally drench his face with sweat. As the seconds passed, he felt overcome by a sudden desire to turn around and join Alexandra. The next thing he knew, he did exactly that. He swore she was beyond gorgeous laying there-he sure did pick a real winner in her and a couple seconds later he took a couple steps forward. This was as far as he managed to get as he was caught by surprise by Alexandra's sudden, "what the hell is that?"

Curiosity over what she was making reference to caused him to turn, and that's when he saw it, a silvery white ovalish creature twelve inches in equal width and length with only an enormous mouth filled with huge *stalactite* teeth for facial features.

Sheer terror pulsated in him. He could not believe such a creature existed! What the hell was it? What were its intentions? Clearly to him, it could not be good, given its appearance.

Out of nowhere, whatever this creature-possibly a monster-was darted forward and it stopped when it was near him. The next thing he knew, which caused his eyes to widen with pure fear, it began to eject a blueish gelatinous substance which gave off a rancid stench from its mouth onto him.

"What the hell?" he cried as it streamed down him, his neck and bare torso to be exact. And then he began to feel a sudden hot, burning sensation strike.

Alexandra felt instant riveting horror the moment she laid her eyes on this bizarre creature emerging from the ocean, surrounding them and the yacht they were on. What the hell was it? Were there going to be more of them? What were its intentions?

"Hey what the hell is that?" she yelled out to Jack seconds later.

She didn't receive an answer from him. Instead, she watched whatever this strange creature was zip over Jack's head. And then the worst possible thing she ever saw in her life happened to Jack, the great love of her life, the man she was going to marry soon after graduating from Crestenmore.

As the substance flowed down him, much to Jack's shock, his skin began to peel off. It exposed the unsightly sections of his body, and as a result, his blood stained the deck, causing him to feel sickened nausea.

This feeling was catapulted into full blast misery as he realized, death was on the way. This would leave Alexandra alone and unprotected against whatever the hell this creature was. A sudden jolting blast caused him to cease thinking about this; he realized he developing a sudden desperate hunger for Alexandra's flesh. He was reminded of zombies. Like hell he was about to eat his lover's flesh. He'd sooner hurdle himself into the ocean than subject Alexandra to this.

Even though it would leave Alexandra alone and at the mercy of the creature, he turned away and began to rush back to where he stood a few minutes ago. All the while the creature remained still and unmoving in the same location. It was as this thing was uncertain what to do next.

Alexandra felt a strong rush of nausea witnessing the creature attack Jack. She could not believe Jack was still alive, much less able to walk in this condition. Still, even so, it didn't dispel the way she desired him. Nothing could cause that. She loved the hell out of him and always would.

It didn't help that his next act was to turn away from her seconds later and make his way over to the edge of the deck where he'd stood minutes earlier. She was intelligent enough to realize his reasoning, he intended to toss himself into the sea and she'd lose him forever.

Like hell I will.

Standing up, Alexandra rushed for Jack to prevent this.

As she did, she started to grow fearful since she'd have to pass underneath whatever the hell this creature was. Her fear didn't last long as she suddenly had the desire to suffer the same fate as Jack. Life really wasn't worth living without him in it. As she passed underneath it, the creature failed to give her this.

A few seconds later, she stood inches away from Jack. Reaching out, she wrapped her hand around his forearm to prevent him from jumping. She was filled with queasiness, yet she refused to let go.

"Jack, don't you dare even consider it."

Seconds later, Alexandra felt tears fill her eyes and stream down her face.

Jack wasn't the least bit surprised, Alexandra's being so close increased his craving for her flesh. It made him realize, more than ever, he had to take a dive into the ocean and fast, otherwise, chances were incredible he'd act on his desires.

"Alexandra please let me go, I have to do this!" he cried, turning to face her. "What happened to me has caused a craving for your flesh to develop, you know like a damn zombie. I want to die before it gets so bad I have no choice but to act on it. If you care about me, you won't allow that to happen."

Jack saying this, that he had developed a hunger for human flesh just like a zombie caused her fear of them to surface. It also caused her to start thinking about Gemma and her obsession for all things living dead. She was absolutely certain her roommate and fellow sorority sister would be excited beyond belief over it. Get a real kick out of it. Maybe even give

Jack permission to bite into her flesh or brain to have the experience of knowing how it felt to become a zombie's meal. The thought of Jack doing this to her and having a zombie furiously devour her flesh/brain chilled her to the bone and elevated her fear of them.

But do I want Jack to continue suffering his hunger for flesh or brains?

And for the next few seconds afterwards, Alexandra strongly considered getting over her fear of what Jack had become, allow him to feast on her flesh or brain, whichever he preferred and had a craving for. In the end though, her fear of zombies won out and she decided against forcibly convincing him to forget about not wanting to harm her in any way, shape or form.

"I do," she whispered, thinking about this in her mind. She released the grip on his arm, lifted it up, and placed it against his face. She felt nausea over the touch, yet still continued to keep it placed there. It would be the last time she'd ever have the chance.

At the same time, she felt her heart break into a million pieces. It was right there and then she realized she couldn't let him go without one last act of physical affection. She wrapped her arms around his neck, staining them with his blood and pulled his head in for their last kiss ever. Not a simple peck but heavy duty. She could taste hot copper blood as she did so, not that it mattered given how she felt about him.

"Now what are you waiting for, I can't stand to see you in this condition any longer." She pulled away from his lips, hers stained with his blood. She turned-from him, unable to witness his tossing himself over. She heard a loud, thunderous splash and she lost him forever.

An instant later, she made a certain decision. She wanted to suffer the same fate as Jack and she began to approach the creature. It took only seconds for her to reach it, and wanting to snag its attention, she screamed out a "come on damn you, kill me like you did my boyfriend!"

As she stood there, she shut her eyes tight, expecting to receive the same bluish gelatinous substance spat on her, resulting in her skin melting off. This didn't happen. What shocked the crap out of her, her ears were filled by an unnerving, bone chilling wail. It made her open her eyes to see it was coming from the creature.

"Stop it, stop it!" she cried frantically.

The creature didn't, kept it right up. It made her realize, for whatever reason, it had no intention of doing to her what it did to Jack. Seconds later, she decided to hide out in her cabin and if need be, plug up her ears to prevent this wail from filling them.

It was while she was making her way to her cabin, the creature started to pursue her at a slow pace. It kept up the bone chilling wail, continuing to irritate Alexandra and make her move more quickly in an effort to reach her destination.

The wailing continued to drive Alexandra nuts. Spotting a fire extinguisher mounted on the wall, she wondered if she could use it to propel the creature away from her. How would it react if she attempted it?

There's only one way I can find out, she thought and the next thing she knew, was propelling herself forward. She removed it from the cabinet, and once in her hands, she spun around to meet the approaching creature. She aimed and fired a blast of *foam* at it. She felt incredible relief blossom as this seemed to do the trick and propel the creature backwards. She smiled as it turned and zoomed away from her, retreating under the water.

I hope you stay under there, she thought and resumed heading for her cabin.

***

Reaching the door to her cabin, Alexandra pushed it open and stepped inside. Closing it back, she headed straight for her bed and crawled onto it. She stared up at the ceiling, and as she did, Jack seeped into her mind. It caused her to start thinking about what was happening to his corpse right now. Probably shark food, she realized. Tears soon started filling her eyes, and a few minutes later, her eyes fluttered shut and she drifted off to sleep.

She began to dream. In it a scenario invaded her mind-she decided to allow Jack, who survived sharks devouring him and crawled back on board, to devour her flesh after all.

"Jack, I refuse to let you throw yourself into the ocean once again," she informed him as they stood face-to-face on the yacht's deck. Her fear of zombies not bothering to show up. "If that means agreeing to let you devour my flesh, then so be it."

"Are you sure now?" He asked.

"Uh-huh, I am. Now come on, snap to it, get with the eating." And to prove she was serious about wanting him to do this, she moved even closer to him so he could get started.

Seconds later, she was introduced to what it felt like to have her flesh devoured. Gripping her right arm, Jack moved it straight towards his mouth. The next thing Alexandra knew, she felt real live bright pain as he bit hard into her forearm. Her blood immediately started to flow as a result, some of it painting the deck floor red.

"Are you okay?" Jack asked, his voice flavored with nervous concern.

"Uh-huh, I can handle it. Now keep on going."

And he sure the heck did!

Within seconds, he had the rest of her arm's flesh stripped off and devoured. Her left arm was next to suffer; and then to make her legs accessible, she got down on her back, stretching her arms above her head.

"Now come on, get down here and continue," she instructed him.

He did, sitting beside her legs, his splayed out in front of him.

"So how do I taste?" She asked as he devoured the flesh off her legs, one after the other, further staining the yacht floor with her blood. And then for the first time since he started devouring her flesh, she began to grow light headed and dizzy from the loss of blood.

"You taste absolutely delicious," his instant answer as he began moving his head towards her bare stomach to get started on it. The pain grew worse as Jack bit harsh into the side of it, her blood flowing like mad. It dispatched the dizziness and lightheadedness right the heck out of her.

"I love you so much Jack!" She cried feverishly, moving her head repeatedly from left to right as he bit hard into her stomach right above her navel, no doubt to remove and devour her intestines.

As the minutes progressed, the dizziness and lightheadedness reestablished itself in her. She had her liver and kidney removed and devoured as well.

"Okay, now remove and devour my brain and heart, take my life and devour the rest of my flesh," she said.

He obliged her this as he positioned himself prone on her so they were face-to-face. He bit hard into the left side of her neck like a freaking blood sucking vampire. As the seconds wore on, the dizziness and lightheadedness grew stronger. Her eyes began to fall shut and she felt Jack bite into her forehead, no doubt to start extracting her brain. Bright, intense pain followed.

The dream ended with her opening her eyes. The creature's bone chilling wail was right outside her door.

Alexandra considered heading out there to find out if this time around, the creature had a willingness to spit the blue substance on her so she could join Jack in death. However, in the end she didn't. An idea infiltrated her mind; it might be a real smart idea to warn the world of this creature.

Yes, that's what I need to do, she decided.

As soon as she made this decision, the creature started to smash itself furiously against the door.

Realizing the creature might succeed in breaking in, Alexandra threw herself off the bed and made a mad dash for the fire extinguisher. Swiping it up, she aimed it straight at the door, expecting the creature to burst in any second.

But what if it wasn't out there alone? Had one or more of these creatures returned from the sea with it? If this was the case, would she be able to repel them all with the fire extinguisher? Was she about to have her flesh flayed off by the bluish substance? Not by the first one, who seemingly was disinterested in it for some reason, but one of the other ones. If in fact there were now more than one out there. The thought of this caused genuine fear to blossom in her, and her eyes started searching frantically for some weapon to use against them. She frowned when she didn't see anything.

Alexandra had her answer as to whether or not there were multiple creatures lurking out there as the frantic smashing erupted against multiple locations on the door.

It caused her to erupt with, "if you freak creatures burst in here, I swear you'll get a face full of fire extinguisher foam!"

It didn't dissuade the creatures from ceasing their frantic pounding against the door. As moments progressed, her eyes widened with even more fear as the creatures continued smashing the door causing it to be thrown open.

It allowed her to see the exact number of creatures out there. Four in total, and it was only seconds before they were darting in and straight for her. Fear for her life triggered Alexandra into aiming the fire extinguisher in hopes blasting them with foam would send them retreating away from her like it had the first one.

She frowned as it seemingly had no effect on them. Not knowing what else to do, she made the decision to use the fire extinguisher like a baseball bat. Within seconds the quartet of creatures closed the distance on her. It caused her to start smashing them as hard as she could.

At first, it seemed to be effective and she was knocking them backwards like baseballs. They reacted to it by singing out the bone chilling wails, but unlike the initial time she received an earful, these were furious in tone. It was like, well, she was seriously pissing them off by doing it.

And then it happened, she began to grow fatigued, and it didn't help she was unnerved by the wails. She began to falter as a result, and she stopped temporarily; her hands dropped down. This was a fatal mistake as it allowed the creatures to zoom in and get at her.

She was introduced to those dangerous teeth as they began to furiously bite into her bare, exposed flesh; making her seriously regret wearing a bikini. Her face brightened with riveting pain and at the same time, she felt her warm sticky blood race down her body. The pain was so harsh and intense that she had no choice but to release a powerful wordless scream.

***

And then she awoke with a jolt, her eyes wild and frantic with incredible fearful nervousness.

Glancing around and not seeing any of the creatures, the door shut tight, Alexandra quickly realized what she had experienced was one heck of a really freaking scary nightmare.

Resting her head back down against the pillow, Alexandra began to contemplate. Even though it was a nightmare, the creature or creatures were real and still around, either in the ocean or on board. If it was the latter and there were more of them like in her nightmare; rest assured chances were good she'd experienced what would happen if she dared to step from her cabin. But if she didn't, and remained hiding in here, it would disallow her the chance to warn the island inhabitants and the world of these creatures. Not only that, but eventually she'd starve. She realized there was no way around it. She'd have to venture out and make her way to that island. Out of fear the creature or creatures might be out there, Alexandra made the decision to cover up her bikini, disallow them the chance to bite into her like in the nightmare she'd suffered.

Launching herself off the bed, she made a mad dash straight for her suitcase, unzipped it, and started rummaging through it. She pulled out a size extra-large beige knitted sweater and hurried to slide it on. It dropped down mid-thigh, long enough to mask all of her bikini and she made her way towards the door.

***

With incredible caution, unsure of what she'd meet out there, Alexandra stepped out. Looking right and left, she breathed a sigh of relief as she didn't see any of the creatures.

Let's hope I continue not to see or have a run in with any of them, she thought as she headed right, reached the stairs, and started heading up them.

Making a return to the deck, Alexandra saw it was creature free, relieving the heck out of her. The next thing she knew, she was heading over to the edge. Reaching it, she looked out towards the island, and that's when she saw it.

Next to the yacht, surprising the heck out of her, sat a rowboat void of anyone on it. All she could make out was a rifle, on its side.

Nervousness instantly grew in her. She hadn't seen the boat there before, meaning it arrived while she was in her cabin or making her way to it.

A worse thought invaded her mind, had whoever was on it made his or her way onto the yacht? And if there was someone with her, would they be hazardous like the creature? One thing was sure, the rowboat was close enough for whoever it was to successfully swim for and climb aboard.

The thought of this possibility made Alexandra spin around and start scanning with sudden, nervous eyes in all directions. She didn't see anyone on the deck, which meant they were lurking somewhere else on the yacht, hiding. And when she discovered them, they'd spring out to attack or something far worse.

As she continued to stand there, Alexandra began to wonder if she should go searching for him or her, them. One she could probably handle, but two or more, forget it, she wouldn't stand a chance.

Before she had a chance to come up with a decision, a masculine voice filled her eyes, unnerving her. "I can see you beautiful!"

It came from somewhere behind her, and spinning around, she saw something she desperately wished she hadn't. Sure enough it was a man, but he had suffered the same as Jack. It meant he, whoever the heck he was, had an unfortunate meetup with the creature prior to coming aboard. Or maybe it happened while she was in her cabin. Making her way to or from it? Whichever the case, it happened.

"I know what happened to you. You had an unfortunate run in with the creatures calling the ocean home."

"Yeah, you'd better believe I did, sweet darling," he answered her in a taunting tone. "They didn't always call the ocean home. No, babe, that thing is a freaking space creature who arrived on Earth hundreds of thousands of years ago believe it or not. And unluckily for you, having its' space vomit spat on my head, resulting in melting my skin off has turned me into a freaking zombie. And are you smart enough to know what a zombie craves?"

"Human flesh," Alexandra answered him quickly and in a quiet tone.

"Correct!" he bellowed in full blown enthusiasm.

"What's your name?" the next words to escape her lips.

"Sean Callermare, and I swear sweetheart, the hunger for it is pulsating in me really bad and I can't wait to devour yours!"

And the next thing Alexandra knew, Sean was charging forward to satisfy his appetite. He reached her in seconds.

"You are such a gorgeous sweetheart," he leaned in and whispered into her right ear. "I'm going to take such delight in devouring your flesh."

And this is exactly what he did. He didn't start right away. Oh no. He started off by reaching down to the bottom of the sweater she had on and gripping it, he frantically began to yank it up. For some unknown reason-maybe perhaps she desired to join Jack in death, forget about warning the world about the creatures, she willingly lifted her arms up, allowing him to do it. She said nothing as he tossed her sweater down onto the deck and she continued to remain silent as he moved his head forward to her left shoulder. The next thing Alexandra knew, she felt bright biting pain as Sean bit hard, and pulling out, ripping away flesh, blood, her blood began to stain her bare torso.

"Uh-uh, we're not finished yet," Sean said in a gloating tone.

The next thing he did was continue devouring her flesh, gripping her right bicep and lowering himself to the floor, taking her with him.

"Get down on your back," he instructed in a demanding tone.

She did as ordered.

As soon as she did, Sean was kneeling beside her on the right. He leaned in, biting furiously into the side of her bare stomach. More of her blood came pouring out of her, staining the yacht's deck.

"I repeat, your flesh is delicious sweetheart," Sean taunted, staring right at her.

Over the course of the next several minutes, Sean continued devouring her flesh. She started to look exactly like him and Jack after the creature spat the bluish substance on him. All except the flesh of her head.

"And now sweetheart, it's time for the main course," Sean said, focusing his eyes on her head. "But first."

Before Sean commenced with devouring the flesh covering her face and then went to work extracting her brain to devour it as well-the main course as he termed it, he placed his lips against hers, kissing them heartily. Seconds later, Alexandra was overcome by a dose of intense biting pain as Sean bit into her forehead to try and extract her brain. More of her blood exploded as a result.

Another few seconds later, sickened ghastly disgust was racing through her as she saw Sean gripping her brain. He bit harshly into it like someone would to a delicious piece of mouthwatering fruit.

"Um, delicious," Sean teased in amusement between intervals of devouring it.

There's not a chance in hell I'm about to let you do that to me, Alexandra thought, returning to reality.

And to prevent Sean from reaching her, Alexandra turned the fire extinguisher upside down to meet his rapid advance.

"Like hell I'm about to let you clobber me upside the head with that thing," he snarled, closing the distance on her. "And then trust me, I'm going to take such delight in tasting that delicious flesh you wear, babe."

And to prove he was being sincere about this, he stuck out his tongue, moving it over his lips in a teasing manner.

The sight of it, and knowing the reason behind it caused a nauseated, revolting sensation to cascade through her. Increasing the desire to smash him right upside the head with the fire extinguisher and hopefully put an end to him by decapitation.

Another few seconds later he closed the distance on her. It triggered her into putting all her strength into swinging the fire extinguisher in an effort to do it. He was completely opposed to her doing this as he reached out his hands to attempt ripping the weapon from her.

"No, I refuse to be turned into a meal for you!" she screamed, doing her best to hold onto the fire extinguisher for dear life.

"The feistiness is seriously getting my appetite for you up and running baby!" he bellowed, putting in more of an effort to rip the fire extinguisher out of her hands.

And for the next several seconds, Alexandra felt a blast of incredible nervousness as she could feel herself losing her hold on the fire extinguisher.

No, I refuse to become a meal for a skinless freak zombie wannabe! She thought and began putting all her strength to keep her weapon from being ripped from her hands. Unfortunately, he proved to be the stronger of the two. It bestowed her with the despondent sensation she was about to suffer one of the worst things imaginable.

This was until her mind was invaded by the perfect solution on how to prevent it. And it was a good thing she came up with this idea when she did; as a couple seconds later, he was successful in tearing the fire extinguisher from her hands. She brought her knee up to target his crotch area. She made contact with it and she smiled as it did the trick. He released his hold on the fire extinguisher and she thanked her quick reflexes for being able to grab hold of the fire extinguisher before it struck the ground. She wasted no time in turning it upside down and began smashing it against the left side of his head, which produced a thick, sickening splat.

Again and again, she repeated the act before he had a chance to recuperate and mount a defense.

Not letting up resulted in the sickening removal of his pulverized head from his neck. It caused nausea to rage in the pit of her stomach, and she was surprised she didn't let loose with acidy bile over it.

Even though she succeeded, she didn't cease with her attack. For some reason, his body remained standing, and she continued to smash his body, propelling it backwards sending it over the deck and into the cold dark waters of the ocean.

As Alexandra stood there, she shot a glance down onto his decapitated head lying on its side. Almost immediately the nausea returned stronger than ever and not caring she'd touch it with her bare toes, bringing her right leg forward, she started treating it like a freaking soccer ball, sending it straight into the ocean to join the rest of him.

Moving forward, Alexandra stared down onto the ocean.

As she did, she began to wonder what the heck was doing under there. Was it watching her? Did it plan on returning to the yacht, and this time around, spit the flesh melting substance on her? Or like in her nightmare, would others of its species, provided there was more down there, do the job instead? Or with it?

As she continued to think about it, a certain idea invaded Alexandra's mind. Did the creature melt the skin off the life down there like it did to humans? If so, did it turn sea life cannibalistic as well?

Distracting her from her thoughts, the water suddenly erupted with a harsh frothing. The sight of it made Alexandra take a couple nervous steps backwards.

In a rush, Alexandra aimed the fire extinguisher in the direction of the ocean water to meet the creature or creatures in hopes to propel it back into the ocean's depths before it or they had a chance to reach her.

The moments progressed, the ocean water growing more frantic with the frothing. It resulted in her bold, "come out and get out here and receive a face full of foam."

Almost immediately the creature exploded from the frothing water. It reminded her of a spitball being spat out of a straw. It wasn't alone, like in her nightmare, three more had joined, and with it, nervous panic grew like mad in her. Would she be able to handle all four of them, or was she about to have her flesh dispatched off her body?

No, I have to handle them, I have to! She thought frantically and let loose with the foam. It resulted in them singing out the unnerving wailing, coming out in an irritated tone. Oh yeah, her spraying them with foam clearly pissed the creatures off big time. And the next thing she knew they were darting frantically out of the path.

Quick as a flash she again aimed the fire extinguisher at the fast-approaching creatures, blasting them with more foam. She frowned, realizing they had wizened up as they moved out of the way and resumed zooming in towards her. Still, she continued to blast the foam at them, the ones on the right, the left, repeating the act over and over. They again started singing out the irritated wails and it was more powerful and potent than ever.

Striking them with another couple blasts of foam only made them zoom out of the way. Making matters worse, they were joined by three more of the creatures. Fear dominated her over their arrival. She was barely able to handle four of these creatures, and now there were seven in total.

I'm so freaking dead, there's not a chance I'll be able to handle all of them.

Resigning herself to this horrendous fate, forgetting about making her way to the island and warning about the threat of these creatures, Alexandra squatted down in a rush, placing the fire extinguisher onto the floor thereby making herself defenseless against their attack. The moment she stood back up, the creatures zoomed in towards her and she shut her eyes tight, unwilling to witness them spit the substance on her.

Alexandra could hear the wailing get closer and closer.

As the moments progressed, she could feel tears start to sting her eyes. Not only was she about to suffer the worst fate imaginable, she wouldn't be able to warn the islanders and world about these creatures.

And then out of nowhere a sudden thought was driven into her mind. No, there wasn't a chance she could allow human beings to become skinless freaks with an appetite for flesh.

Quick as a flash her eyes opened and she was racing to grab up the fire extinguisher. Back in her hands, she aimed it at the rapidly advancing creatures, blasting the foam at them. Like before, they were intelligent enough to dart out of the way, and the next thing Alexandra knew, the creatures had her surrounded. Three came in from the left, four from the right, and they began to close in on her.

Another attempt to fire foam on them proved futile as they darted out of the way.

Just as it began to sink in there was no hope left for her; the perfect solution as to how she could escape them invaded her mind. The rowboat. It had oars and the rifle. Would bullets work on these creatures? She had to find out and darted for it. No surprise, the creatures began zipping after her, letting loose with the wailing.

She stood at the deck, staring down at the rowboat down below. Not caring if she'd be injured, tucking the fire extinguisher under her arm, Alexandra began to climb over as the creatures made their arrival.

She dropped, landing hard on her back, the fire extinguisher slipping from underneath her arm and rolling away.

Ignoring this, she shot a glance back up, saw the creatures hovering above. Suddenly they took a nose dive for her.

Reaching down, Alexandra scrambled to pick up the rifle, she had it in her hands in no time. Checking it, she was overcome with relief as she saw it was loaded. She pointed it up, aiming it. Good thing she did as the creatures made their arrival and she began firing like mad at them.

Alexandra discovered bullets were indeed effective against these creatures. They caused them to explode into a disgusting white goo.

Continuing to fire, ignoring the sudden nausea, she managed to take out a couple more before they wisely retreated back underneath the ocean. She wasn't taking any chances and pointed the rifle at the water;

expecting them to reemerge at any given moment. One minute, two, and nothing.

Three minutes into it and she anchored herself down in a sitting position. Five minutes and Alexandra realized for the time being, the creatures wouldn't be back out.

"Island, here I come," Alexandra said. She reached out, took hold of the oars and started to row.

***

Alexandra had her guard up, the rifle and fire extinguisher in reach as she continued to row for the island.

For all she knew, the creatures might come bursting back out of the ocean at any time.

As the minutes passed, Alexandra shot a glance down and was caught by shocked surprise. She saw something swimming next to her. It was clearly a great white shark, but there was something different about it. Downright freaking scary as she received her answer as to whether or not the creatures spat the substance onto sea life.

Widening her eyes with pure dread, she saw it was red and skinless. She rowed even faster to try and escape it, all the while releasing a shocked whisper, "oh you poor, unfortunate bastard."

Alexandra quickly discovered this was a serious mistake. Out of nowhere, over and over again, it began to smash itself hard and frantically against the side of the rowboat.

Feeling a rush of sudden nervous fear and irritation caused her to reach out and grab the rifle to put an end to this. She never received the chance as it abruptly ceased with the smashing and lurched up and out of the water. Its head exposed, Alexandra was riveted with a rush of pure terror.

Like the creatures, the shark had no eyes, only an enormous mouth filled with the huge *stalactite* teeth.

Another similarity between it and the creature was revealed as it began to sing out the unnerving wailing.

Alexandra stood up in a rush, desperate to get her hands wrapped around the rifle. She quickly discovered this was a tremendous mistake as it began to smash its head against the side of the boat. There was no doubt in her mind its intentions to try and knock her into the water. Why, either to take a bite out of her or spit the substance onto her. She was caught off-guard and filled with a rush of immense fear and released a yelp of surprise as she was knocked straight into the water. In a rush, she scrambled like mad to climb back onto it, before the hybrid shark/creature had any chance to reach her.

Grabbing hold of the edge, Alexandra used all her strength attempting to pull herself back into it; all the while her eyes focused on the shark. They widened with fear as it began swimming frantically straight for her. And then she felt it, something brushed against her leg.

Looking down, she felt a rush of nervous panic as she saw a second shark. It began to swim for her as well, which triggered her into putting more of an effort to pull herself back into the boat before they reached her.

Halfway in and to safety, she suffered a jolting shock as something collided against the bottom of the boat and she was knocked back into the water.

By now, the pair of sharks were closer than ever, and as two more sharks broke through the water Alexandra began to wonder if she should forget about trying to pull herself into the boat, forget about warning the islanders about the creatures, remain in the water and allow the sharks to spit the substance on her or devour her.

Well maybe I won't suffer so bad, she thought, the sharks tightening in around her. The next thing she knew, hot tears began to form in her eyes and roll down her face.

No! She screamed furiously in her mind and she again reached out for the edge of the boat and started to scramble to pull herself back in before the sharks reached her. The sharks were almost upon her now, and then a miracle—she was able to pull herself back into the rowboat.

She knew in an instant the sharks were seriously pissed as they began to furiously smash themselves against the boat. It sent Alexandra scrambling to grab the rifle, and her hands wrapped around it, she spun back around and started shooting away at them. Her act blew sickening chunks out of them, it spilled their blood, staining the ocean red, and she smiled as their corpses sank back under.

Continuing to make her way for the island came with relief as the creatures didn't emerge from the ocean again nor did she have any shark difficulties.

Part III

It wasn't long before Alexandra was closing in on the island. Another few minutes later, she reached the shore, and climbing out, she successfully managed to pull the rowboat onto the white sand. She had to admit the island was really gorgeous, the white sand oh so comfortable against her bare feet as she started to move forward. Reaching into the boat, she wrapped her hands around the rifle, lifting it out. She turned and started heading away from the boat.

Over the next few minutes, Alexandra felt the temperature rise several degrees, making her grow unbearably hot and uncomfortable. Alexandra was given no choice but to remove the sweater she had on to beat the heat.

She placed the rifle onto the sand. Straightening back up, Alexandra gripped the bottom of her sweater, and lifting it over her head, she had it off in no time, and was scrambling to get the rifle back in her hands in case a skinless human turned flesh and brain hungry zombie decided to introduce themselves to her.

For the next several minutes of heading forward, the rifle pointed out in front of her, Alexandra was alarmed by not running into a single person. It made her wonder if perhaps, and it drilled her with intense nervousness, the inhabitants of the island were forced to abandon it thanks to the creatures invading it. Or worse, much worse, they met up with the most horrible fate imaginable and were turned skinless and infected with a ravenous appetite for human flesh. It was this that made Alexandra wonder if she had made a mistake in setting foot on this island.

No, there's not a chance the creatures could have turned everyone living on the island, she decided and continued to move forward.

"Hey, hello, can anyone hear me?" she called out, receiving only silence for an answer. "Well, better go see if I can find someone and tell them exactly what's going on."

After a while of traveling the island, still not finding any life, human or skinless zombie, Alexandra arrived at a section dominated by heavy foliage. Like the rest of the island so far, it looked absolutely gorgeous and for this reason, she had no difficulty continuing to head forward.

Alexandra's arrival on the island hadn't gone unnoticed. Who had caught sight of her arrival, Christine Havers, born twenty-seven years ago in Glasswind, had caught sight of her arrival. Like Alexandra and Jack, she was looking forward to spending her weekend on the island. Unlike Alexandra and Jack, she and her friends, all in their early twenties; Melissa Cavens, Nicholas Westers, Jessica Masters and Tim Davis, formed a thriller horror writing group. They met up on a weekly basis in the living room of her house after work; and arrived on the island a couple of hours before Alexandra, by motorboat, Tim, a pro in piloting one; had lucked out and hadn't run into the creatures right away.

It happened when they went exploring the island. Surprisingly, they stumbled onto the silvery spacecraft which had transported the creatures to Earth. Silvery in color, it was shaped like a cigar. They found it hidden in the enormous forest Alexandra had now stepped into. These creatures were swarming all around it and despite trying their hardest to escape them, they weren't fast enough. As a result, Melissa, Nicholas, Jessica and Tim thrust blame on her for not only their becoming skinless zombies, but talking them into coming here as well.

"It sure the hell wouldn't have happened if you hadn't," Nicholas informed her in an angered tone. "I can't speak for Jessica, Tim, and Melissa, but our friendship as well as being a member of your writing group is over and done with from this moment forward."

And as the seconds progressed, Melissa, Jessica and Tim went right along with Nicholas and his decision to end their friendship and being in the writing group-thereby dissolving it.

Where they were now, traveling the rest of the island in search of human flesh to devour.

Setting her sights on Alexandra, Christine had every intention of devouring the woman's flesh before her now former friends became aware of her presence. It sure as hell didn't matter the woman was armed with a damn rifle, her appetite for her flesh was strong enough to risk getting shot to try and get her. And maybe bullets had no effect on what she had become.

Christine began trailing after the woman.

After several minutes of doing so, she witnessed the woman stop briefly and strip off the sweater she had on. This revealed the bikini she had on underneath and receiving an eyeful of the woman's bare skin only increased her desire to devour her flesh.

Another several minutes of heading after the woman passing, Christine watched her arrive at the forest and head into it. She reached the forest two minutes later and set foot inside as well.

As she continued her pursuit of the woman, the desire to devour her flesh increased. Out of nowhere, and surprising the heck out of her, Christine's mind was invaded by a scenario of how it would go down when she caught up to the woman.

Having no desire to have the woman put up a fight against her as soon as she reached her, she would wrap her right hand around the woman's left bicep.

"Let me the hell go, you skinless zombie freak!" the woman would scream.

She wouldn't. Instead, she'd do the exact opposite. She'd yank the woman close to her and waste no time in biting furiously into the left side of her neck to disable her. This would result in the woman blasting out one hell of a painful, bloodcurdling scream.

The woman's flesh would taste delicious, filling her with a strong desire to devour the rest of her-her bikini clad body stained with her own blood, and as Alexandra's eyes rolled into her head and unconsciousness took over, she would lower her onto her back to finish her off.

Snap!

Dispatching Christine from her thoughts, not watching where she walked, she stepped on a branch, alerting the woman she was there and pursuing her.

Alexandra felt dominated by a rush of tremendous panic, caused by the snap of a branch get stepped out somewhere behind her. Did the creatures introduce themselves to some of the island residents? Turn them into skinless zombies like Jack and Sean? Had one or more of them noticed her arrival on the island and were pursuing her, desperate to make a meal out of her? Desperate to find this out, Alexandra turned around. Her panic blossomed hot in her as she saw, sure enough, an unfortunate woman had been introduced to the creatures and had the bluish substance spat on her.

Like hell I'm going to let you devour my flesh, you skinless zombie bitch!

Alexandra's next act was to aim the rifle straight at her pursuer. She fired off a shot at her.

At the last second, Christine decided not to risk finding out whether or not bullets would cause any damage to her. A miracle was bestowed on her as with each time the woman fired at her, she successfully managed to avoid getting shot. The miracle continued as the woman frowned as she emptied the rifle on her.

"Damn it to hell!" Alexandra screamed as she no longer had any bullets left in the rifle. It caused her to run with a sudden burst of speed to try and escape her flesh and brain hungry pursuer. Hide somewhere, anywhere. She kept shooting nervous glances to make sure her living dead pursuer remained a safe distance behind her. She saw the forest was separated and there was a path up ahead.

Maybe I can find somewhere to hide, and then smash this zombie bitch in the head with my rifle! Yeah, that's what I need to do. Alexandra put on an extra burst of speed. In a minute she reached the clearing and ran through it.

In doing so, Alexandra was struck by a sudden jolting surprise when she discovered was waiting for her. Brown and soupy, almost immediately, she made the incredible mistake of stepping into the sludge and sank down mid-calf in it. It caused her to release her hold of the rifle and made her not want to retrieve it-that and it no longer had bullets, making it worthless to her. Watching it vanish underneath the crap, she was overcome with nausea-this substance whatever the hell it was felt absolutely gross touching her bare skin. This made her seriously regret removing her sweater to beat the heat. And then out of nowhere, her mind was invaded by what it possibly was.

Quicksand.

If it was, she realized, rest assured, she had stumbled into something just as dangerous as the skinless zombie in fast pursuit of her. Rest assured she was now stuck in a dangerous death trap. Fear replaced the nausea. It didn't help that she continued to disappear into this sickening gross ass substance at a slow, slothful pace. About two minutes later she was buried to her waist in it.

I am so screwed.

As Alexandra continued her slow descent into whatever disgusting crap this was, she began to wonder if someone had made the mistake of falling into it before she had. It sure would have really sucked if they had. Seconds later she was struck by a alarming surprise. Something underneath brushed up against her leg. It immediately told her that yeah something was underneath this substance, in it with her, and because of it, her nervous fear elevated.

What the hell am I stuck in this crap with? She asked herself.

Whatever it was, it could not be good, possibly downright dangerous. A few seconds later, and sinking down a few more inches, Alexandra again felt whatever it was touch up against her leg. And then out of nowhere, something began to attempt breaking out from underneath. More seconds passed and a hand stained with the substance broke through the surface. Another one a few inches away from the first one. Another. Another. Second hands. More of what was underneath escaped out from all around her. They were clearly human and they might be more of the skinless zombies, victims of the blue spitting substance creatures. If this was the case, rest assured they were coming out to claim her, to devour her flesh.

"So hungry for flesh!" The first one to escape wailed out in a gruff, masculine tone, revealing to her that yes these in fact were the skinless zombies.

"We're going to devour you!" Yet another zombie bellowed in a youthful, twenty-something tone at the same time she went under a few more inches.

The next thing Alexandra knew, the gruff masculine sounding zombie propelled himself closer to her. It brought them practically next to each other face-to-face and then, focusing his eyes on her bare shoulder, pushed his head forward to it.

Seconds, and Alexandra was the recipient of feeling the absolute worst pain imaginable and this skinless zombie bit harshly into her shoulder. She had no choice but to sing out the most painful scream she had ever done in her life. Her blood began flowing from the wound once the skinless zombie pulled his teeth out of her shoulder and stained the substance crimson red. She barely had any time to react to it as another skinless zombie positioned somewhere close behind her came up and bit into her other shoulder. It reacted the same way, singing out another one of those painful screams.

"You're so delicious sweetheart!" he bellowed triumphantly, the tone of his voice gruff and masculine like the first zombie. He followed this up by shoving her downward and the last thing she saw before disappearing under completely; the first and second zombie shoving themselves back under. And when they joined her underneath, they'd continue devouring her flesh. That much was clear to her.

Snapping out of this, Alexandra returned to reality. She realized this was nothing but a scary as all heck daydream and she'd imagined the whole thing. The zombies were buried underneath the quicksand, not the quicksand itself. She was still a prisoner in it and she sank down a few more inches. Seconds later she saw her female zombie pursuer make her arrival.

Christine couldn't believe her misfortune. Whatever the hell this crap was, was guilty of robbing her of the woman whose flesh she had her heart set on devouring.

As she stood there and watched Alexandra disappear into whatever the hell the substance was at a slow rate of speed; it struck her hard in the face—quicksand, it had to be. The next thing Christine knew, she was asking herself if she should make an attempt to try and rip the woman out so she wouldn't lose her to it, miss out on the chance to sink her teeth into her flesh and brain and devour them one right after the other, starting with the woman's flesh and wrapping things up with her brain.

The problem she saw, the woman might resist her trying to do it. Why exactly, preferring to slip down into the quicksand instead of being devoured by a skinless zombie. Christine knew for a fact if she was in the woman's position, she would definitely go for the non-painful way of dying. Disappointment dominated her, and she realized getting her hands and teeth into her flesh were now out of the question; Christine took a couple steps backwards. She turned and started distancing herself away from the woman, leaving her to continue to be taken by the quicksand.

While the skinless zombie starving for her flesh silently observed her stuck in this horrible predicament, the substance rose over Alexandra's stomach, heightening the nausea.

I can't believe this is how I'm going to die, sucked down into putrid, gross quicksand, Alexandra thought as depression took over and she continued her descent. Out of nowhere, surprising the hell out of her, her mind was invaded by an idea. She would falsely promise the skinless zombie she could devour her flesh in exchange for giving her a helping hand.

Yeah, that's exactly what I need to do, Alexandra decided as she descended farther, to her armpits, her arms stretched out before her. It was a good thing she did this when she did. Another few minutes later there was no doubt in her mind she'd go under completely.

"Please I'm begging you, if you help me out of this crap, I promise you can devour my flesh!" Alexandra cried out to the skinless zombie in a sincere, believable tone.

The first thought to invade Christine's mind, the woman had no intention of actually doing this. That as soon as she assisted her, she would either run off or try her hardest to push her into the quicksand.

"Yeah, you must think I'm damn stupid," Christine said, turning to face the woman. "As soon as I help you out, you'll go back on that promise and run off. Either that or attempt to yank me into that quicksand you're stuck in."

"I won't!" Alexandra screamed, her voice drenched with fear.

I sure the hell know I'm going to regret this, Christine thought right before she decided that yes, she'd help rip the woman out of the predicament she was stuck in.

The next thing Christine knew, she was making her way back to the quicksand to try and accomplish the rescue.

"Come on, give me your arm," escaped her as soon as she arrived. "And you'd better hope you don't weigh a lot and that quicksand wants to release you, or believe me this will really suck for you." And with that, Christine stretched her arm out to the woman. She wasn't the least bit surprised when the woman frantically elevated her arm from resting on the surface of the quicksand; she reached out and gripped her hand like her life depended on it. Touching her flesh, Christine was overcome with sudden depression by the fact she was now a freakish skinless zombie and there wasn't a chance in hell she could return to the way she was before arriving on the island. Meeting up with that creature and having it spit its skin-removing blue substance not long afterwards. Jealousy that this woman still had her flesh intact replaced the depression and it strengthened Christine's desire to devour her flesh.

Christine went into action putting all her strength into yanking the woman out so she could devour her flesh. At first, the woman remained stuck-it was as if the quicksand refused to give her up. But as the seconds passed and she put more of a strong effort into it, the quicksand began to relent and release its hold on the woman. A couple minutes passed and she doubled that effort, the quicksand let go a bit more. The first thing to rise up the woman's shoulders-followed seconds later by her torso. An excited, victorious feeling dominated Christine. Another few minutes later, the woman was home free and safe, the two of them standing face-to-face.

Alexandra felt incredibly grateful that the woman successfully managed to rip her out of that quicksand. It was because of this that she wondered if she should forget about trying to escape when the opportunity presented itself. Instead, show her gratitude and let her devour her flesh after all. But of course, it would have to be after she warned the inhabitants of this island-those who hadn't met up with the creatures and transformed into skinless zombies as well. But were there any left? Had everybody here suffered? Was she the only non-transformed one on this island? If this was the case, rest assured once they became aware of her, they'd be ravenous for her flesh. Like Sean. Like this woman most likely.

Well, if I'm destined to become a meal for a skinless zombie, it's going to be the one standing face-to-face with me. Why, to show my gratitude for her having a heart and ripping me out of that disgusting quicksand.

"So uh thanks are in order for you having a heart and ripping me out of that quicksand. Even though you probably did it so you'd have the opportunity to devour my flesh."

"So you know about what I've become?" Christine asked.

"My boyfriend Jack was transformed." Alexandra wasted no time answering her. "It was the worst thing I'll ever experience and my heart broke into a million pieces when he threw himself into the ocean so he wouldn't let his appetite for flesh get the best of him and eat mine."

"That must have sure sucked for you," Christine said.

"Yeah, you'd better believe it. So since all signs point to us getting chummy-chummy, tell me your name."

"Christine Havers, now it's only fair for you to do the same."

Alexandra Hexingmore. So what's your story Christine? How'd you become what you are now?"

"My former thriller horror writing group, friends from high school, arrived here from Glasswind..."

"Yeah that's where Jack and I are from. He and I called it our hometown our entire lives."

"Yeah the same. Anyway, we met up with those blue-spitting bastard creatures almost immediately after setting foot on this island and were transformed."

"You didn't by chance go exploring the island, did you?"

"It's how my former friends and writing group were transformed. We ventured into this forest and made our way not far from here and that's where we discovered the reason why those creatures are here. An actual spacecraft, they were swarming all around it and caught up to us before we could escape them. My friends disown and hate me for talking them into coming here resulting in them being transformed into skinless zombies."

"I bet that sure sucks."

"Uh-huh, it does. Anyway, those things are damn extraterrestrials Alexandra. It means in some universe beyond our own there's a planet full of these bastard creatures and their skinless zombie-creating blue substance."

Alexandra was overcome with instant terror. If these deadly creatures existed, what else was there in the same universe they called home? For all she knew, there might be other extraterrestrial species more dangerous living in this universe that have more deadly abilities than the blue substance. Would the human race be able to survive if they decided to visit Earth? Or would humans be wiped out and become ancient history?

The fact that humans might be on the way out and eradicated from existence caused incredible depression to dominate Alexandra. For this reason, being devoured by Christine to escape growing old and witnessing this potentially horrible future seemed welcoming. Seconds later, Alexandra made the snap decision that hell yes, she was going to let Christine do it.

"The human race is really damn screwed if there's more extraterrestrials with dangerous abilities like the ones who are here now," she admitted to Christine seconds after making this decision. "There's not a chance in hell I'm going to stick around, grow old and watch the eradication of humans. I'd rather die young and go out by having a skinless zombie devour my flesh."

"You can't be sure that's actually going to happen," Christine replied. "For all we know, these extraterrestrials here now might be the only ones who are going to be visiting Earth."

"I'm not taking any chances Christine," Alexandra said in a bold tone. "You can be the one who does it to me, as a way of thanking you for ripping me out of that disgusting quicksand. If you don't want to, I'll hunt down one of your former writing group members and friends to do it. I'm sure they'll have no problem saying yes to it. Them or one of the island inhabitants, since I have no doubt some or all of them have been transformed by now."

"Since you put it that way, I'll be the one who steps up to the plate and does it to you," Christine said. "So, with that out of the way, should I do it right here and now?"

"Sure, be my guest if you want to get a mouthful of quicksand."

"Hell no, I sure don't want that."

"It's why we should head back to the ocean and I can wash it off, and then my flesh and brain is yours."

One thing was clear to Christine as she trailed behind Alexandra as they made their way through a different section of the woods. She could barely wait to get down to business, bite into Alexandra and devour her flesh. Out of nowhere and surprising the crap out of her, the thought invaded her mind that Alexandra might want to see the creatures' spacecraft before it happened.

No, who the hell am I kidding, that's damn stupid! Why would she want to lay her eyes on the spacecraft of her boyfriend's murderer?

***

"It won't take long," Alexandra said as soon as they were back on the beach and she launched herself towards the ocean.

As she was immersed in the water to wash the quicksand off, Alexandra began to contemplate. How would it go down when Christine devoured her flesh. One thing was quite clear to her, it would be painful as all heck, and for the next few seconds she wondered if she really should go through with it.

No, whom am I kidding! I'd rather die young like I decided. Be spared witnessing the human race, all those I love and care about potentially being wiped from existence by extraterrestrials with dangerous abilities! Or worse skinless zombies! Like what was currently happening!

Another couple minutes later, the quicksand washed off, she stepped out of the ocean water and started making her way back to an awaiting Christine. There was no doubt in Alexandra's mind, this woman's appetite for human flesh-her flesh-must be overwhelming in her. Again, the question she asked herself as she got closer and closer to Christine would it be as painful and brutal as what she experienced in that horrible quicksand zombie daydream? She began to wonder if she actually wanted to go through it after all.

No, who the hell am I kidding, of course I do! I have to do it in order to escape the possibility of dangerous extraterrestrials arriving on Earth! To turn the human race into skinless zombies! Or if not that, something far worse! Like I made the decision before, I refuse to grow old and witness with my own two eyes the human race become extinct, wiped out by these space monster beings!

I'll be seeing you soon Jack, Alexandra whispered to herself as she began to speed up to reach Christine even faster. She hurriedly closed the distance on her.

Watching Alexandra washing the quicksand off, Christine's desire to devour her flesh and brain increased. And who could blame her for this? Alexandra looked so mouthwatering delicious.

I sure can't wait to bite into you and taste that delicious looking flesh covering you Alexandra, she thought.

"So I sure hope your appetite for my flesh and brain is alive and kicking!" Alexandra called out as she closed the distance.

Yeah, you'd better believe I can't wait to devour you! Christine thought.

The two of them stood face-to-face, and with it, laying eyes on Alexandra's bare flesh, her appetite for it was increased to almost one hundred percent.

For the next few seconds, the fear of having to suffer tremendous pain with what was about to go down made Alexandra once again question if she wanted to go through with this after all.

No! Hell no! I'm not backing out of it, and that's that!

"Okay, well, I won't keep you waiting any longer," Alexandra said. "Now come on, snap to it, I'm all yours."

No more words escaped Christine. Instead, she reached out and gripped Alexandra's biceps. Her intention was to devour her brains first and work her way down until there was nothing left. Yeah, she was that damn starving for this woman. And the next thing she knew, she was moving her mouth straight for Alexandra's forehead.

"A heads up, what I do next is incredibly painful," she alerted Alexandra.

"Yeah, don't worry, I can take it," Alexandra answered her in a fearless tone.

About to bite down, Christine was caught by sudden surprise. Racing from the forest, Alexandra, Melissa, Nicholas, Jessica, and Tim. Incredibly crushing disappointment began to dominate her as she realized they had their sights and appetite set on Alexandra. They were fully intending to steal Alexandra from her to exact revenge against her. And with them outnumbering her four to one, there pretty much wasn't anything she could do to prevent them stealing Alexandra away from her. There was a single possible way to prevent them from taking Alexandra; she'd alert her and they could try and get the hell out of there. But where? And was Alexandra a fast runner? She sure the hell wasn't, despite her being thin and in shape.

"Hey, are you a fast runner?" She asked as her former friends were closing the distance on them.

"What, why?" Alexandra asked, her voice flavored with sudden nervousness.

Christine didn't receive a chance to answer Alexandra as Melissa, Nicholas, Jessica, and Tim finally made their arrival. Wasting no time, the four of them reached out to grab Alexandra. It resulted in her yelling out, "hey what the hell?" as she was hoisted up and they raced her off back towards the forest. A few minutes later they were out of sight.

Christine collapsed down onto the sand in defeat.

***

Tremendous fear rushed through Alexandra as she was carried off by not one, but four skinless zombies. The members of Christine's writing group no doubt. Unlike Christine, they really didn't respect or care for her and were more interested in using her to satisfy their appetite.

Damn it, the pain I'm going to suffer as they devour my flesh is going to be four times painful and intense. Oh well, that's my bad break, she thought miserably. *I'm just going to have to accept it.*

Within a matter of a few short minutes, these skinless zombies had her in the forest. Dropping her, the four of them followed her down and frantically rushed to tear off her bikini. They began aggressively biting into her bare body everywhere-oh hell yeah, they sure had an appetite for her flesh all right. She screamed out in horrific pain as her blood began to flow.

I'll be seeing you soon Jack, and *the good thing about this happening, at least I won't be around to witness extraterrestrials destroy the human race,* Alexandra thought as she grew weaker and weaker; they continued to devour her. Her eyes fell shut as her life and blood left her body.

About the Authors

Shawn Putnam

Shawn Putnam is a man on the short south side of fifty who has been writing since high school, married for almost thirty years with a twenty-one-year-old son and two puppies. Only recently has he felt secure enough to submit his works for publication, and he is somewhat gratified that persons other than his family have found a kernel of worth in his humble stories.

R.C. Mulhare

R.C. Mulhare once successfully defended her day-job workplace from zombies, through some judicious use of clearance-rack garden tools and survived a fight with Yog-Sothoth cultists in a hallway of a hotel in Providence; she's also picked up extra work editing the product blog of Umbrella Corporation...

In actuality, R.C. Mulhare was born in Lowell, Massachusetts and grew up in a nearby town, in a hundred-year-old house up the street from an old cemetery. Her interest in the dark and mysterious started when she was quite young, when her mother read the faery tales of the Brothers Grimm and quoted the poetry of Edgar Allan Poe to her, while her Irish storyteller father infused her with a fondness for strange characters and quirky situations. Between writing projects, she moonlights in grocery retail. She's also fond of hiking in the woods of the White Mountains of New Hampshire and browsing the antiques shops one finds all over New England. A two-time

Amazon best-selling author, contributor to the Hugo Award Winning Archive of Our Own, and member of the New England Horror Writers, she has one hundred twenty stories in print through dozens of independent publishers including Atlantean Publishing, Macabre Maine, DBND Publishing, Hellbound Books, Nocturnal Sirens Publishing, FunDead Publications, Deadman's Tome, NEHW Press, Lovecraftiana Magazine, Tales of Wonder and Dread, and Weirdbook Magazine, with more stories in the works. She shares her home with her family, a vintage music-loving baby parakeet, about fifteen hundred books and an unknown number of eldritch things that rattle in the walls when she's writing late in the night. She's happy to have visitors through her page at: https://linktr. ee/rcmulhare

JOSIAH SANTOS

Josiah Santos works as a Supply Chain Asst. Manager, but found that his passion lies in entertaining others through writing. Although he grew up afraid of anything creepy and watching horror movies from behind a pillow, he grew to appreciate how the horror genre could be used to confront fears and explore where they come from. Through encouragement from his amazing wife, he embraces the uncomfortable and the painful moments in life through writing, and although some of his works may be dark at times, they never come from a dark place.

MARK MACKEY

Mark Mackey is a long-time resident of Chicago, Illinois, with no plans to relocate elsewhere, either city or state and has written tales included in various anthologies and co-written *The Soulless*, a harrowing horror novel commencing on an ocean liner and concluding on a mysterious island. https://www. amazon.com/stores/Mark-Mackey/author/B0054

About the Editor

Aaron Crocker

Aaron was raised in the small town of El Dorado Springs, Missouri and later moved to Virginia where he currently resides. He holds a few degrees, the most applicable being a B.S. in English, Linguistics, and Communications from the University of Mary Washington.

In 2016, he wrote his first piece "Suburban Suicide" which took second place in a national divergent literature competition. From there he picked up a few more national and international awards in short and micro fiction competitions, sat on various short fiction judging panels, and has spoken at several writing events—the most notable being an invitation to address the Library of Congress in 2020 (virtually).

Over several years, Aaron published two moderately successful, limited-edition fundraising anthologies, and this is where he gained an appreciation for and enjoyment of publishing. From there, he dreamed up and founded Campfire Publishing, and although he quickly became aware of the editing skills required of such an endeavor, he is nothing if not dedicated and open to learning.